Glyn Severn's Schooldays

By

George Manville Fenn

Glyn Severn's Schooldays
by George Manville Fenn

ISBN: 978-93-61422-00-3

Published by

DOUBLE 9 BOOKS

2/13-B, Ansari Road
Daryaganj, New Delhi – 110002
info@double9books.com
www.double9books.com
Tel. 011-40042856

ABOUT THE AUTHOR

George Manville Fenn was a very productive author of novels, a writer, an editor, and an educator from England. He was born on January 3, 1831, in Pimlico, London. He mostly learned on his own; he taught himself Italian, French, and German. During the years 1851–1854, he went to Battersea Training College for Teachers and then became the head of a state school in Alford, Lincolnshire. In the early 1850s, Fenn started to write short stories and pieces for newspapers and magazines. The Old Forest Ranger, his first book, came out in 1856. Afterward, he wrote more than 100 books, many of them for teenagers and young adults. He was one of the most famous writers of his time, and his books were well-liked and read by many people. He also worked as a reporter and writer for Fenn. Among the newspapers and magazines, he worked for was The Boy's Own Paper, which he ran from 1866 to 1874. He worked hard to make children's books better and was a strong supporter of education and reading. The Englishman Fenn passed away on August 26, 1909, in Isleworth.

CONTENTS

Chapter One
The New Boys

Slegge said it was all "bosh;" for fifty years ago a boy at school had not learned to declare that everything which did not suit his taste was "rot." So Slegge stood leaning up against the playground wall with a supercilious sneer upon his lip, and said it was all "bosh," and only fit for children.

The other fellows, he said, might make idiots of themselves if they liked, he should stop in and read; for Dr Bewley, DD, Principal of the world-famed establishment—a grey, handsome, elderly gentleman in the truest sense of the word—had smilingly said after grace at breakfast that when he was a boy he used to take a great deal of interest in natural history, and that he presumed his pupils would feel much the same as he did, and would have no objection to setting aside their classical and mathematical studies for the morning and watching the entrance of the procession when it entered the town at twelve o'clock.

The boys, who were all standing and waiting for the Doctor to leave the dining-hall, gave a hearty cheer at this; and as the ragged volley died out, after being unduly prolonged by the younger pupils, instead of crossing to the door from the table, the Doctor continued, turning to the mathematical master:

"I think, Mr Morris, you might be kind enough to tell Wrench to get the boy to help him and place a line of forms by the wall, so that the young gentlemen can enjoy the privilege of having a prolonged private box above the crowd; or, shall I say, a high bank in this modern form of the classic amphitheatre?"

"Hear, hear!" said Mr Rampson, the heavy, solid-looking classical master, impressed by the Principal's allusion to the Roman sports; and he grumbled out something in a subdued voice, with his eyes shut. What it was the boys did not hear, but it was evidently a Latin quotation, and ended in *ibus*.

The Doctor then marched slowly towards the door, with his black gown floating out around him, and carrying his mortar-board cap by the limp corner; for while everything about him was spick and span—his cravat of the stiffest and whitest as it supported his plump, pink, well-shaven chin, and his gown of the glossiest black—a habit of holding his college cap by its right-hand corner had resulted in the formation of a kind of hinge which made the University headpiece float up and down in concert with his stately steps as he turned his head from side to side and nodded benignantly at first one and then another of his junior pupils.

The masters followed, looking very severe indeed; and, following the example set by Mr Morris, they all frowned and shook their heads at the great waste of time that would follow the passing of the procession.

"So childish of the old man," said Morris to the French master, Monsieur Brohanne, a particularly plump-looking Gaul. "The boys will be fit for nothing afterwards."

"*Certainement!*" said the French master.

"But I suppose I must give orders for these seats to be placed;" and as soon as he was outside he summoned Wrench—the pale-faced and red-nosed official whose principal duty it was, with the assistance of a sturdy hobbledehoy (Mounseer Hobby-de-Hoy, as the boys called him) to keep well-blackened the whole of the boots in the big establishment—and gave orders to carry out and run a line of forms all along the outer wall of the great playground, which was continued farther on by the cricket-field hedge.

"A great waste of time," said Morris; but he gave very strict orders to the man-servant that the biggest and strongest form was to be chalked "Number One," and reserved for the masters only.

There was a buzz in the dining-hall which grew into a roar as the door closed. The boys, who had sat down to breakfast rather wanting in appetite—from the fact that their consciences were not very clear regarding studies in English and French or certain algebraic solutions or arrangements in angles specified by "A B C" and "D E F," according to the declarations of a well-known gentleman named Euclid—felt in their great relief as if they would like another cup of coffee and two slices more, for the holiday was quite unexpected.

It was about this time that Slegge gave his opinion to his following, which was rather large, he being the senior pupil and considering himself head-chief of the school, not from his distinguished position as a scholar, but from the fact that his allowance of cash from home was the largest of that furnished to any pupil of the establishment, without counting extra tips. Slegge, Senior—not the pupil, for there was no other boy of the same name in the school, but Slegge *père*, as Monsieur Brohanne would have termed him—being sole proprietor of the great wholesale mercantile firm of Slegge,

Gorrock and Dredge, Italian warehousemen, whose place of business was in the City of London, and was, as Slegge insisted, "not a shop."

"You fellows," he said, "can do as you like. Some of you had better set up a wicket and the net, and come and bowl to me. Ha, ha! look at Thames and the Nigger! It will just suit them. Those Indian chaps think of nothing else but show. I shan't be at all surprised if the nigger goes up to dress and comes down again in white muslin and a turban.—I say! Hi! Thames! Rivers! What's your stupid name? It's going to be a hot day. You ought to come out with the chow-chow."

"No, no," whispered a boy beside him, "chowri."

"Well, chow-chow, chowri; it's all the same," said the big lad impatiently. "Horse-tail to whisk the flies away.—Hi! do you hear?"

"Are you speaking to me?" said the tall, very English-looking lad addressed.

"Of course I am."

"Well, you might address me by my name."

"Well, so I did. Thames. No, I remember, Severn! What idiots your people were to give themselves names like that!"

"Well, it's as good as Slegge anyhow," said the lad.

There was a little laugh at this, which made the owner of the latter name turn sharply and fiercely upon the nearest boy, who shut his mouth instantly and looked as innocent as a lamb.

"Look here," said Slegge, turning again to the lad he had addressed, "don't you be cheeky, sir, or you'll find yourself walked down behind the tennis-court some morning to have a first breakfast; and you won't be the first that I have taught his place in this school."

"Oh," said the lad quietly, "you mean fighting?"

"Yes," said Slegge, thrusting out his chin, "I mean fighting. You are new to this place, and you have been coming the stuck-up on the strength of your father being a poor half-pay Company's colonel. Honourable East India Company indeed! Shabby set of sham soldiers got-up to look like the real."

The face of the boy he addressed changed colour a little, and he drew a deep breath as he compressed his lips.

"And don't you look at me like that," continued Slegge, who was delighted to find a large audience gathering round him to listen while he gave one of the new boys a good setting down, "or you may find that, after

I have done with you, you won't be fit to show your ugly mug in the row of grinning boobies staring over the wall at a twopenny-halfpenny wild-beast show."

"I don't want to quarrel," said the lad quietly.

"Oh, don't you!" continued Slegge, with a sneering laugh. "Well, perhaps I do, and if I do I shall just give your master one for himself as well."

"My master," said the lad staring.

"Yes, your master, the nigger—Howdah, Squashee, or whatever he calls himself. Here! hi! you, Aziz Singh-Song, or whatever your name is, why don't you dress up and go and get leave from the Doctor to ride the elephant in the procession? Your father is a mahout out there in India, isn't he?"

The boy he addressed, who had just come up to lay his hand upon the shoulder of Severn, to whisper, "What's the matter, Glyn?" started on hearing this address, and his dark face, which was about the tint of a *young* Spaniard's, whom he resembled greatly in mien, flushed up and the lips closed very tightly, but only to part again and show his glistening white teeth. "My father—" he began.

"Bother! come on," cried Severn, putting his arm round the other and half-pushing, half-dragging him through the crowd of lads who were clustering round in expectation of a coming set-to.

There was a low murmur as of disgust as the two lads elbowed their way through, whilst Slegge shouted after them.

"Sneaks!" he cried. "Cowards! But I haven't done with you yet;" and as they passed out through the door into the great playground he drew himself up, giving his head a jerk, and then moistening his hands in a very objectionable way, he gave them a rub together, doubled his fists, and threw himself into a fighting attitude, jerking his head to and fro in the most approved manner; and, bringing forth a roar of delight from the little crowd around him, as quick as lightning he delivered two sharp blows right and left to a couple of unoffending schoolfellows, picking out, though, two who were not likely to retaliate.

"That'll be it, boys, the pair together—one down and t'other come on. Both together if they like. They want putting in their places. I mean to strike against it."

"Hit hard then, Sleggy," cried one of his parasites.

"I will," was the reply. "There you have it;" and to the last speaker's disgust he received a sharp blow in the chest which sent him staggering back. "Now, don't you call me Sleggy again, young man. Next time it will be one in the mouth.—Yes, boys," he continued, drawing himself up, "I do mean to hit hard, and let the Principal and the masters see that we are not going to have favouritism here. Indian prince, indeed! Yah! who's he? Why, I could sell him for a ten-pun note, stock and lock and bag and baggage, to Madame Tussaud's. That's about all he's fit for. Dressed up to imitate an English gentleman! Look at him! His clothes don't fit, even if they are made by a proper tailor."

"It's he who doesn't fit his clothes," cried one of the circle.

"Well done, Burney!" cried Slegge approvingly. "That's it. Look at his hands and feet. Bah! I haven't patience with it. The Doctor ought to be ashamed of himself, taking a nigger like that! Why didn't he come dressed like a native, instead of disguised as an English lad? And he's no more like it than chalk's like cheese. Yes, I say the Doctor ought to be ashamed of himself, bringing a fellow like that into an establishment for the sons of gentlemen; and I'll tell him so before I have done."

"Do," said the lad nearest to him; "only do it when we are all there. I should like to hear you give the Doctor a bit of your mind."

Slegge turned round upon him sharply. "Do you mean that," he said, "or is it chaff?"

"Mean it? Of course!" cried the boy hastily.

"Lucky for you, then," continued Slegge. "I suppose you haven't forgotten me giving you porridge before breakfast this time last year?"

"Here, what a chap you are! I didn't mean any harm. But I say, Slegge, old chap, you did scare them off. I wish the Principal wouldn't have any more new boys. I say, though, you don't mean to get the wickets pitched this morning, do you?"

"Of course I do," cried Slegge. "Do you want to go idling and staring over the wall and look at the show?"

"Well, I—I—"

"There, that will do," cried Slegge. "I know. Just as if there weren't monkeys enough in the collection without you!"

At this would-be witticism on the part of the tyrant of the school there was a fresh roar of laughter, which made the unfortunate against whom it was directed writhe with annoyance, and hurry off to conciliate his schoolfellow by getting the wickets pitched.

Chapter Two
Declaration of War

Meanwhile the two lads, who had retired from the field, strolled off together across the playground down to the pleasant lawn-like level which the Doctor, an old lover of the Surrey game, took a pride in having well kept for the benefit of his pupils, giving them a fair amount of privilege for this way of keeping themselves in health. But to quote his words in one of his social lectures, he said:

"You boys think me a dreadful old tyrant for keeping you slaving away at your classics and mathematics, because you recollect the work that you are often so unwilling to do, while the hours I give you for play quite slip your minds. Now, this is my invariable rule, that you shall do everything well: work hard when it's work, and play hard when it's play."

The two lads, Glyn Severn and his companion of many years, Aziz Singh, a dark English boy in appearance and speech, but maharajah in his own right over a powerful principality in Southern India, strolled right away over the grass to the extreme end of the Doctor's extensive grounds, chatting together as boys will talk about the incidents of the morning.

"Oh," cried the Indian lad angrily, "I wish you hadn't stopped me. I was just ready."

"Why, what did you want to do, Singhy?" cried the other.

"Fight," said the boy, with his eyes flashing and his dark brows drawn down close together.

"Oh, you shouldn't fight directly after breakfast," said Glyn Severn, laughing good-humouredly.

"Why not?" cried the other fiercely. "I felt just then as if I could kill him."

"Then I am glad I lugged you away."

"But you shouldn't," cried the young Indian. "You nearly made me hit you."

"You had better not," said Glyn, laughing merrily.

"Yes, of course; I know, and I don't want to."

"That's right; and you mustn't kill people in England because you fall out with them."

"No, of course not; I know that too. But I don't like that boy. He keeps on saying nasty things to us, and—and—what do you call it? I know—bullies you, and says insulting things to me. How dare he call me a nigger and say my father was a mahout?"

"The insulting brute!" said Glyn.

"Why should he do it?" cried Singh.

"Oh, it's plain enough. It's because he is big and strong, and he wants to pick a quarrel with us."

"But what for?" cried Singh. "We never did him any harm."

"Love of conquest, I suppose, so as to make us humble ourselves to him same as the other fellows do. He wants to be cock of the school."

"Oh—oh!" cried Singh. "It does make me feel so hot. What did he say to me: was I going to ride on the elephant?—Yes. Well, suppose I was. It wouldn't be the first time."

"Not by hundreds," cried Glyn. "I say, used it not to be grand? Don't you wish we were going over the plains to-day on the back of old Sultan?"

He pronounced it Sool-tann.

"Ah, yes!" cried Singh, with his eyes flashing now. "I do, I do! instead of being shut up in this old school to be bullied by a boy like that. I should like to knock his head off."

"No, you wouldn't. There, don't think anything more about it. He isn't worth your notice."

"No, I suppose not," said the Indian boy;—"but what makes me so angry is that he despises me, and has treated me ever since we came here as if I were his inferior. It is not the first time he has called me a nigger.—There, I won't think anything more about it. Tell me, what's this grand procession to-day? Is it to be like a durbar at home, when all the rajahs and nawabs come together with their elephants and trains?"

"Oh, no, no, no!" cried Glyn, laughing. "Nothing of the kind."

"Then, why are they making all this fuss? It said on the bills we saw yesterday in the town, 'Ramball's Wild-Beast Show. Grand Procession.'"

"I don't know much about it," said Glyn; "only here in England in country places they make a great fuss over things like this. I asked Wrench yesterday, and he said that this was a menagerie belonging to a man who lives near and keeps his wild-beasts at a big farm-like place just outside the town."

"But why a procession?" said Singh impatiently.

"Oh, he takes them all round the country, going from town to town, and they are away for months, and now they are coming back."

"Menagerie! beast show!" said Singh thoughtfully. "They are all tame, of course?"

"Yes, of course," said Glyn. "It said lions and tigers and elephants and camels, and a lot more things on the bills. I should like to see them."

"You English are a wonderful people. My father used to have tigers—three of them—a tiger, a tigress, and a nearly full-grown cub. But they were so fierce he got tired of keeping them, and when the tigress killed one of the keepers, you remember, he asked your father about it, and they settled that it would be best to kill them."

"Of course, I remember," said Glyn; "and they had a tiger-hunt, and let one out at a time, and had beaters to drive them out of the nullahs, and shot all three."

"Yes," said Singh thoughtfully; "and my father wouldn't let me go with him on his elephant, because he said it wouldn't be safe. Then these will all be tame tigers and lions? Well, I shall like to see them all the same, because it will make me feel like being at home once more. I say, when is your father coming down again?"

"Don't know," said Glyn quietly. "I did ask in my last weekly letter."

"Ah!" said the Indian boy with a sigh, "I wish I were you."

"Well, let's change," said Glyn laughing. "You envy me! Why, I ought to envy you."

"Why?" said Singh, staring.

"Why, because you are a maharajah, a prince; and when you grow old enough you are going back to Dour to rule over your subjects and be one of the biggest pots in Southern India."

"Well, what of that?" said Singh quietly. "What good will that do me? But of course the Colonel will come too."

"Ah, that remains to be seen," said Glyn. "That'll be years to come, and who knows what will happen before then?"

"I don't care what happens," cried Singh hotly. "He's coming back to India when I go. Why, he told me himself that my father made him my guardian, and that he promised to look after me as long as he lived. He said he promised to be a father to me. It was that day when I got into a passion about something, and made him so cross. But I was very sorry afterwards," said the boy quietly, "he's such a good old fellow, and made me like him as much as I did my own father."

"Well," said Glyn merrily, "you have always had your share of him. It has made me feel quite jealous sometimes."

"Jealous! Why?" said Singh wonderingly.

"Because he seemed to like you better than he did me."

"What a shame!" cried Singh. "Oh, I say, you don't mean that, do you, Glyn, old chap? Why, you don't know how fond he is of you."

"Don't I?"

"No; you should hear what he says about you sometimes."

"Says about me? What does he say about me?"

"Oh, perhaps I oughtn't to tell you," said Singh, showing his white teeth.

"Yes, do, there's a good fellow," cried Glyn, catching the other by the arm.

"Well, he said he should be proud to see me grow up such a boy as you are, and that my father wished me to take you for an example, for he wanted me to become thoroughly English—oh, and a lot more like that."

Glyn Severn was silent, and soon after, as the two boys turned, they saw a group of their schoolfellows coming down the field laden with bats and stumps, while one carried a couple of iron-shod stakes round which was rolled a stout piece of netting.

"Here," said Glyn suddenly, "let's go round the other side of the field. Old Slegge's along with them, and he'll be getting up a quarrel again. I don't want to fight; but if he keeps on aggravating like he did this morning I suppose I shall have to."

"But if we go now," said Singh, "it will look as if we are frightened. We seemed to run away before, only you made me come."

"Oh, it doesn't matter what seems," cried Severn irritably. "We know we are not frightened, and that's enough. Come on."

The two boys began to move slowly away; but they had not gone far before Slegge shouted after them, "Hi, you, sirs! I want you to come and field."

"Then want will be your master," said Severn between his teeth.— "Come on, Singh. Don't look round. Let's pretend we can't hear."

They walked steadily on for a few paces, Severn making-believe to be talking earnestly to his companion, when:

"Do you hear, there, you, sirs? Come here directly. I want you to field!"

"I dare say you do; cheeky great bully!" said Glyn softly. "I shan't come and field for you. The Doctor did not give us a holiday to-day to come and be your slaves."

"Hi, there! Are you coming, or am I to come and fetch you?" shouted Slegge, without any effect, and the big lad turned to Burney and gave him an order. The next minute the boy, armed with a stump, came running at full speed across the grass, shouting to the two companions to stop, but without their paying the slightest heed or increasing their pace.

The consequence was that the lad soon overtook them, to cry, rather out of breath, "Did you hear the captain call to you to come and field?"

Singh glanced at Glyn, who gave him a sharp look as he replied, "Yes, I heard him quite plainly."

The messenger stared with open eyes and mouth, as if it was beyond his comprehension.

"Then, why don't you come?" he cried.

"Because we are going up to the house," replied Glyn coolly, "to our dormitory."

"That you are not," cried Burney. "The rules say that the fellows are not to go up to their rooms between hours, and you have been here long enough to know that. Now then, no nonsense. Here, you, Singh, you've got to come and field while old Slegge practises batting, and Tompkins has got to bowl."

As the boy spoke in an unpleasant dictatorial way he made a thrust at Singh with the pointed stump he held; but quick as thought and before it was driven home, this third-part of a wicket was wrenched from his hand by Severn and sent flying through the air.

"How dare you!" shouted Burney, and he made a rush at Glyn to collar him and make him prisoner; but before he could reach the offending lad a foot was thrust out by Singh, over which he tripped and fell sprawling upon his face.

"Oh!" he shouted, half-beside himself with rage; and, scrambling up, he made a rush with clenched fists at the two boys, who now stood perfectly still awaiting his onslaught.

It was a thoroughly angry charge, but not a charge home; for Burney stopped some three or four yards short of the distance, with his rage evaporating fast and beginning to feel quite discreet.

For quite a minute the opponents stood gazing fiercely, and then what had threatened to become a cuffing encounter became verbal.

"Look here," cried Burney, "you two will get it for this. What am I to say to the captain?"

"Tell him to bowl for himself," said Singh sharply.

"Here! Hi! Burney, bring 'em along!" came from across the field and from between Slegge's hands. "Tell these beggars they had better not keep me waiting much longer!"

"All right!" shouted back Burney; and then to the two lads, "There, you hear. Come on at once, and as you are new chaps I won't tell on you. You had better come, or he'll pay you out by keeping you on bowling so that you can't go and see the show."

"Yes," said Glyn quietly. "Go back and tell him what Singh said."

"What!" cried Burney, staring with wonder. "Tell the captain he's to bowl for himself?"

"Yes," said Glyn coolly, "as long as he likes.—Come along, Singh;" and, throwing his arm over his Indian companion's shoulder, the two lads fell into military step and marched slowly towards the Doctor's mansion-like house.

"I am afraid it means a fight, Singh," said Glyn quietly. "Well, I dare say we can get over it. I am not going to knuckle down to that fellow. Are you?"

"Am I?" cried the boy, flashing a fierce look at his English companion. "What do you think?"

Glyn laughed softly and merrily.

"Shall I tell you?" he said.

"Yes, of course," cried the Indian boy hotly.

"Well, I think you will."

"What!"

"When you can't lift hand or foot, and your eyes are closing up so as you can hardly see."

"And I won't give up then!" cried the boy passionately.

"Well, don't get into a wax about it, old chap," said Glyn in a dry, slow way. "I don't suppose you'll have to, for the big chuckle-headed bully will have to lick me first, and I dare say I can manage to tire him so that you can easily lick him in turn."

"You are not going to fight him," cried Singh hotly.

"Yes, I am."

"You are not. He insulted my dead father. A mahout indeed!"

"So he did mine," said Glyn. "A shabby half-pay military officer indeed! I'll make *him* look shabby before I have done."

"Now, look here," cried Singh, "don't be a beast, Glynny, and make me more angry than I am. I am bad enough as it is."

"So am I, so don't you get putting on the Indian tyrant. Recollect you are in England now. This is my job, and I know if father were here he'd say I was to have the first go in. He's such a big fellow that I believe he'll lick me easily. But, as I said before, I shall pretty well tire him out, and then you being the reserve, he'll come at you, and then he'll find out his mistake. And I say, Singhy, old chap, I do hope that my eyes won't be so closed that I can't see. Now then, come up to our room. It's a holiday, and the rules won't count to-day. Come on, and we'll talk it over."

"But—" began Singh.

"Now, don't be obstinate. You promised father you'd try and give way to me over English matters. Now, didn't you?"

"Well," said the lad hesitatingly, "I suppose I did."

"Come on, then. You see war's begun, and we have got to settle our plan of campaign."

The young Maharajah nodded his head and smiled.

"Yes," he said, "come up to our room. We ought to dress, oughtn't we, to see the procession? I say, I don't know how it is, I always like fighting against any one who tries to bully. I am not sorry that war has begun."

"Neither am I," said the English lad quietly, "for things have been very unpleasant ever since we came here, and when we've got this over perhaps we shall be at peace."

Chapter Three
The Prince's Regalia

The bedroom shared by Glyn Severn and Singh was one of a series, small and particularly comfortable, in the new annexe the Doctor had built expressly for lecture-room and dormitories when his establishment began to increase.

The comfortably furnished room just sufficed for two narrow beds and the customary furniture; and as soon as the two lads had entered, Singh hurried to his chest of drawers, unlocked one, took out a second bunch of keys to that he carried in his pocket, and was then crossing to a sea-going portmanteau standing in one corner, when Glyn, who was looking very thoughtful and abstracted, followed, and as Singh knelt down and threw open the travelling-case, laid his hand upon the lad's shoulder. "What are you going to do?" he said shortly. "Only look out two or three things that there's not room for in the drawer."

"What for?"

"Why, to dress for the procession."

"Stuff and nonsense! You are quite right as you are," cried Glyn half-mockingly. "You must learn to remember that you are in England, where nobody dresses up except soldiers. Why, what were you going to do?"

"I was going to put on a white suit and belt."

"Nonsense!" cried Glyn. "This isn't India, but Devonshire. Why, if you were to come down dressed like that the boys would all laugh at you, and the crowd out in the road shout and cheer."

"Well, of course," said Singh; "they'd see I was a prince."

"Oh, what a rum fellow you are!" cried Glyn, gripping his companion's shoulders and laughingly shaking him to and fro. "I thought that I had made you understand that now we are over here you were to dress just the same as an English boy. Why, don't you know that when we had a king in England he used to dress just like any ordinary gentleman, only sometimes he would wear a star on his breast."

"Oh, but surely," began Singh, in a disappointed tone, "he must have—"

"Yes, yes, yes; sometimes," cried Glyn. "I know what you mean. On state occasions, or when he went to review troops, he would wear grand robes or a field-marshal's uniform."

"But didn't he wear his crown?"

"No," cried Glyn, bursting out laughing. "That's only put on for a little while when he's made king."

"What does he do with it, then, at other times?"

"Nothing," cried Glyn merrily. "It's kept shut up in a glass case at the Tower, for people to go and see."

"England seems a queer place," said Singh quietly.

"Very," cried Glyn drily. "You never want those Indian clothes, and you ought to have done as I told you—left them behind."

"But the Colonel didn't say so," replied the boy warmly. "He said that some day he might take me with him to Court. It was when I asked him for the emeralds."

"What do you mean—the belt?" said Glyn quickly.

"Yes."

"You never told me that you had got them."

"No; the Colonel said that I was not to make a fuss about them nor show them to people, but keep them locked up in the case. Here they are," cried the boy; and, thrusting down one hand, he drew from beneath some folded garments a small flat scarlet morocco case, which he opened by pressing a spring, and drew out from where it lay neatly doubled, a gold-embroidered waistbelt of some soft yellow leather, whose fastening was formed of a gold clasp covered by a large flat emerald, two others of similar shape being arranged so that when the belt was fastened round the waist they lay on either side. It was a magnificent piece of ornamentation, but barbaric, and such as would be worn by an Indian prince.

Apparently it was of great value, for the largest glittering green stone was fully two inches in length and an inch and a half wide, the others being about half the size, and all three engraved with lines of large Arabic characters, so that either stone could have been utilised as a gigantic seal.

"I don't see why one shouldn't wear a thing like this," said Singh. "My father always used to wear it out at home wherever he went, even when he wore nothing else but a long white muslin robe. On grand Court days he would be covered with jewels, and his turban was full of diamonds."

"Yes," said Glyn drily and with a half-contemptuous smile upon his lips; "but that was in India, where all the rajahs and princes wear such things."

"Well," said the boy proudly, "I am still a maharajah, even if I have come to England to be educated; so why shouldn't I put on a belt like this on a grand day if I like?"

Glyn took the brilliant belt from his companion's hand and held it towards the light, inspecting curiously the beautiful gems, which were of a lustrous green marked with flaws.

"Ah," he said, "it looks nice, and is worth a lot of money I suppose."

"Of course," said the young Indian; and he added haughtily, "I shouldn't wear it if it were not."

"Well, you can't wear it," said Glyn, passing the embroidered leather through his hands and turning it over in the bright sunlight which came through the window.

"But why?" cried Singh, frowning slightly at having his will challenged.

"Well," said Glyn, "first of all, as I told you, because the boys would laugh at you."

"They dare not," cried the boy proudly.

"What!" cried Glyn laughing. "Why, English boys dare do anything. What did Slegge say this morning?"

"Slegge is what you call a blackguard," cried Singh angrily.

"Well, he isn't nice certainly," said Glyn; "but he'd begin at you again directly, and chaff, and say that you ought to ride on the elephant."

"Well," said the boy, "and that would be my place if there were a howdah. Of course I shouldn't ride on the great brute's neck."

"Yes, in India; but can't you recollect that you are still in England?"

"Of course I can," cried the boy, with flashing eyes; "but I can't forget that I am a prince."

"Now, look here," said Glyn, "what did dad say to you when the Doctor left us with him in the drawing-room? I mean before father went away. Have you forgotten?"

"Of course not. He said, 'Never mind about being a prince. Be content with the rank of an English gentleman till you go back to your own country.' And that's what I am going to do."

"Well done," cried Glyn merrily. "Then, now, put this thing away; you don't want it. But stop a moment. I never had a close look at it before."

"No; the Colonel told me to keep it locked up and not to go showing it about so as to tempt some *budmash* to steal it."

"Well, we haven't got any *budmashes* in England," said Glyn merrily, as he began to inspect the emeralds again and took out his handkerchief to rub off a finger-mark or two and make the gems send off scintillations of sunlight which formed jack-o'-lanterns on the ceiling. "But we have plenty of blackguards who would like to get a chance to carry it off."

"What, among our schoolfellows?" cried Singh hastily.

"Bah! No! There, put it away. But I should like to know what that writing means."

"It's out of the Koran," said the boy as he took the jewelled belt back reverently and held it up to the light in turn. "It's very, very old, and means greatness to my family. It is a holy relic, and the Maharajahs of Dour have worn that in turn for hundreds of years."

"Well, you put it away," said Glyn; "and I wouldn't show it to anybody again, nor yet talk about it. I wonder the dad let you have it."

"Why?" said Singh proudly. "It is mine."

"Yes, of course; but it is not suited for a boy like you."

"A boy like me!" cried Singh half—angrily. "Why, I am as old as you."

"Well, I know that; but my father doesn't give me emeralds and diamonds to take with me to school. He could, though, if he liked, for he's got all those beautiful Indian jewels the Maharajah gave him."

"Yes," said Singh, "and that diamond—hilted tulwar."

"Yes, that's a grand sword," cried Glyn, with his eyes sparkling. "I should like to have that."

Singh laughed mockingly.

"Why, you are as bad as I am," he cried.

"That I am not! Why, if I had it, do you think I should buckle it on to go and see a country wild-beast show?"

"Well, no, I don't suppose you would," said Singh quietly, as he gravely replaced the emeralds in their receptacle and curled the belt around them before shutting down the velvet-lined and quilted cover with a loud snap. "But some day, when we have both grown older, and we are back in India—I mean when I am at home in state and you are one of my officers—you will have to get the Colonel to let you wear it then."

"Ah," said Glyn, slowly and thoughtfully, "some day; but that's a long time off. I suppose I shall be a soldier like the dad is, and in your army."

"Why, of course," cried Singh. "You will be my greatest general, just the same as your father was when mine was alive. He was always a great general there, though he was only colonel in the Company's army. There, I suppose you are right. I like to look at that belt, but I won't show it about; but I say, Glyn, I shall be glad when we get older and have both begun learning to be—no, what do you call it?—not learning—I mean, being taught to be soldiers."

"Training," said Glyn.

"Yes, training—that's it; and we shall go together to that place where your father was, not far from London. You know—the place he used to talk to us about, where he was trained before he came out to India."

"Addiscombe," said Glyn quietly, as he stood watching his companion thrust the case back into the bottom of the portmanteau and rearrange the garments he had moved, while his hand lingered for a few moments about a soft white robe, which he covered over with a sigh before closing the lid and turning the key of the great leather case.

"Yes," he said, "Addiscombe. What stories he used to tell us about the young officers there! What did he call them? I forget."

"Cadets," said Glyn thoughtfully.

"That's it. I wish I didn't forget so many of those English words; but," continued the boy, "I liked it best when he told us about the battles out at home, when all the chiefs around were fighting against my father the Maharajah, so as to slay him and divide his possessions. You know, my father has talked about it to me as well—how he was so nearly beaten and weakened, and so many of his bravest officers killed, that it made him apply to the great Company for help, and they sent your father. Oh, what a brave man he was!"

"Who said that?" cried Glyn, flushing up.

"My father the Maharajah. He said so to me many times, and that he was his best and truest friend. Oh yes, I used to like to hear about it all, and he used to tell me that the Colonel would always be my truest friend as well, and that I was to love him and obey him, and always believe that what he told me to do was right. And I always do."

"Of course you do," said Glyn flushing. "Yes, Singh, he is some one to be proud of, isn't he? But I am like you; I don't much like coming to this school, though the Doctor is very nice and kind to us both."

"Yes, I like him better than the masters," said Singh; "but I don't like the boys, and I don't think they like me."

"Oh, wait a bit," said Glyn. "It's because everything seems so different to being in India; but, as father says, there is such a lot one ought to learn, and we shall get used to it by-and-by; only, I say, you know what the dad said?"

"You mean about trying to be an English gentle man and leaving the maharajah till I get back home?"

"Yes, that's it," cried Glyn eagerly.

"Yes; but it's hard work, for everything is so different here, and the boys are not like you."

"Oh yes, they are," cried Glyn merrily; "just the same. Here, come on; let's go down and see whether Wrench has put up those forms by the wall. We want to see the show."

"Yes," cried Singh. "It puts one in mind of Dour again, and I have been thinking that we don't get on with the other boys through me."

"What do you mean with your 'through me'?" said Glyn.

"Well, I don't quite know. It's because I am an Indian, I suppose; and when they talk to me as they do, and bully me, as you call it, it makes my heart feel hot and as if I should like to do something strange. But I am going to try. And look here, Glyn," said the lad very seriously, "I shall begin at once."

"Begin what?"

"Trying to make them like me. I shall make friends with that big fellow Slegge, and bear it all, and if he goes on again like he did this morning I have quite made up my mind I won't fight."

"Oh," said Glyn drily. "Well, come on down the grounds now. We shall see."

Chapter Four
The Elephant cries "Phoomp!"

Plymborough was out in street and road excepting those who lived on the line of route and had windows that looked down upon the coming procession, which was to be timed to reach the town, after a long march from Duncombe, at noon precisely.

Small things please country people, and there was not much work being done that day. It was an excuse for a holiday, as eagerly seized upon by the townsfolk, old and young, as by the young gentlemen of Dr Bewley's establishment.

But that was not all. The villages near Plymborough were many, and the people for miles round flocked into the place to see the procession and stop afterwards about the market-place to visit the exhibition of beasts and listen to the band.

The day was gloriously fine, and all promised a famous harvest of sixpences for the great Ramball himself, a man as punctual in his appointments as he was in the feeding of his beasts, this being carried out regularly at certain times, but, unfortunately for the animals, in uncertain quantities dependent upon the supplies.

Dr Bewley's boys took their places along the forms quite an hour before noon, this punctuality having something to do with getting the best places, as they put it, though—as the forms were in a line under the brick wall, which was low enough with their help for the shortest boy to see over, and the procession would pass close beneath—it was hard to see any difference in the positions, or why the form reserved for the masters was any better than that at the extreme end.

But certainly the masters' form was considered the best from the fact that it stood first, while the nearest end of the next form was taken up in spite of his declaration by Slegge, whose greatest admirers got as close to him as they could or as he would allow.

"Let's go and stand with them," said Singh, as they crossed over to the wall.

"Oh, I don't know," replied his companion. "I vote we go right to the other end along with the juniors."

"Very well," said Singh with a laugh; "but they'll say it's because we're afraid."

"Yes," replied Glyn coolly; "but let them. I don't think we are." And leading the way, he made for the last form, which they had all to themselves, and stood there quietly looking down at the crowd below and along the Duncombe road, which was pretty well lined with people standing about or seated in cart or chaise waiting for the coming sight.

The masters were not in such a hurry, and they remained in the house talking together, so that they were not present to see the skylarking and listen to the banter going on, a good deal of which was set going by Slegge, who was in a high state of glee, and scattered a great deal of chaff, to the great delight of his parasites, who eagerly conveyed insulting messages from their chief to the two new pupils at the other end of the line—at least, they bore those that were not too offensive; others that seemed likely to produce some form of resentment from the lads they attacked were sent on by the youngest boys.

All this palled after a time, and a certain amount of whispering beginning close at hand, Slegge asked sharply what the whisperers were talking about, when silence ensued, no one present daring to repeat the remark which Burney had made, which was to the effect that old Slegge had said that he was not going to stoop to see the miserable procession, but all the same he had taken the best place.

The consequence was that Slegge guessed pretty correctly that something was being whispered dealing with him, and he was just growing fiercely insistent and threatening what he would do if somebody did not confess, when the masters came upon the scene and took their places; while directly after there was a loud cheer, for from out of the distance came the faintly heard throbbing of a drum.

Everything else was now forgotten. Eyes and ears were strained, and minutes elapsed before the pulsations caused by the beating of two balls upon the tightly stretched skin began to grow nearer, and Mr Rampson commenced a discussion to fill up the time by throwing quotations from the old Roman authors at his fellow-tutors and the older boys.

It was a favourable moment for calling a drum a tympanum and giving descriptions of the different forms, curves, and lengths of the various trumpets used by the Roman soldiery in their warlike processions, all of which Slegge voted bosh, and intimated his opinion to the next boy that old

Rampson had better go to the other end of the forms and pour it out on the two new fellows.

At last, though, the pulsations of the well-belaboured drum came nearer and were mingled with the mournfully plaintive notes of the wind instruments being blown by the band, the performers seated in a tall triumphal car decorated in scarlet and gold, and ornamented by a gilt carving meant to represent the giant anaconda of South America embracing and crushing the twenty bandsmen of Ramball's show, gentlemen who, by the way, wore a richly worsted-embroidered uniform of scarlet baize, the braid being yellow ochre of the deepest dye.

The carving round the car was either a two-headed anaconda or a combination of two performing an evolution in twists about the musicians, tying them up apparently, from the spectators' point of view, in horrible knots and giving them a terrible aspect of suffering, the apparent pressure of the serpents' folds causing their faces and cheeks to swell out in an appalling way, and their eyes to start from their sockets, while their sufferings seemed to produce wails, shrieks, and cries for help or mercy, mingled with groans, as the men worked hard with a perfect battery of old-fashioned key-bugles, supported by ophicleide and bassoon.

Most painful were the shrieking, strident cries produced by a pair of clarinets, and altogether there came from out of the knots of the serpents a hideous chaos of sound, drawn onward by a team of six horses, and received with wild cheers by the crowd, for it was really the new triumphal march freshly down from town, but in which the bandsmen were not perfect as regarded their parts.

"Is that music or the roarings and cries of some of the beasts?" whispered Singh.

There was a burst of laughter from the boys who heard the native remark, which made Singh turn round upon them angrily; but at a touch from Glyn he smiled good-humouredly, and then laughed aloud.

"Well, it was a stupid thing to say," he cried. "Of course it's the music."

"I say, Singh," burst in Glyn, and he nodded towards the huge drum that was suspended at the back in the highest part of the car, hung, as it were, between the curling tails of the two gilt serpents. "I say," he cried, "wouldn't that astonish the people at Dour? What would they say to that for a tom-tom?"

"Ah!" cried Singh, "I'll buy one like that, and take it back with us when we go home."

"No, I say, don't," cried Glyn. "They make noise enough there as it is."

"Noise!" echoed Singh. "They don't call that noise."

As they were speaking the great six-horse car rumbled slowly by, with the drummer beating hard and the buglers and trombonists blowing their best; while the crowd, taking up the cheer started by the boys, sent it echoing along towards the main street, where, coming slowly along, and stretching as far as eye could reach, there was a long line of caravans, all exceedingly plain and of a uniform yellow colour, with the names of their contents painted on them in black letters.

The place of honour was given to the king of beasts, for the first of the cars bore the word "Lions;" but probably his majesty was asleep, for not so much as a muttering purr on a large scale came from the narrow grating at the top.

Tigers followed; the next car held leopards, each carriage being of the same uniform level, with the black letters; and, coming slowly after them, were about two score, kept a good distance apart so as to lengthen the line as much as possible.

But at first there was nothing else to see, and Singh turned impatiently to his companion, and said: "When does the procession begin?"

"Why, that's the procession," said a small boy close to him, taking the answer upon himself. "The wild beasts are inside. Didn't you know?" And then he proceeded to display his own knowledge. "They draw all the vans up in a square," he began excitedly, "out there in the home-field behind the 'King's Arms,' and then they open the sides of the vans, which are like great shutters on hinges at the top and bottom, so that when they are opened one shutter falls down and covers the wheels, and the other is pulled up, leaving the side all iron bars. Don't you see? Then, instead of being vans, they are turned into dens and cages."

"Is that so?" said Singh quietly.

"Oh, I suppose so," replied Glyn. "I have never seen one of these affairs; but it seems a very reasonable way for building up a place all dens and cages in very short time."

"Oh, look here!" cried another of the boys. "Here's a game! Look at that nigger!"

Singh started as if he had been stung, and was about to turn furiously upon the boy, under the impression that he was the nigger in question; but at the same moment he caught sight of a full-blooded, woolly-headed West Coast African leading a very large camel by a rope, the great ungainly beast mincing and blinking as it gently put down, one after the other, its soft, spongy feet, which seemed to spread out on the gravelled road, while their high-shouldered owner kept on turning its bird-like head from side to side, muttering and whining discontentedly, as if objecting to be seen by such an elongated crowd, and murmuring against being made the one visible object of the show.

The camel was not an attractive creature, for, in addition to its natural peculiarities of shape, it was the time of year for shedding its long hairy coat, and this was hanging in ragged ungainly locks and flakes all along its flanks and about its loping, unhealthy-looking hump.

This was something to look at, and the excited boys shouted, cheered, and gave forth remark after remark such as must have been painful to the dignity of the melancholy-looking beast, which kept on turning its half-closed, plaintive-looking eyes at the noisy groups, wincing and seeming to protest against the unkindly and insulting remarks.

"Oh, I say, isn't he a beauty?" cried one.

"Yes; it's just like a four-legged bird," shouted another.

"That's right. They've caught Sindbad's roc and clipped his wings."

"Cut them right off," said Glyn laughingly, joining in the mirth. "Poor fellow, look how he's moulting!"

There was a burst of laughter at this, and as it ceased another boy shouted:

"Ought its hump to wobble like that, and hang over all on one side?"

"That isn't its hump," cried Burney; "that's its cistern in which it carries its drinking-water. Don't you know they can go for days without wanting any more? Can't you see it's empty now?"

"Poor camel!" said one of the boys.

"Yes, poor, and no mistake! Why, it's all in rags," cried Burney, and the unhappy-looking beast went mincing on, to be followed by another van labelled "Birds." Then came one labelled ominously and in very large letters, "Serpents;" those next in succession containing antelopes, nylghaus, crocodiles, eagles, rhinoceroses, zebras, monkeys, orang-outangs, chimpanzees, rib-nosed baboons, and so on, and so on, cage after cage, den after den, a procession of so many painted yellow vans drawn by very unsatisfactory-looking horses, till, as the last one came into sight far on the right, it was observed by the boys as they stood leaning their elbows on the wall that there was something special being kept for the finale, for the crowd was closing in behind and coming on surrounding this last van.

"Oh, I shall be so glad when it's all over," said Singh. "I would have said let's go away ever so long ago, only the Doctor might think it disagreeable after he had given us leave to see."

"Yes, it would have looked bad," replied Glyn. "It seems to me such a shame," he continued, "getting us all here to see a procession of wild beasts, and all we have seen is a camel."

"But don't you see—" began Singh.

"Of course; I said so. I have seen a camel. But if the man let the people see all his wild beasts they wouldn't pay to go into his show."

"Oh," cried Singh, "that's it. I never thought of that. Of course. But what are the people all crowding up for behind that last van?"

"Because it's the end," said the small boy who had spoken before.

"No; but there's something they can see, for they are all pressing close up, and the boys are stooping down to look underneath."

"Yes, and there's a man with a whip trying to keep them back."

That was all plain enough to view as the great van, drawn by four stout cart-horses, came nearer, with the whip-armed carter who walked by their side varying his position to cross round by the back, making-believe to use his whip and keep the boys from getting too close.

"Well, they can see something," said Glyn, as the great vehicle came nearly abreast; and as it did the lad gripped his companion by the shoulder.

"Look, look!" he cried. "My word, it is queer!"

"What is?" said Singh excitedly.

"Two pairs of giants' trousers walking underneath the van. There, can't you see? Oh, isn't it comic. And they don't fit."

"Nonsense," cried Singh excitedly. "It's a big elephant underneath there, and he's so heavy he has broken through the bottom of the wagon."

It certainly gave a stranger that impression; but the young Indian was not right. It was only the showman's ingenious device to convey his huge attraction from town to town unseen save just so much as would whet the spectator's curiosity and make him wish to see more.

"Dear me," said a rich, unctuous voice just behind the lads; and the boys started round at the familiar tones, to see the benignant-looking Doctor blinking through his gold-rimmed spectacles and commenting upon the spectacle for the benefit of his younger pupils. "You see, my dear lads," he began, "a monstrous animal like that must weigh tons, and would be too heavy for the horses to—"

The Doctor's words were drowned by the roar of laughter that arose from behind the wall, for Glyn's comment had been taken up quickly, and ran from end to end of the line, with the result that, like a chorus dominating their laughter, the boys joined in one insane shout of:

"Trousers! trousers!"

The next moment it was over the wall and running through the crowd, who caught it up and began to yell out the name of the familiar object of attire, staid elderly men holding their sides and laughing, boys shrieking with delight and pointing under the van at the two pairs of huge pillar-like legs with the loose skin hanging about them like some specimen of giant frieze, till, as the van moved on, the driver grew frantic and began to smack his whip; while, to add to the tumult, there arose from within a peculiar hoarse trumpeting roar that can only be put into print by the words: *Phoomp! phoomp! phoomp!*

There was a crash, and the next moment the monstrous beast stood panting and trumpeting by the side of the ruins.

"Ha!" cried Singh excitedly, and he gripped at Glyn's arm so sharply that he made him wince. "Hark at him! Hark at him!" he whispered hoarsely in the boy's ear. "The jungle! the jungle! Why, it must be a big bull elephant. Oh, we must go and see him to-night!"

Singh saw him the next minute; for, startled by the terrific roar behind them, and probably knowing well the power of the utterer, the four draught horses began to suffer from panic. One began to rear and plunge, and before the driver, who was close to the hind wheels, could force his way through the crowd and seize its rein, it made a dash for the sidewalk farthest from the Doctor's wall. Like gregarious beasts, its companions went with it; the front of the van was wrenched round and the off fore-wheel ascended the path, while at the same moment, as the furious trumpeting continued, there was a crash, one side of the van was heaved up as if by an internal earthquake, and the next moment, amidst the noise of splintering wood, the plunging of horses, and the elephant's deafening roar, the great yellow vehicle lay over on its side, and the monstrous beast, fully ten feet high, stood panting and trumpeting with uplifted trunk by the side of the ruins, glaring round as if seeking which enemy to charge.

Chapter Five
An Al-Fresco Lunch

There were plenty of those whom the great beast looked upon as foes lying prostrate, for with yells of dismay the crowd dashed off helter-skelter, trampling each other down in their efforts to escape, clearing the way as rapidly as they could; but the only object that offered itself for attack was one of the big van horses, which had swung round in the alarm, to stand right in the elephant's way.

And now, flapping its ears, giving its miserable little tail a twist in the air, and uttering a pig-like squeak, the elephant charged, catching the horse in the ribs and knocking it over on to its side; and then, without stopping to trample upon the poor animal, the monster indulged in a peculiar caper resembling a triumphant war-dance, a movement which but for the suggestion of danger would have been comical in the extreme. Then, stopping short as if to make a survey of its position with its piercing eyes, the elephant looked at the ruined van, then at the villa residences opposite the Doctor's great mansion, then at the blank wall (which seemed to puzzle it, with what looked like a palisade of boys' heads), and next up the road.

At last, turning sharply round to point with uplifted trunk down the road in the direction from which it had come, it went off in its curious shuffling shamble as if in pursuit of the flying crowd; while, now in a state of the greatest excitement, about a score of the wild-beast van-drivers, headed by the man who had the elephant in charge, cracking his whip and shouting for it to come back, started in pursuit.

The Doctor's pupils, evidently feeling that they were safe behind the wall, for the elephant displayed no intention of using his trunk to pick their heads as if they were gigantic cherries, all stood fast, most probably too much startled to stir; and having an excellent view of this unexpected episode in the procession, had the satisfaction of seeing the principal actor trotting away the whole length of the playground wall, his hind-quarters looking more than ever like an enormous pair of ill-made, ill-fitting trousers.

"Will he catch them—overtake any of them?" cried Glyn, as the elephant passed the spot where he and Singh were watching the proceedings, the latter with his dark eyes glittering and nostrils quivering, as the whole business brought back something he had once seen in his native state.

But as he spoke the loud shouting of the frightened crowd tearing away down the road suddenly ceased, as those nearest became conscious of the fact that their pursuit by the great beast had ceased.

Soon after passing the end of the Doctor's wall, the elephant, now fully at liberty, found itself by the tall, well-clipped mingled hawthorn-and-privet hedge that enclosed the lawn-like, verdant cricket-field, at the far side of which there was a grand row of old elms which brought back to the escaped animal memories of Indian forests and pendant boughs covered with fresh green leaves that could be torn down and eaten; and, stopping short in the rapid pace which it had pursued, swinging its massive head from side to side, it once more turned itself "half-right," as if upon a pivot, stared at the tall green hedge for a few moments, and then, curling its trunk right backwards over its neck, it uttered another trumpeting note which was no longer angry, but sounded cracked and partook of the nature of a squeak. Then it did not charge the hedge, but just walked through it; and as soon as its great circular feet began to feel the soft, yielding grass into which they sank, for the ground was moist, the great brute began to twitch its tail in the most absurd way, squeak with delight, and indulge in the most clumsily ridiculous gambol ever executed by monster ten feet high.

It was for all the world such a dance, magnified, as a fat, chubby little Shetland pony would display when, freed from bit, bridle, or halter, it was turned out to grass. And now, as the elephant began careering right across the cricket-field in the direction of the row of elms, there was a shout of dismay from the row occupying the forms; and, headed by Mr Morris, a retreat was made to a place of safety, that being represented by the doors opening on to the playground—Mr Morris, the mathematical master, charged as he was with his long study of Euclid, evidently considering it to be his duty for the benefit of his pupils to describe a straight line.

But he was soon distanced by the boys, whose wind was much better. The last, as if he considered it his duty to protect the rear, was the Doctor himself, looking exceedingly red in the face and breathing very hard. But, truth to tell, he—not being either a general, admiral, or even captain of a vessel of war—was not influenced by any brave intention to leave the field or vessel only after the last of his men. The Doctor's proceedings were caused by inability to keep up.

But he was not the last. The sight of an elephant cantering across country, or in its customary shuffling gait, was nothing new to Singh and Glyn. Experience gained in more than one hunt, and in a land where these mammoth-like creatures are beasts of burden, as well as perhaps a feeling that if they did happen to be pursued youth and activity would enable them to get out of the brute's way, caused the two boys to stand fast alone upon the last form, thoroughly enjoying the acts of the performer, and wondering what he would do next.

"Oh, Glyn," cried Singh, clapping his hands as hard as he could, "and I was grumbling! Why, this is a procession! I haven't seen anything like this since we left home."

"No," panted Glyn, who was as excited as his companion. "Why, it's like old Rajah Jamjar, as we used to call him, on the rampage. Here come the men," he continued. — "Hi! I say, the Doctor won't like you breaking through his hedge," he shouted, though his words were not heard. — "He's broken a way for them, though."

"Here," shouted Singh, with his hands to his mouth, "you mustn't go after that elephant with whips. He's raging, and if you go near he'll turn upon you perhaps, and kill you."

But the men could not hear his words, and, each with his big carter's whip, they followed slowly across the field, unheeded by the elephant, and evidently without the slightest intention of overtaking the fugitive.

The great brute turned neither to the right nor left, but stopped as soon as he reached the row of elms, beyond which were the garden and grounds of the most important resident in Plymborough, a very wealthy retired merchant, who took great pride in his estate, and whose orchard annually displayed a vast abundance of red and gold temptations of the kind beloved by boys in other counties as well as sunny Devon.

It was pleasant and shady beneath the elms, and a faintly heard grunt of satisfaction came to the two boys' ears as they saw the great fugitive reach up, twist its indiarubber-like trunk, and gather together a bunch of twigs, which it snapped off, and then, reversing its elastic organ, stood tucking them into its peculiarly moist mouth.

"Oh, he's quiet and tame enough," said Glyn.

"No, he isn't," cried Singh; "he's in a fury."

"But it's a regular tame one," said Glyn. "I dare say they might walk up and drive it in now. I'll go and help them if you will."

"Well," said Singh, slowly and thoughtfully, "I don't know. It's a strange elephant; he's been scared, and I saw as he passed that he was in a temper; but I dare say we know as much about elephants as they do."

"Yes, let's go."

But as they were speaking, and the elephant stood refreshing itself with another bunch of green leaves, it appeared to catch sight of the group of drivers, who, whip-armed, had now stopped together to consult in the middle of the field, where they were being joined by a fat, chuffy-looking little man, who was hurrying to them, hat in one hand, yellow silk pocket-handkerchief in the other, with which he kept on dabbing his very smooth and shiny white bald head.

The elephant was evidently watching, and had recognised this white shiny head, for he raised his trunk and let fall the twigs, blew a defiant blast upon his natural trumpet, and, wheeling round once more, did not charge, but made a crashing sound as he walked right through the park-palings which divided the two estates, where beneath the trees a green hedge would not grow.

As the elephant disappeared in the next field, only a glimpse being obtained of it through the one panel of the split oak fence, every one seemed to recover his departed courage. The men, now joined by the bald-headed personage, who was really the proprietor of the great show, began to follow the fugitive to the boundary of the Doctor's grounds.

The two boys sprang off the form and ran to join them, while away to the right, bodies began to appear from the Doctor's premises where heads only had been seen; and chief amongst these was Mr Morris, the mathematical master, who, influenced by his conscience, and reminded of the fact that he had gone on drawing that line very straight till he reached the shelter of the house, an act which he felt must have rather lowered his reputation for bravery amongst the boys, now came out a few yards into the playground; and, as the boys began to gather round him, he moved on again a little way, making a point of keeping himself nearest to the danger, if any danger there were, but not going so far as to preclude an easy retreat.

Now, in naval law, during an action there is a tradition that the safest place for a sailor, and where he is least likely to be hit, is the hole through which a cannon-ball or shell has crashed into the ship. Possibly, being a mathematician, Mr Morris may have calculated the possibilities against the elephant that had marched through that piece of fence coming back through it again. And so it was that as the Doctor's grounds were clear, the enemy having departed, he followed farther and farther out into the cricket-field, and then headed a cluster of the first-form boys who, unknown to the Doctor, were making for the broken fence. The fact that they soon saw the elephant's pursuers pass through, and with them the bald-headed man, with their fellow-pupils Glyn and Singh on each side leading, had doubtless something to do with the forward movement.

Slegge, too, was the biggest and loudest there. He was looking very white, almost as white as Ramball's bald head, but he said it was all a "jolly lark;" and then for want of something else to say to express how he was enjoying himself, he made the same remark again, and then laughed aloud. But it was the same sort of laugh as would be uttered by the victim of a practical joke who has suddenly sat down upon a tin-tack or a pin.

Mr Morris, too, grew braver and braver, and he smiled a ghastly smile which rather distorted his features as he addressed his pupils.

"Come along, boys," he said. "This is a holiday indeed. We are going to search for the unknown quantity. An elephant hunt in the Doctor's grounds! It is quite a novelty."

"But it isn't in the Doctor's grounds now, sir," said Burney.

This was meant to be facetious; but it turned Mr Morris's smile into a glare, and brought down upon the boy's head a rebuke from Slegge.

"Here, don't you be so fast, youngster," cried the latter, with the wisdom of a sage in his stern look. "Just remember whom you are talking to, if you please." Then, to curry favour with the master, "I beg your pardon, Mr Morris, would this be an Indian or an African elephant?"

"Well, Mr Slegge," said the mathematical master, with his ghastly smile coming back, "now if this were a question of a surd in a compound equation I should be happy to tell you; but as soon as the captive is taken again, and the 'lark,' as you call it, is over, I should recommend you to ask Mr Rampson. He'll tell you, and give you some information as well respecting the Carthaginian army and the elephants with their towers that they marched against the Romans. My mathematical studies take up all my brain-power, and I never venture upon another master's ground. By the way, who are those boys that we just saw walk through that fence with the show-people? Trespassers, of course. We don't want any of the town boys here. No violence, mind; but I think you might give them a lesson and turn them out."

"But they were the two new pupils, sir."

"What! Severn and the Prince?"

"Yes, sir," came in chorus.

"Dear me! The Doctor would be very angry if he knew. He strongly objects to his young gentlemen making friends with strangers."

"Yes, sir," said Burney; "and they have gone out of bounds."

"Will you keep your mouth shut?" whispered Slegge; and, dropping a pace behind the master, he clenched and held up one fist very close to Burney's nose as if it were a curiosity that the boy might like to see.

"Ah, well," said Mr Morris, "perhaps they thought that it would be the safest place behind the elephant's keepers. These tamed animals have a great dread of the whip."

All was beautifully calm now out in the field. The grass seemed greener than ever. There was an excited crowd in the main road by the damaged hedge, and quite a cluster of pupils, masters, and servants up by the house; but Morris and his little party were alone, and all seemed so safe that they grew thoroughly brave, and quite nonchalantly edged their way on towards the broken panel which looked temptingly clear.

All was still, and there was no suggestion of danger, while as they slowly went close up there was no sound of voice. It was perfectly evident that the elephant must have been followed far away, and had probably gone right on through the neighbouring grounds and made his way somewhere out at the back.

They were approaching diagonally, and as they came very near to the opening a curious electric kind of feeling such as is called by old women "the creeps," manifested itself in what doctors term the "lumbar regions" of every one's back.

But they were all very brave, and Morris suddenly became conscious of the fact that the boys were all looking at him in a very questioning way, so he could not help feeling that there were drawbacks to being the leader of a party when there is possible danger somewhere ahead, and it is impossible for the sake of one's credit to retreat.

This is especially the case in connection with dogs that are supposed to be mad and have to be driven away, or in haunted rooms, and the walking of ghosts and other vapours of that kind which a puff of the wind of common-sense would always blow away.

Somehow or other, Morris began to talk very loudly to his young companions as he screwed his courage up to the sticking-point, feeling as he did that at all hazards he must go right up to that opening and just look through. And with this intent, followed not quite closely by the boys, he went so near that he had but to take one more step to be able to look through into the next field; in fact, he was in the act of stretching out his hand to lay it upon one of the big oaken splints that hung from its copper nail, when there was a sharp report as if a pistol had been fired just on the other side, and in an instant the whole party were in retreat.

"Ha, ha, ha!" laughed Morris. At least it was supposed to be a laugh; but the sounds were very peculiar, and he looked strangely white as he shouted, "Stop, boys, stop! What are you afraid of? It was only one of those carter fellows who cracked his whip.—Well, my man," he continued, in a husky voice that did not seem like his own, to one of the van-drivers who now appeared in the opening, "have you caught the elephant?"

As the man replied the boys began to collect again from their ignominious flight, and it was observable that they were all laughing at one another in an accusatory manner, each feeling full of contempt for the pusillanimous behaviour of the others, while the looks of Morris might have given the whole party a conscious sting.

But there was the van-driver answering as the boys clustered hurriedly up.

"No, sir, and I've had enough of it," said the man. "It aren't my business. I'm monkeys, I am; and got enough to do to keep they mischievous imps in their cage. I don't hold with elephants; they are too big for me, and I know that chap of old."

"Indeed!" said Morris, eager to cover his last retreat by drawing the man into conversation.

"Yes, sir, he's a treacherous beggar. Pretends to be fond of a man, and gets him up against a wall or the side of a tree, and then plays pussy cat."

"Plays what?" cried Slegge.

"Pussy cat, sir. You know: rubs hisself up again' a man same as a kitten does against your leg. But it aren't the same, because if the pore chap don't dodge him he gets rubbed out like a nought on the slate."

"Dear me! Extraordinary!" said Morris. "But—er—er—where is the fugitive beast now?"

"Ah, you may well call him a fugity beast, sir. I don't quite know what it means; but that's a good name for him, and he desarves it. Oh, he's over yonder now, right in the middle of yon orchard, and nobody durst go near him. Every time any one makes a start he begins to roosh, and then goes back in amongst the trees, and when I come away I never see anything like it in my life. It was bushels then."

"Bushels—bushels, my man?"

"Yes, sir, he was a-picking the apples with that trunk of his, and tucking them in as fast as ever they'd go. A beast! he'll fill hisself before he's done. He won't leave off now he's got the chance, and he'll kill anybody who goes nigh him. You see, the master keeps him pretty short to tame him down and keep him from going on the rampage. It's all a mistake having a thing like that in a show. You take my word for it, sir. If you goes in for a mennar-gerry you take to monkeys. They don't take nothing to keep, for the public feeds them on nuts and buns, and if it warn't for their catching cold and going on the sick-list they'd be profit every ounce."

"Er—thank you, my man," said Morris haughtily; "but I don't think it probable that I shall venture upon a peripatetic zoo—eh, young gentlemen?"

"Oh no, sir!" came in chorus.

"Can we see the huge pachyderm from here?"

"Packing apples, sir? No, no, don't you alter that there, sir. You called him fugity beast just now, and you can't beat that.—No, you can't see him. He's in there among them apple-trees."

"Why, he's got into old Bunton's orchard, sir," cried Slegge, and he stepped forward to the opening. "Yes, you can't see the elephant, sir, but you can see the men all round. I think they are tying him up to a tree, sir."

"Yes, that's likely," said the man grimly. "I dare say they've all got a bit of string in their pockets as will just hold him."

"Er—do you think we could go up a little closer, my man, without the young gentlemen getting into danger?" said Morris, in the full expectation that he would be told it would be dangerous in the extreme.

"Go closer, sir? Yes, of course you can. He won't hurt none of you so long as you don't try to take his apples away. If yer did I shouldn't like to be you."

"Let's go, then, sir," cried Burney eagerly, and the desire seemed to be growing in the other boys' breasts.

"Well, I don't know," said Morris; "that is, if you will promise not to go too close."

"Oh, we won't go too close, sir," cried Slegge warmly, and he looked as if he were speaking the truth.

The result was that the master, trying very hard to carry off his disinclination to go with the remark, "We don't often have such an opportunity as this, boys," led the way across the park-like field of the Doctor's neighbour towards an extensive orchard, in which, nearly hidden by the trees, the escaped monster was having his banquet of apples, and turning a deaf ear, or rather two deaf ears of the largest size, to all orders to come out.

Chapter Six
Glyn and Singh to the Rescue

As the party from the school drew nearer they could hear the occasional crack of a whip and a loud order given in a rather highly pitched tone to the beast, bidding him come out.

Then followed the snapping of twigs and a peculiarly dull grumbling sound as if the elephant were muttering his objections to the orders of his master, the bald-headed man, who still held his hat in one hand, his yellow handkerchief in the other, and dabbed the big white billiard-ball-like expanse as if he felt that it was very warm work.

Then there was a *crunch, crunch, crunch,* as if pippins were being reduced to pulp, and more twigs were heard to snap.

"Let him hear the whip again, Jem," shouted Mr Ramball.

"Oh, he won't come for that, sir," growled the man addressed; but he made the long cart-whip he carried crack loudly three times in obedience to the order; and as the fresh party drew as near to the orchard as they cared to go, after all had given a furtive glance round for a way to escape, the low grumbling muttering grew louder; while as the animal moved right into sight so did those who were watching him, and Slegge and his companions saw Glyn and Singh approach.

There was another movement on the part of the elephant, whose towering form came through the thickly growing orchard trees to one whose burden was of a deep rich-red, and here it stood bowing its head up and down, and slowly shaking it from side to side, while the trunk swung and turned and turned and swung here and there, till its owner had selected the fruit most pleasing to its little pig-like eye, when with serpent-like motion it rose in the air, and the end curled round the selected fruit, which was lowered and tucked out of sight on the instant.

"Now, look here, my lads," cried the proprietor of the menagerie to his men, "I can't have you all standing here gaping like a set of idiots as if you had never seen the brute before. Go in round behind him with your whips and drive him out."

There was a murmur of grumbles from the men, that seemed to be echoed by the elephant, which went on swinging its head up and down as if it were balanced on a spring. But no one stirred.

"Do you hear me?" cried the proprietor, his highly pitched voice growing quite shrill. "Here, I shall have no end of damages to pay for what he's doing. They'll be putting it in the lawyers' hands, and they'll be charging me a shilling for every apple he eats.—Eh! what's that? Not safe?"

"No; he's got one of his nasty fits o' temper on," said the driver of the great van which had come to grief.

"Tchah! Nonsense! You are a coward, Jem."

"Mebbe I am," grumbled the man; "but, coward or no, he knocked me flat over on my back, and once is quite enough for one day."

"Yah!" shouted his master. "You are ready enough to come on Saturday night for your pay; but if I want anything a little extra done, where am I?—Here, give me the whip." And he snatched it from the man's hand and walked towards the great beast, half-hidden among the trees.

"Say, you boys," growled the driver, "if I was you I'd just be ready to run. You've only just got to dodge him. Stop and make sure which way he's going, and then get in among the trees."

"Yes, quick: in amongst the trees," cried Morris, and he set the example.

"Nay," growled the man. "Not yet. Wait and see first which way he means to go."

Morris set the example of running in another direction, followed by his boys and by the voice of the driver.

"Why, that's worse," he cried. "That's about the way he'd go."

"Then which—what—why— Here, what are you two laughing at?" This to Glyn, who was stamping about with delight.

"Oh, I couldn't help it, sir," cried the boy, and before he could say more there was another loud crack of the whip as Ramball made his way round behind his rebellious beast and shouted at him to "Come out of that."

He had hardly uttered the words when there was a crashing and breaking of wood as if the elephant were making its way quickly through the trees in obedience to the command; and as the sounds ceased, the menagerie proprietor came staggering out without his handkerchief or whip, to stand in the middle of his men looking half-stunned and confused.

"Did he ketch you, sir?" said the driver, with a laugh of satisfaction in his twinkling eyes.

"Brought down his trunk across my back," panted the proprietor. "My word, he can hit hard!"

"Yes, sir; I know. Knocked me flat on my back, he did."

"Knocked me on my face," cried the proprietor angrily. "Look here," he said, "is there any skin off my nose? I fell against a tree."

"Took a little bit of the bark off," grumbled the man, who did not seem at all sympathetic. "Hadn't you better let him fill hisself full, sir, and have a rest? He'll come easy, perhaps, then."

"Do you want me to stand still here and see a devouring elephant go on eating till he ruins me? We must all join together and drive him out."

"But he'll drive us out, sir," said the man in a tone full of remonstrance.

"Then we must try again. I am not going to be beaten by a beast like that."

"Look here, my man," said Morris, "hadn't you better tie him up to one of the trees and leave him till to-morrow? They do this sort of thing abroad, I hear, by tying the elephant's legs or ankles to the trunks of trees."

"What!" shouted Ramball. "Why, he'd take them all up by the roots and go cantering through the town, doing no end of mischief, with them hanging to his legs. Think I want to have to pay for the trees as well as the apples?"

"Then—er—lasso him and lead him home."

"Lass which, sir?"

"Lasso him, my man, with ropes."

"Why, he ain't a wild ostrich of the desert, sir. Look at him!—Here, one on yer run off and fetch the longest cart-rope. This 'ere gentleman would like to have a try."

The boys were roaring with laughter by this time, the mathematical master's parasites joining in as heartily as Glyn and Singh.

"Don't be rude, fellow," said Morris.

"Don't be rude?" cried Ramball, who was fuming with disappointment and rage. "Rude yourself. If you give me much more of your sarce I'll set the animile at you."

As this was proceeding, the elephant, whose taste for apples had been satiated, came slowly out into the open, to stand bending and bowing his massive head, which he swayed slowly from side to side and blinked and flapped his ears, as he watched the assembly with his little reddish eyes in a way which made the mathematical master grip Slegge by the arm.

"I am getting uneasy," he whispered, "about you boys. Don't run, but follow me slowly back to the fence. Tell the other boys, and we will go at once."

"Can't you coax him out, sir?" said Glyn, as he approached the proprietor.

"No, I can't coax him out," cried Ramball snappishly; "but you mind your own business, I know mine. I have had enough of you putting your spoons in my porridge."

"Here, Mr Severn! Mr Singh!" shouted the mathematical master. "This way! We are going back to the college." But he did not go far.

"But I want to see the elephant brought out, sir," replied Singh. "He oughtn't to be left like this. He may do mischief."

"Oh, now you've begun, have you?" yelped the proprietor, whose voice in his anger had gradually reached the soprano. "I suppose you would like to have a try?"

"Oh, I don't want to interfere," replied Singh coolly. "Where do you want the elephant to go?"

"Where do I want him to go? Why, home of course, before he does any more mischief. I wish he was dead; that I do! And he shall be too. Here, Jem, run back to Number One—here's the key—and bring my rifle and the powder-flask and bullet-bag. I'm sick of him. He'll be killing somebody before he's done—a beast!—Tigers is angels to him, sir," he continued appealingly to Morris. "He's the wickedest elephant I ever see, and I've spent more on him in damages than I paid for him at first; but he's played his last prank, and if I can't drive him I can shoot.—'Member that lion, my lads, as killed the gentleman's hoss?"

"Ay, ay, ay!" came in a low murmured growl.

"Got out, sir," continued the proprietor, waving one hand about oratorically, and dabbing his bald head with his hand. "Here, some of you, where's my yellow handkerchy? Oh, I know; I left it in that there apple-wood, and I'd lay sixpence, he's picked it up and swallowed it because it's yellow and he thinks it's the skin of a big orange. Got out of his cage, he did, sir, that there lion—been fiddling all night, I suppose, at the bolts and bars—and we followed him up to where he got in the loose-box of a gentleman's stable; and there was the poor horse down—a beauty he was—and that there lion—Arena his name was—lying on him with his face flattened out and teeth buried in the poor hoss's throat, so that when I got to the stable door there he was, all eyes and whiskers, and growling at you like thunder. I knowed what my work was, sir," continued the proprietor, addressing his conversation entirely to Morris, "and you can ask my men, sir; they was there."

"Ay, ay, ay!" was growled.

"It warn't the time for showing no white feathers when a lion's got his monkey up like that. I brought my gun with me—fine old flint-lock rifle it is, and I got it now—and the next minute that there dead horse had got a dead lion lying beside him. But I sold his skin to a gent for a ten-pun note, to have it stuffed, and it's in his front hall now, near Lungpuddle, in Lancashire.—Well, you, are you going to fetch that there rifle, or am I to fetch it myself?" he yelled at his man.

"Oh, I wouldn't shoot him, guv'nor," growled the man.

"What's it got to do with you?" almost shrieked his master.

"Oh, I aren't going to lose nothing, guv'nor, only a bit of a chum. He's knocked me about a bit, and tried to squeeze all the wind out of me two or three times; but that was only his fun. I shouldn't like to see him hurt."

"Then perhaps you'd like to go and fetch him out of that there urcherd?" cried his master.

"He aren't in," said the man sturdily; "and if he were, no, thank you, to-day. To-morrow morning perhaps I shouldn't mind; but I do say that it'd be a burning shame to shoot the finest elephant there is in England. The one at the Slogical Gardens in London is nothing to him, and you know, master, that that's the truth."

"You fetch my rifle."

"I wouldn't talk quite so loud, guv'nor, if I was you," replied the man. "Elephants is what they call 'telligent beasts, and you don't know but what that there annymile is a-hearing every word you say and only waiting till I'm gone to make a roosh, knock you down, and do his war-dance all over you."

"Hah! The same as they trample the life out of the tigers at home."

Every one turned sharply upon the speaker, whose voice sounded clear and ringing, as he stood there frowning angrily at the elephant's master.

"Bah! Stuff!" cried the man in his high-pitched voice. "I have read anecdotes about animals, and I know all them stories by heart. They look as if they could; but them beasts can't think, and the stories are all lies.—You be off and fetch that rifle before I send somebody else; and look here, Jem, if you don't obey my orders you take a fortnight's notice to quit from next Saturday, when you are paid."

"Then you are going to shoot the elephant," cried Glyn, "because you don't know how to manage him?"

"What!" half-shrieked the man. "Here, I say, where do you go to school? Things are coming to a pretty pass when boys like you begin teaching me, who've been nigh forty year in the wild-beast trade! What next?"

"Glyn Severn's right," said Singh sternly.

"Here's another of them!" cried the man, looking round from face to face.

"Quite right," continued Singh. "Why, the poorest coolie in my father's dominions would manage one of the noble beasts far better."

"Ho!" said Ramball sarcastically. "Then perhaps the biggest swell out of my father's dominions would like to show me how to do it himself."

"I don't know that I can," said Singh quietly; "but I dare say the poor beast would obey me if I tried."

"Oh, pray try, then, sir.—Only, look here, governor," continued the man, addressing Morris, who was not far off, "I don't know whether he's your son or your scholar—I wash my hands of it. I warn you; he's a vicious beast, and I aren't a-going to pay no damages if my young cock-a-hoop comes to grief."

Singh laughed a curious, disdainful laugh. Then he took a step in the direction of the elephant, but Glyn caught him by the arm.

"Don't do that, Glyn," said the boy quietly. "I don't believe he would hurt me. Come with me if you like. You know what he'll do if he's going to be savage, and you run one way and I'll run the other."

This was in a low voice, unheard by any one but him for whom it was intended; and the next moment, amidst a profound hush, the two boys moved towards the elephant, who was swaying his head slowly from side to side, and looking "ugly," as the man Jem afterwards said.

Then out of the silence, urged by a sense of duty, Morris cried in a harsh, cracked, emotional voice, not in the least like his own, "Severn! Prince! Come back! What are you going to do?"

His last words came as if he were half-choked, and then like the rest he stood gazing, with a strange clammy moisture gathering in his hands and upon his brow, for as the two boys drew near, the elephant suddenly raised its head, threw up its trunk, and uttered a shrill trumpeting sound.

As the defiant cry ceased, Singh stepped forward in advance of his companion, and shouted a few words in Hindustani.

The elephant lowered its trunk and stood staring at the boy, as if wonderingly, before coming slowly forward in its heavy, ponderous way, crashing down the green herbage beneath the orchard trees, and its great grey bulk parting the twigs of a tree that stood alone, and beneath whose shade the monster stopped.

The boys stood still now, and Singh uttered a short, sharp order in Hindustani once more.

'Come on, Glyn,' he cried. 'It's all right. Take my hand.'

Instantly, but in a slow, ponderous way, the great beast slowly subsided, kneeling in the long grass, while Singh went up quite close, with the animal watching him sharply the while, and laying out its trunk partly towards him, so that when close up the boy planted one of his feet in the wrinkling folds of the monstrous nose, caught hold of the huge flapping ear beside him, climbed quickly up, and the next minute was astride the tremendous neck and uttering another command in the Indian tongue. The result was that the elephant raised its ears slightly so that Singh could nestle his legs beneath; and as he settled himself in position a merry smile spread about his lips.

"Come on, Glyn," he cried. "It's all right. Take my hand."

Glyn obeyed, and as if fully accustomed to the act, he rapidly climbed up and settled himself behind his companion.

There was another sharp order, and the great beast slowly heaved himself up, muttering thunder, and grumbling the while.

"Well, I *am* blessed!" cried the proprietor. "You, Jem, did you ever see such a game as this?"

The man addressed did not say a word, but gave one thigh a tremendous slap, while the elephant stretched out his trunk towards them, took a step or two in their direction, and uttered a squeal.

Singh shouted out a few words angrily, and the long serpent-like trunk hung pendent once again, with the tip curled up inward so that it should not brush the ground.

"Now then," cried Singh to the proprietor, "where do you want him to go?"

"Right up into the show-field, squire," cried the man excitedly. "Think you can take him?"

"Try," replied the boy with a scornful laugh; "but I ought to have an *ankus*. But never mind, I can do it with words.—I say, Glyn," he continued, speaking over his left shoulder, "we are going to ride in the procession after all. If the Colonel knew, what would he say?"

"But—but—" cried Morris. "My dear boys, pray, pray come down! Think of the consequences to yourselves—and what will be said to me."

"Oh, it's all right, Mr Morris," cried Glyn confidently; "we must take the elephant now. Singh and I have ridden on elephants hundreds of times, though we have never acted the parts of mahouts.—There, go on, Mr What's-your-name, and Singh here will make him carry us back right to where you wish."

There was no further opposition. In fact, it would have been a bold man who would have dared to offer any; but the proprietor came as close as he thought prudent, panting hard, as the huge beast swept along in its stately stride.

"I beg your pardons, young gents—beg your pardons! Honour bright, sirs, I didn't know. Oh, thank you; thank you kindly. You are saving me a hundred pounds at least, and if you'd like a nice silver watch apiece, or a monkey, or a parrot, only say the word, and you shall have the pick of the collection. And look here, gentlemen, I'll give you both perpetual passes to my show."

"Thank you! thank you!" Glyn shouted back. "We will come and see it;" while Singh sat as statuesque as a native mahout, and an imaginative Anglo-Indian would have forgotten his Eton costume and pictured him in white cotton and muslin turban; while, as they neared the great elm-trees where the gap showed grimly in the fence and the boughs hung low, the amateur driver uttered a warning cry in Hindustani, with the result that his great steed threw up its trunk, twined it round a pendent branch that was in their way, snapped it off, and trampled it under foot.

Chapter Seven
"Salaam, Maharajah!"

The menagerie proprietor hurriedly led the way straight across the cricket-field; for, full of excitement, he was eager to get right away with the depredating animal before the owner of the damaged fence and orchard came upon the scene.

"I can talk to him better when I get on my own ground," he said to himself; and, making straight for the gap in the Doctor's hedge, the elephant, in obedience to word after word from his mahout, followed with long, swinging strides.

There was a crowd outside the hedge in the road, and they would have been across the field long before; but, in obedience to an order from the Doctor, Wrench was on guard and kept them back. His rather difficult task ceased as the elephant drew near, for the crowd scattered to avoid the monster, and the Doctor's man gave way too, the only difference being that the little mob drew away outside the hedge while the man made way in; for, seeing who were mounted on the great animal's neck, he ran towards the house to meet the Doctor, who, followed by the other masters, was now coming toward the gap with a small opera-glass in his hand.

"Here, Joseph," he cried breathlessly, "am I right? Are those two of my pupils?"

"Yes, sir; a-riding striddling on the elephant's neck."

"Dangerous! Madness! So undignified too! What will people think? Run and tell them to get off directly and come to me."

The man hurriedly retraced his steps; but before he could reach the gap in the hedge the elephant strode through and out into the road, and the Doctor and his aides hurried back into the house to reach one of the front windows just as, headed by the proprietor and followed by a crowd, the elephant strode by, the two boys taking off their caps to salute those at the window.

The Doctor turned with a look of blank amazement upon his countenance, to stare for a few moments at the classical and French masters, who had followed him in.

"Gentlemen," he exclaimed angrily, "did you ever see such extraordinary behaviour in your lives? Oh, this must be stopped!"

But it was not stopped, for the elephant was striding away along the main street of the town, with a crowd regathering as they saw that the powerful monster seemed to be well under control; while the boys, now thoroughly enjoying their exciting ride, needed no persuasion from Ramball to keep their places and take their mount right up to the show-field, where several of the yellow vans were already in place, their drivers having commenced the formation of the oblong square which was to form the show.

Here, shortly afterwards, the elephant stopped of its own volition close to a great iron picket which was being driven into the soft earth, and by which a truss of hay had been placed ready for its refection.

Here, as the elephant stood still, it paid no heed to a couple of Ramball's men, who in obedience to their master's orders set to work to fasten a strong chain to the monster's leg and attach it to the iron picket.

For, evidently satisfied with its fruity lunch, and calmed down from the excitement brought on by the accident, possibly too from a certain feeling of satisfaction at hearing the native tongue of some old mahout ringing in its great ears, the huge beast now began to take matters according to its old routine. It commenced by gathering up portions of the hay, which it loosened with its trunk, sniffing at it audibly, and then beginning to scatter it about, the boys making no attempt to quit their lofty perch.

"Here, one of you, bring a bucket of water," cried Ramball. "He ain't hungry now. Don't let him waste that hay. Have you fastened the chain?"

Without waiting for the men to answer, the menagerie proprietor examined the great fetters himself.

"Look sharp," he shouted; "quick with that water before he spoils all the hay."

One man had hurried off to the pump with a couple of empty buckets, while the others seized upon the truss which the elephant was disturbing, but only to drop it directly, for the captive just lightly waved its trunk right and left, and the men were sent flying in different directions.

Phoompf snorted the tyrant, and immediately went on picking up and scattering the hay all around it, thickly covering the grass.

"Well, I suppose we had better get down now, hadn't we?" cried Glyn.

"Yes, sir—no, sir. Just wait a little bit, please," cried Ramball. "You're a-keeping of him quiet; only I don't want this 'ere to be made a free gratus exhibition for everybody to see. It's a cutting off my profits. Hi, there, some of you! why don't you shut them gates?" he shouted to certain of his men who were driving in the latter half of the line of yellow vans.

"Can't get the rest in if we do, sir," came back.

"No, of course they can't," grunted their master, looking up at the two lads. "Things is going awkward to-day, and no mistake.—Oh, here comes the water," he continued, speaking now to Singh. "I dare say that will cool him down. Just say a word to him, sir, and tell him to drink."

"Tell the men to put the buckets down before him," replied Singh; and as the water-bearer drew near the elephant evidently scented the refreshing fluid, and uttered a sonorous snort.

Directly after, as the man nervously set down the brimming buckets, anxiously watching the waving trunk the while, and leaping away as he saw it coming towards him, the tip of the great hose-like organ was thrust into the first vessel, there was a low sound of suction as many quarts were drawn up, and then the end was curled under, thrust right back into the huge creature's mouth, and then there was a loud squirting sound like a fire-engine beginning to play to put out the animal's burning thirst.

Back went the trunk into the bucket again, the curving inward followed for a second discharge, there was repetition, till in a very brief space the first bucket was empty, and then, with a disdainful swing of the trunk, the vessel was sent flying, and the emptying of the second commenced, to be ended by the satiated beast picking it up to hold it on high as if to drain out the last drops, and then begin to swing it to and fro as if to hurl it at its master.

"Hah–h–h–h–ah!" cried Singh, and the great creature ceased swinging the bucket to and fro, and dropped it on the hay.

"Come, Singh, we have had enough of this," cried Glyn impatiently. "Let's get back, or we shall be having the Doctor sending to see what has become of us."

"Don't you be afraid about that, young gentlemen," cried Ramball. "I'll speak up for you both."

"Thank you," said Glyn drily; "but you've done with us now."

"Done with you, young gentlemen! I only wish you'd stop and join my troupe. I'll make it right and pleasant for you, and be glad too. Pay you better, too, than any one else would when you leave school. Why, bless your heart, you—the dark one I'm talking to—if you like to come I'll spend any amount up to a hundred pounds for getting you a thorough Indian corstume all muslin and gold, and a turban with jewels in it—imitations, of course, it wouldn't run to real, but the best as is to be had—with a plume of feathers too, ready for you to ride in procession same as you did to-day. What do you say?"

"Yes, Singh," cried Glyn laughing, as he sat close behind his companion, and catching him by the shoulders he began to shake him to and fro. "There's an offer for you. What do you say?"

"I am going to get down," said Singh with a haughty curve to his lip. "Well, I won't tell him I'm not an English boy." Then sharply resuming his native tongue, he uttered an order which made the great beast kneel down in the hay with its trunk stretched straight out before it, and raising its ears a little, ready for its two riders to climb down forwards and spring off.

"Ha!" cried Singh, as he approached close to the elephant and planted his right foot upon the upper portion of its trunk. "I should rather like to have you," he said, speaking softly, so that his words only reached his companion's ear. "You are the first in England to show me that you know what I am."

"But you can't have him, Singh," said Glyn laughing. "No more elephants till we get back to Dour, and that won't be for years to come."

"No," said the boy sadly; "that will not be for years to come.—Huh!" he cried to the elephant, as he removed his foot and drew back. "You're a fine old beast after all."

The monster rose at his command, and stood blinking at him and swinging his trunk to and fro.

"Mind, sir!" shouted Ramball, who had been looking on anxiously. "Don't you trust him. He's brewing mischief. He always is when he looks quiet like that; and the way he can knock you over with that trunk—my word!"

"Oh, he's not going to knock me over with his trunk," said Singh, smiling; and, uttering a few words in Hindustani, he stood close up to the elephant and reached one hand up to its great ear and laid the other upon its trunk.

"Salaam, Maharajah!" he cried, and the animal threw up its head, curled up its trunk, and trumpeted loudly, before going down upon its knees before the lad.

"Good! Up again!" cried Singh in Hindustani, and added a few more words, the result of which was that the monster stood calmly by its great picket-peg, making its chain jingle as it began slowly swaying its head from side to side again.

"Well done, sir!" cried Ramball. "Thank you, sir. You'll shake hands with me, won't you?"

"Oh yes," said Singh quietly; "I'll shake hands," and he extended his own.

"You are a gentleman and no mistake," cried the man. "I say, think that offer of mine over. I'll make it worth your while. I will, honour bright!"

Singh shook his head gravely, and there was a mocking smile upon his lip.

"No, no, thank you," he said. "I am going back to school, and some day back to India; but I should like to come and see you and the elephant again."

"Of course you would, sir, and come you shall," cried Ramball. "Perpetual passes! You don't want no pass. Just you show your face here, both of you, whenever you like, and bring as many of your schoolmates with you too, and you will be as welcome as the flowers of May. Look here, young gentlemen, I am going to keep the show open here for three days, and then we go off to my farm three miles out of the town to lay up for a bit of rest and do repairs, and get the animals into condition, before we take the road again. You come and see me there, and pick out what you'd like to have, monkeys or parrots, as I said. I don't offer you anything big, because I don't suppose you could keep it at school; but I have got some of the amusingest little monkeys you ever see, and a parrot as can talk—when he likes, mind you," continued the man, laying a fat finger against his nose, "and that ain't always. But when he is in the temper for it he can say anything, and you wouldn't know but what it was a human being.—Going, gentlemen?"

"Yes, we are going now," said Singh.

"Yes, it's time we were off," said Glyn; "but I say, Mr Ramball, what about that rifle?"

"Rifle? Oh, you mean my gun?"

"Yes," said Glyn. "You don't mean to shoot that grand beast?"

"Shoot him, sir? Not me. It put me in such a temper and made me say that. But, young gentlemen, do think over what I said. Why, if you joined my troupe, I'm blessed if I wouldn't buy another as big as him, and then you'd have a elephant apiece."

Chapter Eight
Doctor Bewley changes Sides

As the two lads reached the main street, chatting over their adventure, something occurred which made Glyn turn his head sharply, and as he did so a small boy shouted, "Hooray!"

It was the little spark applied to the touch-hole of a cannon, and a loud roar followed.

"Here, let's go back," cried Singh. "The Rajah's broken loose again."

"No, no," cried Glyn. "They are shouting at us."

"What for? What have we done?"

"I suppose it's because we rode the elephant. Here, come along; let's turn down here and get round by the fields."

The young Indian generally gave way to his English friend; and, obeying directly, they hurried down the first turning, but in vain. A crowd of men and boys were after them, cheering loudly, and this crowd was snowball-like in the way in which the farther it rolled the more it grew. So that in spite of all their efforts they were literally hunted right up to the Doctor's gates, where they arrived hot and breathless to find a larger crowd than before which had gathered to satisfy themselves with the rather empty view of the damaged hedge, the big footmarks, and a wheelwright and some of Ramball's men getting the great bottomless elephant-van into condition for dragging to the show-field.

As soon as the two boys came in sight there was a rush made for them, and amidst deafening cheering and vain efforts to hoist them shoulder-high and carry them into the playground, they managed to reach this resort at last, and join their schoolfellows in keeping out the excited mob, some of whom, the youngest of course, began to decorate the brick wall with their persons like so many living statues. And then to the two lads' disgust, the whole school, with the exception of Slegge, and half-a-dozen of his party who wanted to join in the ovation but did not dare in the presence of their tyrant, began to cheer them as loudly as the boys without. Several of the younger juniors began to idolise them in a very juvenile way by hanging on to them, slapping their backs, and shaking hands.

Altogether it was a strange mingling of the pleasant and unpleasant, the former predominating with Singh, who for the first time since he had joined the school found himself thoroughly liked.

Slegge and his following stood aloof, the latter listening to the former's sneering remarks, some of which reached Glyn and made him feel hot; while just in the midst of the loudest cheering, Wrench the man-servant made his appearance, followed by a big tom-cat which passed most of its time in the pantry rubbing its head against Wrench's legs while he was cleaning the plate or washing tea-cups, probably in gratitude for past favours. When it was a kitten some young Plymborough roughs had hurled it into the little river, and were making of it what they termed a "cockshy," pelting it with stones, fortunately ineffectually, and trying to beat it under water, when the Doctor's footman, who was crossing the bridge, saw what was going on and made an unexpected charge upon the young ruffians, effectually scattering them. One tripped and fell headlong into the river, out of which he crawled as thoroughly wet as the unhappy little kitten, which Wrench received as it swam ashore, rolled up in his handkerchief and took home to his pantry, where it grew rapidly, waxed fat, and was never so happy as when it could find a chance to rub its head against its master.

Hard on Wrench's heels came also one Sam Grigg, page-boy, who on particular occasions wore a livery jacket with three rows of plated pill-like buttons, but who was now in the fatigue-dress of rolled-up shirt sleeves and a very dirty apron, while his left-hand was occupied by a boot, the right by a blacking-brush, which seemed to have been applied several times to an itching nose, his chin, and one side of his face, rather accounting for the plural nickname given him by the boys of "Day & Martin."

These had come out to join in the ovation, Wrench adding several proud encomiums, one of which was, "My eyes, gentlemen! You did do it fine!"

The Doctor's footman had hardly uttered these words when there was the loud ringing of a bell.

"The Doctor!" he ejaculated, and he hurried into the house, his exit from the playground being followed by a fresh burst of cheering and a peculiar triumphant dance on the part of the page, accompanied by the waving of boot and blacking-brush, till, in his disgust, Slegge made a rush at him from behind, grabbed him by the scruff of the neck, and ran him rapidly to the boot-house, sent him flying in with a savage kick, and banged the door after him.

"A blackguard!" he cried haughtily. "That's why our boots are not half cleaned. How dare he! The dirty, contemptible scrub! The Doctor ought to be told of this."

Slegge stood sniffing and snorting and glaring round fiercely at the worshippers of the two heroes of the hour, who stood flushed and worried, ready to beat a retreat to the dormitory.

But an end was put to their reception in a very unexpected way, for Wrench suddenly made his appearance, looking very solemn as he hurried off to the two lads with, "The Doctor wants to see you both, sirs, directly, in the study."

Slegge's face lit up with a malicious grin.

"Haw, haw!" he laughed. "Three cheers, boys! The Doctor wants to see them both in his study. Impositions! Hooray! Cheer, you little beggars! Why don't you cheer?"

The adjuration fell flat, for not a boy uttered a sound, save one who exclaimed, "Oh, what a shame!" and then went off to the cricket-field, trying hard, poor little fellow! to suppress the natural desire to cry out and sob, for Slegge had "fetched him," as he termed it, a sounding slap upon the cheek, which echoed in the silence and cut the boy's lips against a sharp white tooth.

"What's the Doctor want?" whispered Singh, as they followed the footman into the house.

"A wigging, I'm afraid, gentlemen," said the man who heard his words. "But don't you mind. You write out your lines and do your imposition like men. It was fine! What you did this morning has made every one think no end of you, and it will never be forgotten so long as this 'ere's a school."

A tap of the knuckles, which sounded hollow and strange, for they had reached the study-door.

"Come in!" in the Doctor's deepest and most severe tones, and the next moment the two boys were standing separated from their preceptor by the large study-table, while he sat back in his revolving chair with his finger-tips joined, frowning at them severely from beneath his up-pushed gold-rimmed spectacles.

There was silence for quite a minute, and it was not the Doctor who spoke first, but Glyn, who, under the impression that the Doctor was deep in thought and had forgotten their presence, ventured to say, "I beg your pardon, sir; you sent for us," and put an end to the mental debate as to the form in which the subject should be approached.

"Yes, sir," said the Doctor sternly. "I have sent for you both, as it is better that any lapse from the strict rules of my establishment should be dealt with immediately; not that I wish to be too severe, for you are both new pupils and strange to the regulations of a high-class school in England. You gather, of course, that I am alluding to your very undignified conduct in the sight of all your fellow-pupils."

"Yes, sir," said Glyn; "about our riding the elephant?"

"Of course. It was disgraceful. You, to whom I should have looked for the conduct and demeanour of a gentleman, being the son of an eminent officer in the army, behaving like some little common street-boy, and leading your fellow-pupil, in whom from his ignorance of English customs and etiquette such a lapse might be excused. It was only the other day that your father the Colonel, sir, told me that you would set an example to the young Prince, and here I find you directly snatching at the opportunity to behave as you have done."

"I beg your pardon, sir," cried Glyn, in a voice full of protest, "it was—"

"Silence, sir!—Yes, what is it?" cried the Doctor angrily, for there was a quick tap at the door, and the footman appeared. "Have I not told you, sir, that when I am engaged like this I am not to be interrupted?—Eh? Who?"

"That showman, sir, wants to see you, sir."

"That showman?" cried the Doctor angrily. "What showman? What about?"

"Come about the damages, sir; the broken fences. He said he wouldn't keep you a moment, sir, if you would see him."

"Oh," said the Doctor, cooling down. "Yes, the damages, the torn-up hedge and the broken fence. A most annoying affair. You can sit down, gentlemen, while I dismiss this man.—Where is he, Wrench?"

"In the hall, sir; on the mat."

"Ho!" said the Doctor, rising; and he marched slowly out, leaving the boys looking at one another and then at the busts of the great scholars of Greece and Rome ranged at intervals upon the cornices of the bookcases that covered the study-walls.

Neither felt disposed to speak, for an inner door stood ajar, and from the other side came the faintly heard scratching noise of a pen.

And so in silence some ten minutes or so passed before the Doctor came in, looking very different of aspect and ready to sign to the boys to sit down again as they rose at his entrance.

"A most unpleasant business, young gentlemen," he began, as he seated himself; and sinking back he removed his spectacles, folded them, and used them to tap his knee; "but in justice to you I must hasten to say that this man's coming has given a very different complexion to the affair. A very strange, uncultured personage, but most straightforward and honest. I like the way in which he has offered to bear all the expense of repairing the fences. He speaks most highly of your gallantry—er—er—er—pluck, he called it—most objectionable phrase!—in dealing with this savage beast. H'm, yes, what did he say—tackling it. But I was not aware that you had engaged in roping or harnessing the animal. He, however, talked of your both managing the monster wonderfully, and—er—it had never occurred to me before that you had both had some experience of elephants in India."

"Oh yes, sir," cried Glyn eagerly. "Singh has elephants of his own, and we often used to go out together through the forest upon one as big as that."

"Ha! Very interesting," cried the Doctor. "I was under the impression that your proceedings this morning were—that is—in fact, that you both did it just for the sake of a ride."

"Oh no, sir," cried Glyn. "The men were all afraid of the elephant, and Singh spoke to it in Hindustani, and—"

"Yes, yes, exactly," said the Doctor, smiling. "It was very brave, and—really, I cannot conceal the fact that I felt alarmed myself when the great furious beast came charging across the grounds. Yes, he speaks highly in praise of your conduct, and really, young gentlemen, I—I must apologise for having spoken to you as I did while suffering from a misunderstanding. Er—hum!" continued the Doctor didactically, and he rose slowly to stand waving the gold spectacles through the air, "it is the duty of every gentleman when he finds that he is in the wrong to acknowledge the fact with dignity and good grace. My dear young pupils, I hope I have properly expressed myself towards you both; and let me add that this will be a lesson to us, to me, against speaking in undue haste, and to you both as—er—

"Well, gentlemen," he continued with a smile, "I don't think I need detain you longer from your studies—I mean—er—from your pleasurable pursuits, as this is a holiday, and we will consider the incident as closed."

Smiling benignantly, the Doctor marched slowly round the end of the table again, shook hands warmly with both his pupils, and then showed them to the door.

"Stop! By the way, a little idea has occurred to me. This is a day of relaxation. Mr Singh—er—it is an understood thing, as you know, that your title is to be in abeyance while you are my pupil; for, as I explained to your guardian, Colonel Severn, it would be better that there should be no invidious distinctions during your scholastic career—I should be glad if you and your friend the Colonel's son would dine with me this evening. No dinner-party, but just to meet your three preceptors and a Mr—dear me, what was his name? Really, gentlemen, I am so deeply immersed in my studies that names escape me in a most provoking manner. A gentleman resident in the town here—a Sanskrit scholar, and friend of Mr Morris. Dear me! What was his name? There was something familiar about it, and I made a mental note, *memoria technica*, to be sure, yes—what was it? I remember the word perfectly now. 'Beer.' Dear me, how strange! And it doesn't help me a bit. Really, gentlemen, I am afraid this *memoria technica* is a mistake. How, by any possibility could the name of the ordinary beverage of the working classes have anything to do with the professor's name? Professor Beer—Professor Ale—Professor Porter—Stout? Dear me, how strange! Ah, of course—the great brewers, Barclay—Professor Barclay! At half-past six."

"Thank you, sir. We will come," said Singh, smiling.

"Precisely," said the Doctor, and he stood smiling in the doorway as the boys passed out.

They were at the end of the hall passage when the door closed, and Wrench shot out from somewhere like a Jack from its box.

"Aren't caught it very bad, gentlemen, have you?" he cried eagerly.

"Oh no, Wrench," said Glyn, smiling.

"Thought not, sir, for the Doctor had got a twinkle in his eye when he'd done with the wild-beast man. It would have been hard if you'd caught it after what you did. Pst! There's the study-bell." And the man hurried away, leaving the culprits to stroll out together into the playground, where they found fully half the boys waiting to hear the result of their interview with the Doctor, Slegge and his courtiers hurrying up first.

"Well, beast-tamers," he cried sneeringly, "how many lines of Latin have you got to do?" And he grinned offensively at them both.

"When?" said Glyn coolly.

"When? Why, now, at once."

"We haven't got any lines of Latin to do," said Singh quietly. "To-day is a holiday."

"For us," cried Slegge; "but I know the Doctor. You have both got a pretty stiff dose to do, my fine fellows, and I wish you joy."

"Thank you," said Glyn; "but you are all in the wrong."

"Wrong? Then what did the Doctor say to you?"

"Oh," said Glyn, in a most imperturbable manner, fighting hard the while, though, to keep his countenance as he realised the strength of the shot he was about to send at his malicious persecutor, "he asked Singh and me to come and meet the masters and dine with him to-night."

Chapter Nine
The New Professor

"Let 'em go," snarled Slegge to his courtiers. "It's only another way of getting a hard lesson. I know what the Doctor's dinner-parties are. Let the stuck-up young brutes go. But if I wasn't about to leave the blessed old school I would jolly soon let the Doctor know that this sort of thing won't do. The old humbug told me once that fairplay was a jewel. I don't call it fairplay to be currying favour with a new boy because he's an Indian prince. Indian prince, indeed! Indian bear—cub; that's what I call him, with his leader, currying favour like that! Ha, ha! Ho, ho! Haw, haw!"

This was a melodramatic laugh of the most sarcastic description, prefatory to the letting off of a very ponderous joke. "Currying! Indian curry! That's what he was brought up on. Curry and rice instead of pap. Look at the colour of his skin. But only wait a bit," continued Slegge darkly. "Just wait till the right time comes, and I'll let you all see."

But the Doctor's dinner-party was not quite so ponderous and learned as usual, for the incidents of the day formed the main topic of conversation. The Doctor was in high good-humour, and naturally felt rather proud of his pupils. They had distinguished themselves, and in so doing had distinguished him and his school, and the consequence was that the masters readily took up the subject and were most warm and friendly to the two lads, the other guest in particular, Professor Barclay, as Morris took care that he should be called, much to the annoyance of the classical master, who looked at the new-comer, Morris's friend, rather suspiciously, regarding him as one likely to poach upon his preserves.

During the dinner, the Professor had much to say about Sanskrit, military colleges, and India, and was very attentive to Singh and Glyn, but found the boys quiet and retiring in the extreme.

All, however, seemed to be enjoying themselves but Mr Rampson, who grew more uneasy and suspicious over the coffee, pricking up his ears as he bent over his cup and kept on stirring it, but without drinking, while the Doctor and the Professor were talking together as if discussing some subject in a low tone.

The fact must be recorded against the classical teacher that he was eavesdropping, ungentlemanly as it may sound; but the only thing that reached his ears was the conclusion of the conversation, when the Doctor said, raising his voice slightly, "Certainly, Mr Barclay, I shall give every attention to your testimonials; but my staff of preceptors is complete, and I have always considered Greek and Latin sufficient for my pupils, of course with the modern languages thrown in."

The Professor thanked the Doctor effusively, and in the course of the evening contrived to fix himself like a burr upon Singh, while Mr Rampson made an effort and secured Glyn to himself, jealously taking care that the stranger guest and friend, it seemed, of Morris should not monopolise both the boys.

"It's all a plot," said Rampson to himself—"all a scheme to oust me, and I'll never forgive Morris so long as I live.—I say," he said aloud, "that Mr Barclay seems to have a deal to say to your friend the Prince. Do you know what they are talking about?"

"India, and Sanskrit, and catching elephants," replied Glyn. "Has he been out in India?"

"Oh, don't ask me," said Rampson with asperity; then correcting himself quickly, and with a rather ghastly smile, "I say, you two did distinguish yourselves to-day."

"Oh, did we, sir?" said Glyn, who looked rather tired and bored. "Please don't say more about it."

"Oh no, of course not, if you don't want to hear it. But your friend doesn't seem to mind. Why, the Professor's taking him out into the garden, and the Prince is talking to him as hard as ever he can. Yes, he doesn't seem to mind."

"No," replied Glyn, as he saw Singh, in obedience to a gesture from his new acquaintance, sit down upon one of the garden-seats, and for the next quarter of an hour the boy was talking in quite an animated way, and evidently answering questions put to him by the Professor.

The evening soon glided away, and the boys gladly thanked their host and retired to their own room, utterly wearied out by the events of the day.

As a rule, they lay for some time carrying on conversation and discussing the next day's work; but that night very little was said, and the only thing worth recording was a few sentences that were spoken and responded to by Singh in the midst of yawns.

"Talking about India and Sanskrit?" said Glyn.

"Oh yes; he asked me all sorts of questions about Dour, and he asked me if I had ever seen Sanskrit letters."

"Well?"

"And I told him I had, and he shook his head and asked me where I had seen them."

"Well, what did you say?"

"That I had got some precious stones in my box with some Sanskrit letters cut in."

"Why, you never were so stupid as to tell him about that belt?"

"I don't know that there's anything stupid in it," replied Singh sleepily. "I didn't want him to think I was so ignorant as not to know about a language that your father can read as easily as English, and has talked to us about scores of times. Why, of course, I did."

"Well, of all the old *Dummkopfs* I ever knew, you are the stupidest. Didn't I tell you that—" *Snore.*

"Why, if he isn't asleep!"

Almost the next moment Glyn was in the same state.

Chapter Ten
"English Gentlemen don't fight like that."

The next morning the men sent by Ramball, the proprietor of the world-famed menagerie, were busy at work first thing repairing hedge and fence; and everything was so well done, and such prompt payment made for the estimated damages to the neighbouring orchard, that when a petition-like appeal for patronage was made by Ramball, the owner of the orchard attended with wife, family, and friends; and the Doctor gave permission to the whole school to be present, being moved also, as he told the lads in a brief address, to go himself with the masters and support a very worthy enterprise for the diffusion of natural history throughout the country. The visits were paid to the great yellow-walled prison, and Ramball, in his best blue coat, the one with the basket-work treble-gilt buttons, attended on the Doctor himself to explain the peculiarities of the beasts and give their history in his own fashion.

This was peculiar, and did not in any way resemble a zoological lecture. Still, it was an improvement upon the wild-beast showman of the old-fashioned fairs, and he did not inform his listeners that the tiger was eight feet six inches long from the tip of his nose to the end of his tail, and exactly eight feet four inches long from the tip of his tail to the end of his nose. Neither did he impart knowledge, like another of his craft, and tell people that the boa-constrictor was so-called because he constructed such pleasing images with his serpentine form. But he did inform them that the monstrous reptile he possessed—one which, by the way, was only nine feet long—was always furnished in the cold weather with sawdust into which he could burrow, on account of the peculiarity always practised by creatures of its kind of swallowing its own blankets; and he did deliver an eulogy on his big black bear, and encourage the young gentlemen to furnish it with buns; but he did not confess to the fact that it was his most profitable animal, from the circumstance of his letting it out on hire for so many months in the year to a hairdresser in Bloomsbury, who used, according to his advertisements, to kill it regularly once a week and exhibit it in butcherly fashion hung up and spread open outside his shop, so that passers-by might see its tremendous state of fatness: "Another fat bear killed this morning."

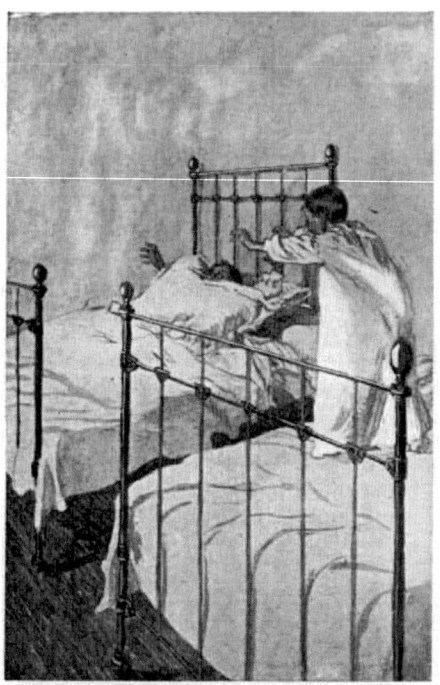

Glyn threw the clothes back, and the next moment the coverings of
his companion were stripped off on to the floor.

It was in the days when the British public were intense believers in
bear's grease as the producer of hair, and no one troubled himself or herself
to investigate the precise configuration of the exhibited animal and compare
it when hung up, decapitated, and shorn of its feet, with the ordinary well-
fatted domestic pig, albeit the illusion was kept up by its being possible to
see through the gratings outside the shop-window Ramball's black bear still
"all alive-o," parading and snuffling up and down in the area.

Glyn and Singh were there, of course, and responded to Ramball's
almost obsequious advances with good-humoured tolerance; but while he
was with the Doctor the boys took notes together, laughing with a good deal
of contempt at the poor miserable specimens—the tiger and two leopards—
compared with those they had seen in their native beauty and grace of
outline in the forests of Dour.

They met one friend there, though, chained by a leg to the massive iron
peg, as he stood swinging his great head from side to side, and stretching
out his enormous trunk for the contributions supplied by the boys.

They were welcomed most effusively by the great beast, which
recognised them at once, and it was only by its attention being taken up by

its keeper, the man who had driven the bottomless van, that the boys got away without being followed by their new friend, which had manifested a disposition to drag the peg out of the ground and follow them like a dog.

It was while the Doctor was delivering an impromptu disquisition upon the peculiarities of the one-horned rhinoceros and the slight resemblance given by the folds of its monstrous hide to the shell of a turtle, that Ramball followed the two boys and made signs to them to come to the other end of the great van-walled booth, when he asked them if they had considered his proposition.

"I never made such an offer before in my life, young gents. It's a good 'un. Don't you let it slide."

But the boys were saved the pain of telling the man that it was quite out of the question by the coming up of the guest at the Doctor's dinner, Professor Barclay, who was effusively civil to Glyn, and fastened himself upon Singh to talk of Indian matters and language till the visit came to an end.

Just before leaving, Ramball came up to them again, but he had to speak in the presence of the Doctor.

"I only wanted to ask the young gents, sir," he said, "if they had made their choice of the two little somethings to keep in remembrance of what they did over the elephant."

"Two little somethings?" said the Doctor loftily. "I am quite sure, sir, that my pupils do not wish to take any two little somethings as a gift from you."

"No, no, sir, not what you call gifts; but just a couple of little trifles as I asked them to pick out."

"Oh, no, no," cried the Doctor. "It is not necessary, my man, and we have no room for such things in my establishment."

"Ah, excuse me, sir," said the man eagerly; "you are thinking I mean something big and awkward; but a nice little monkey, sir, or a bird?"

"Monkeys don't want monkeys," said Slegge, in a whisper to Burney, just loud enough for Glyn to hear, and making him turn sharply upon the speaker.

"Have a baboon, Severn," said Slegge maliciously, for he met the boy's flashing eyes.

"What for?" said Glyn coolly.

"Oh, I don't know," continued Slegge, after a glance at the boys around, who burst into a low series of titters. "I would if I were you. There's a nice brotherly look about that one in the cage, and he hasn't got a tail."

"Mr Severn," said the Doctor, "come here. I want you to tell Mr Ramball that you do not need any recompense for the services you have performed. Mr Singh has already spoken."

"Yes, sir, I'll come," replied the boy quickly, and he did as requested, fully conscious the while that Slegge was saying something disparaging to the nearest boys, and that the Professor had moved up behind Singh and was talking to him again.

"Do you like this Professor Barclay?" said Glyn as they were walking back towards the school side by side.

"Oh, I don't know. He's very pleasant to talk to, of course, for he knows so much about Indian things."

"Oh," said Glyn thoughtfully, for his companion's words sounded reasonable.

"But what was that fellow saying to you?" asked Singh. "He was grinning at you about something. Oh, I should like to do something to him. That nasty look of his always makes me feel hot."

"He wants to get up a quarrel," replied Glyn.

"Well, let him, and the sooner the better. He's always insulting me."

"Then let's insult him," said Glyn.

"Yes," cried Singh eagerly. "What shall we do? Tell him we won't accept a baboon because one's enough in the school?"

"No; treat him with contempt," said Glyn coldly. "We are not going to be dragged into a fight so as to give him a chance to play the bully and knock us about."

"But let's knock him about," cried Singh, "and show him that we can bully too."

"Won't do," said Glyn slowly. "He's too big and strong."

"Yes, he's big and strong; but we shall be two to one."

"Ah, you have a lot to learn, Singhy. English gentlemen don't fight like that."

Chapter Eleven
The Cutting of the Cock's Comb

There was a smart brush at the school a few days later, which resulted in the cutting of Slegge's comb. The Doctor was seated at his study-table, with the open French window letting in the fresh morning breeze and giving him a view, when he raised his eyes from his book, right across the cricket-field to the clump of elms, when there was a tap at the door, responded to by the customary "Come in!" and Mr Rampson entered.

"Ah, good-morning, Mr Rampson," said the Doctor suavely.

"Good-morning, sir. Could you give me a few minutes?"

"Certainly, Mr Rampson," replied the Doctor, sitting back. "Have you something to report?"

"Well, no, sir, not exactly, but—er, but er—I er—thought I should like to ask you if I had given you satisfaction in connection with my pupils."

"Yes, Mr Rampson," said the Doctor, raising his eyebrows; "but why—oh, I see, you want to speak to me and tell me that you have had a more lucrative offer."

"Oh no, sir; I am quite satisfied here, where I have been so long, but—"

"Well, Mr Rampson, what is it? You wish me to increase your stipend?"

"No, sir, I do not; but I don't want to suddenly find myself supplanted by another master through the machinations of a brother-teacher."

"Don't speak angrily, Mr Rampson. Pray, who has been trying to supplant you?"

"Well, sir, I am a blunt man, and I have come to speak out. I am afraid that Morris—why, I know not—has been introducing this Professor Barclay to you to try to get him in my post."

"Indeed, Mr Rampson!" said the Doctor, with a smile. "Well, then, let me set you at your ease at once. Morris did not introduce this gentleman, for he came to me with an introduction from one of the professors at Addiscombe, a gentleman I do not know from Adam. I find that he has been for a few months a resident in the town here, where he is carrying on some study. Morris seems to know him a little, and tells me that he has visited him two or three times at his apartments. I questioned him as to who the man was, and his antecedents, which seemed to be satisfactory. I did so after his presenting his letter of introduction and some testimonials. I thought that it would be only civil to ask him to dinner and explain to him that it was perfectly hopeless for him to expect anything from me; and, in short, one feels a little sympathetic towards a cultivated gentleman who is seeking to obtain an appointment in a none-too-well-paid profession. So now you see, my dear Mr Rampson, that you have not the slightest cause for uneasiness."

"Dr Bewley," cried Rampson excitedly, "you don't know how you have relieved my mind!"

"I am very glad, Rampson; and let me take this opportunity of telling you that— Bless my heart! what is the meaning of this?"

"Of what, sir?" cried Rampson, startled by the speaker's earnestness.

"Look over yonder beyond the elms. Scandalous! Disgraceful! And after all that I have said! I will not have it, Rampson."

"But, sir, I—"

"Don't you see that there's a fight going on? Just as if it were a common school. Come with me at once."

The Doctor set aside his stately march and hurried out through the open window, bare-headed, and closely followed by his assistant.

There, through the elms and close up to the grey park-fence beyond, the whole school seemed to have assembled, and plainly enough at intervals there was the quick movement of two contending figures, while the clustering boys around heaved and swayed as they watched the encounter, quite forgetful in their excitement of the possibility of their being seen from the house.

Dr Bewley did not run, but went nearer to it than he had been since he wrote DD at the end of his name and gave up cricket; while before they were half-way across the cricket-field Mr Rampson was emitting puffs suggesting that the motive-power by which he moved was connected with a modern utilisation of steam.

So intent was the little scholastic crowd beyond the row of tree-trunks which with the park-palings beyond formed the arena, that not a head was turned to see the approach of the masters and give the alarm. The consequence was that the latter were getting close up and able to make out that a fierce fight was going on between Slegge and Glyn Severn, the former seconded by Burney, the latter by the young Prince.

Down came Slegge flat upon his back at the fresh-comer's feet.

There was no shouting, no sound of egging on by the juvenile spectators, only an intense silence, punctuated by a hoarse panting sound, the trampling of feet, and the *pat, pat,* of blows.

The last of these was a heavy one, delivered right from the shoulder with all his remaining force—for the boy was pretty well exhausted—by Glyn Severn; and it was just as the Doctor was filling his capacious chest with the breath necessary after his hurried advance to deliver a stern command to cease fighting. But before he uttered a word his biggest pupil came staggering back towards the ring of boys on the Doctor's side, and as they hurriedly gave way down came Slegge flat upon his back at the fresh-comer's feet.

After delivering his final blow, Glyn Severn nearly followed his impulse, and had hard work to check himself from falling flat upon his adversary. As it was, he dropped only upon one knee, rose again painfully, and stood with bruised and bleeding face gazing blankly at his stern preceptor, who now thundered out in his deepest tones, "What is the meaning of this?"

At the sight of the Doctor a thrill ran through the little throng; and, moved as by one impulse, there was the suggestion of a rush for safety. But the thunderous tones of the Doctor's voice seemed to freeze every young abettor in his steps.

"Do you hear me, sirs?" cried the Doctor again. "What is the meaning of this?"

It was the smallest boy of the school who replied, in a shrill voice full of excitement, conveying the very plain truth:

"Fight, sir. Tom Slegge and one of the new boys."

"Silence!" thundered the Doctor. "You know my rules, and that I have forbidden fighting. Here, somebody, one of the high form boys—you, Burney, let me hear what you have to say. Speak out, sir. Ah, you have been seconder, I suppose?"

"Yes, sir," faltered the lad, whose hands showed unpleasant traces of what he had been doing.

"Ah," continued the Doctor.—"Mr Rampson, see that not a boy dares to move.—Now, Burney, let me hear the whole truth of this from beginning to end. No suppression, sir, from favour or fear. I want the straightforward truth. Who began this disgraceful business?—Stop! Mr Rampson, here. Is that boy Slegge much hurt?"

"A bit stunned, sir, and stupid with his injuries, but he's all right, sir; he's coming round," and in proof thereof Slegge, with the assistance of the master's hands, struggled to his feet, and stood shaking his head as if he felt a wasp in his ear, and then promptly sat down again.

"Now, Burney," cried the Doctor, "speak out. Who began this?"

The boy addressed glanced at the Doctor and then at Slegge, while his lips parted; but he uttered no sound.

"Do you hear me, sir?" roared the Doctor.

"Big Tom Slegge, sir," came from the shrill little fellow who had before spoken.

The Doctor frowningly held up one big white finger at the little speaker, who shrank back amongst his fellows.

"I saw that look of yours, Burney," said the Doctor sternly, "and I read its meaning, sir. It seemed to appeal to your older schoolfellow, one of the principals in this disgraceful encounter, asking him if you might speak out. I'll answer for him. Yes, sir; and beware lest you, as a gentleman's son, lower your position in my eyes by making any suppression. What was the cause of the quarrel?"

Burney's face was working, for after the excitement of the fight and its sudden ending he felt hysterically emotional, and in a broken voice the truth came pouring forth.

"I can't help it, sir, and if he bullies me afterwards for speaking I must tell all. Slegge's been jealous of both the new boys ever since they came. He's been as disagreeable and spiteful as could be, and forced us all to take his side."

"Yes, yes; go on," cried the Doctor, for the boy stopped with a gasp; but he spoke more calmly afterwards. "He's been working it up, sir, for a fight for days, out of jealousy because he thought more was made of Singh and Severn than of him."

"Indeed!" said the Doctor, nodding his head.

"And when it came, sir, to them having such a fuss made over them about their riding the elephant, and you asking them afterwards to dinner, it was bound to come."

The boy stopped, and the Doctor turned to the classical master.

"Do you hear this, Mr Rampson?" he said, in his most sarcastic manner, the one he adopted towards the most stupidly ignorant boys. "I presume then that I ought to ask Mr Thomas Slegge's permission before asking the two new pupils to my board."

"Yes, sir," burst out Burney, who had gathered breath and had now got into the swing of speaking. "It was bound to come, sir. Slegge said he should do it, and I can't help it if I do seem like a sneak for telling all."

"Go on, Burney," said the Doctor. "I'll be the judge of that."

"Well, sir, he told all us seniors to be ready for the first chance there was. He said —"

"Who said?" interrupted the Doctor. "Let us be perfectly correct."

"Slegge, sir. He said we were to be ready, for he was going to begin by giving the nigger fits."

"By giving the nigger fits?" said the Doctor slowly. "And, pray, what did he mean by that?"

"Licking Singh, sir; the new boy from India, sir."

"Oh," said the Doctor sarcastically. "But he has not been giving the nigger fits."

"No, sir; next day he changed his mind, and said he'd let Severn have it first."

"Have it first?" said the Doctor slowly. "Your language is not very correct, Burney. But go on."

"Yes, sir. He sent word round this morning to all the boys except those two that we were to meet down here by the elms; and when we did come, just as he thought, Severn and Singh fancied there was some new game on, and came to see. Then, sir, Slegge began at Severn, insulting him, sir—yes, that he did. I'm not going to say everything he called him; but he told him to stand up like a man and take his punishment."

"Yes; and what did Severn say?"

"He said, sir, he was not going to degrade himself by fighting like a street blackguard; and then Slegge jeered and mocked at him and set us all at him to call him coward and cur; and he ended, sir, by walking straight up to him, and he asked him three times if he'd fight, and Severn, sir, said he wouldn't, and then Slegge gave him a coward's blow—one in the nose, sir, and made it bleed."

"Ah!" said the Doctor. "And what did Severn do?"

"Took out his pocket-handkerchief, sir, and wiped it."

"Exactly," said the Doctor, with grim seriousness, "and a very correct thing too; that is," he continued hastily, as if he had some slight idea of the suggestiveness of his remark, "I mean, that Severn behaved very well in refusing to fight. But he turned upon Slegge, of course, after such an incitement as that."

"No, sir, he didn't; he only stood there looking very red and with his lips quivering, and looking quite wild and reproachful at Singh."

"Oh!" said the Doctor. "Then Singh has been in it too?"

"Yes, sir; Singh came at him like a lion, and said he was a coward and a cur, and that they'd never be friends again. But Severn did not speak a word, and before we knew what was going to happen next, Slegge took hold of Singh's ear and asked him what it had to do with him, and he called him a nigger and an impudent foreign brat; and almost before we knew where we were, Singh hit Slegge quick as lightning, one-two right in the face, and then stepped back and began to take off his jacket; but before he could pull it off, Slegge got at him; and the boys hissed, sir, for while Singh's hands were all in a tangle like in the sleeves, Slegge hit him three or four times in the face; but it only made him fierce, and getting rid of his jacket, he went at big Slegge."

"Ah!" ejaculated the Doctor. "Go on, Mr Burney."

"Slegge made a dash at him, sir; but Singh was too quick, and stepped on one side; and when Slegge turned upon him again Severn sprang in between them, snatched off his jacket, and crammed it into Singh's hands. And then all the boys began to hooray."

"What for?" said the Doctor.

"Because Severn said, sir, out loud, 'Not such a coward as you think, Singhy. I must fight now.'"

"Bad—very bad," said the Doctor; "cowardly too—two boys to one."

"Oh no, sir; Singh didn't do any more. He only laughed, threw down the jacket, and began slapping Severn on the back; and he seconded him, sir, quite fair and square all through, just as if he knew all about fighting, though he is a nig— Indian, sir. And there was a tremendous fight, till, after being a good deal knocked about, Severn was getting it all his own way, and finished off Slegge just as you came up, sir. And that's the whole truth.—Isn't it, boys?"

There was a chorus of the word "Yes," and the Doctor drew a deep breath as it came to an end. Then he uttered the interjection "Hah!" looked very searchingly at Slegge, scanning the injuries he had received, and afterwards made the same keen examination of Severn.

"Disgraceful!" he said at last, shaking his head and frowning. "Young gentlemen, you will resume your studies at once.—Mr Rampson, will you see that these two injured lads go to their dormitory directly. Mrs Hamton will attend to their injuries and report to me whether it is necessary for the surgeon to be called in.—You hear me, boys?" shouted the Doctor. "Disperse at once. There will be a lecture in the theatre in ten minutes' time.—Mr Rampson, there is to be no communication between these two principals and the rest.—You, Burney, and you, Singh, go on to my library."

The next minute the trampled arena was in silence, and the Doctor, with his hands clasped behind him, was marching back alone towards his study, going so slowly that every one who had formed a portion of the little gathering had disappeared by the time he was half-way to the open French window.

There was something peculiar about Dr Bewley's countenance as he slowly marched back. For one minute it was placid, the next stern, and directly after a slight quivering of the facial nerves developed into a mirthful look, which was emphasised by a low, pleasant, chuckling laugh. For the fact was that the tall, stern, portly Doctor's thoughts had gone far back to his old schooldays and a victory he had once achieved over the brutal bully of the school at which he had been placed. And whether he was alluding to the tyrant of his days or to the one who had lorded it for long enough in the establishment of which he was the head must remain a mystery; but certain it was that the Doctor muttered presently to himself, "An overbearing young ruffian! A thoroughly good thrashing; and serve him right!"

The next moment the utterer of these words, which had fallen upon his own ears only, was looking guiltily round as if in dread lest he might have been heard. But there was no one visible but Sam Grigg, who was brushing hard at boots by the entrance to his own particular outdoor den; and he was too far away to hear; while, when the Doctor entered his study, he was met at the door by Wrench, who announced that a lady was waiting in the drawing-room, and he handed a card.

"Ha, yes, Wrench," said the Doctor. "About a new pupil. I will see her directly.—Oh, Singh—Burney, you here? I will speak to you both another time. One moment—this is private, boys. You both know—at least, you do now, Burney, and you from henceforth must remember the same, Singh—I allow no brutal fighting in my establishment; but I am not very angry with you, my lads, for on the whole there was a display of manliness in your conduct that I cannot find it in my heart to condemn. There, you, Singh, can go and see your friend Severn.—And you, Burney, h'm—humph—well, yes, go and see Slegge. You must not forsake your companion now he is down."

Chapter Twelve
"With Faces like this."

Singh's encounter with Slegge had been very short, and when the Doctor sent him in the tokens of the affray were very slight; but a few hours afterwards certain discolorations were so manifest that the Doctor frowned and told him he had better join his companion in the dormitory for a few days and consider himself in Mrs Hamton's charge. Singh hailed the order with delight, and went straight to his bedroom, where the plump, pleasant, elderly housekeeper had just entered before him, carrying a small basin half-full of some particular liniment-like preparation of her own, a sponge, and a soft towel.

When Singh appeared at the door Glyn sat up so suddenly that he nearly knocked over the basin that Mrs Hamton had given him to hold, after spreading the soft towel in his lap, when she began sponging his face with the preparation.

"Oh, my dear child," she cried, "pray, be careful!"

"Ha, ha, ha!" laughed the boy merrily.—"Oh, do look at him, Mrs Hamton. What a guy!"

"Guy!" cried Singh sharply. "What do you mean?"

He dashed to the dressing-table and took his first look at his face in the glass since he had dressed that morning.

"Oh, I say," he cried, "I never thought of this. Why, it's just like my face was that day after the sergeant had shown us how to use the boxing-gloves."

"Yes," cried Glyn merrily; "but what sort of a phiz would you have had if you had fought it out?"

"One something like yours," cried Singh. "Oh, I say, you ought to talk! What eyes! and your lip all cut. Why, your face is all on one side."

"Yes, isn't it shocking, my dear," said the old housekeeper. "I do hope that it will be a lesson to you both. I never could understand why young gentlemen were so fond of fighting."

"Oh, it's because it's so nice, Mrs Hamton," said Glyn, who spoke as if he were in the height of glee.

"I don't believe you mean that, my dear; but there, lie back in the chair again, and let me go on dabbing all your poor cuts and bruises with this lotion and water. It's so cooling and healing, and it will take all the inflammation out.—And don't you go, my dear," she continued, turning to Singh, "till I have done your face over too."

"I am not going," said Singh quietly. "The Doctor sent me up here to stop."

"Has he?" cried Glyn. "Oh, hurrah! Here, Mrs Hamton, another patient for you to make decent.—I say, Singhy, she's just come from old Slegge. I'm afraid I've made his face in a horrible mess."

"You have indeed, my dear," said the housekeeper reproachfully. "But oh, what a pity it is that young gentlemen will so far forget themselves! It grieves me; it does indeed."

"But I don't forget myself," protested Glyn. "I was obliged to fight. You wouldn't have had me lie down and let him knock both of us about for nothing, would you, nurse—I mean Mrs Hamton?"

"Oh, don't ask me, my dear; it's not for me to say; and you needn't mind calling me nurse, for it always sounds nice and pleasant to me. There, now, doesn't that feel cool and comforting?"

"Lovely," cried Glyn softly, and as he looked up in the pleasant face, with its grey curls on either side, his eyes for the moment, what could be seen of them, seemed to be sparkling with mischief and mirth, for there was a feeling of pride and triumph at his success swelling in his breast, and a few moments later, so great was the comfort he experienced under the delicate manipulation of his motherly attendant's hands, that he looked up at her and began to smile—only began, for he uttered an ejaculation of pain.

"Oh, my dear, did I hurt you?" cried the housekeeper.

"No," said the boy, in rather a piteous tone; "it was my face. It's all stiff and queer."

"Yes, I told you that it was one-sided," said Singh merrily.

"Well, never mind, my dear; it will soon be better," said the housekeeper soothingly. "But you must do exactly what I tell you, and be very patient and still."

"But, I say, look here, Mrs Hamton," cried Glyn, catching the hand which was bearing the sponge and holding it to his cheek, to the old lady's intense satisfaction, though somehow there came an unwonted look of moisture in her eyes.

"What were you going to say, my dear? But, dear, dear, what a pity it is that you should go and disfigure yourselves like this! What would your poor father say if he knew?"

"Oh, I say, don't talk about it," cried Glyn.—"Fancy, Singhy, if he could see us now!"

Glyn tried to whistle, but his puffed-up lips refused to give forth a sound; and, seeing this, Singh whistled for him, and then in spite of the pain and stiffness of their faces the two boys laughed till the suffering became intense.

"Oh, don't, don't, don't, Singhy!" cried Glyn. "I can't bear it."

"Well, I never did see two such young gentlemen as you are," said the old housekeeper, smiling in turn.

"You ought both to be lying back looking as melancholy as black, and here you are making fun of your troubles. Ah, it's a fine thing, my dears, to be boys and quite young; but I do hope that you will never fight any more, and that you will both soon go and shake hands with Mr Slegge, and tell him you are very sorry you hit him. I am sure that he must feel very sorry that he ever hit you, he being so much bigger and having so long had the advantage of being taught by the Doctor, who is the best man that ever lived, while you two are so new, and you, Mr Singh, so much younger than Mr Slegge that I do wonder he ever so far forgot himself as to hit you. Now, you will make friends afterwards, won't you?"

"No!" cried Singh sharply. "I hate the coward."

"Oh, my dear!" cried the old lady.

"He doesn't mean it, nursey," cried Glyn, getting hold of her hand again. "He only said it because he feels so sore. He's got a sore face and a sore temper; but it will be all right when he gets well."

"I hope so, my dear; and you will shake hands with him, won't you?"

"Yes," said Glyn merrily, "as soon as he holds out his. I can afford to.—Can't I, Singhy?"

"Oh yes, of course."

"There," said the old lady, "now that's spoken nicely, and I don't think I'll bathe your face any more.—Now, my dear," she continued to Singh, "it's your turn."

"Oh, mine doesn't want doing, does it?" said the boy carelessly.

"Yes, my dear, and very badly too. If it isn't bathed with my lotion it will go on swelling, and be more discoloured still."

"Oh!" cried the boy eagerly.—"Here, you, Glyn, get up out of that chair. It's my turn now, as Mrs Hamton says," and he took another glimpse at the glass. "There, I'm ready. Oh, I say, I do look a wretch!"

Under the care of the good-natured old housekeeper during the next two days a great deal of the swelling went down; but after the old lady's report, and visits from the Doctor himself, they were both still treated as infirmary patients, and relieved from lessons till such time as they should be presentable amongst their fellows.

But on the third day the confinement was growing irksome in the extreme; and the Doctor, after his daily visit, gave Singh permission to come down into the grounds if he liked. But the boy did not like. A glance at his companion in adversity revealed a disappointed look, and as soon as the Doctor was gone he picked up one of the books with which they were well supplied.

"Well," said Glyn gloomily, "why don't you go down?"

"Because I don't want to," was the reply; and no more was said.

But that afternoon soon after dinner, which was brought up to them by the housekeeper on a folding-tray, and just when the irksomeness of their position was pressing hardest upon their brains, there was a quick step on the stairs, a sharp tap at the door, the handle was turned without any waiting for permission, and Wrench's head was thrust in.

"I say, young gents," he cried, "here's a go!"

"What's the matter?" asked Glyn anxiously. "Don't say Slegge's worse."

"I wasn't going to, sir. It's something worse than that."

"What?"

"There's a gentleman along with the Doctor."

"A gentleman!" cried the boys together.

"Yes; a tall, military-looking gentleman, with long white starchers, and such a voice. He seemed as if he wanted to look me through. Fierce as fierce he was when he gave me his card to take in."

"What was on the card?" cried Glyn excitedly.

"Can't you guess, sir?" said the man, grinning.

"Colonel Severn!" shouted Singh.

"My father!" gasped Glyn. "Oh, Singhy! And us with faces like this!"

Chapter Thirteen
Before the "Starchers."

Singh ran across to the glass on the dressing-table.

"Why, Glyn, we can't see him. I'm bad enough, but you are far worse. What's to be done?"

"I dunno," cried Glyn. "Who in the world would have thought he was coming down here to-day!"

"We are supposed to be in the infirmary, aren't we?" said Singh. "I say, couldn't we undress and go to bed?"

"No," said Glyn promptly. "What difference would that make?"

"Why, he'd think we were too ill to be seen."

"Nonsense," cried Glyn. "Wouldn't he come up and see us all the same?"

"Oh dear!" groaned Singh. "What a mess we are in! This comes of your fighting."

"Well, who made me fight? Who began it?"

"Well, I suppose it was I," said Singh; "but I couldn't stand still and let him knock us both about. Oh dear, what a lot of bother it all is!"

"Here, I say, Wrench," cried Glyn excitedly, "were you sent up to tell us that my father was here?"

"No, sir," said the man, grinning; "but I thought you'd like to know. I must go now, in case my bell rings."

The footman went off hurriedly, and the two boys, after a fresh visit to the looking-glass, tried to make the best of their appearance.

Glyn combed his hair down in a streak over one side of his bruised forehead, while Singh poured out some cold water and dabbed and sponged his right eye; but he could not wash away the discoloration that surrounded it, and after applying the towel he plumped himself down in a chair and sat staring at his companion.

"It's no use," he said; "I daren't face guardian, and I won't."

"You tell him so," said Glyn, laughing, "and see what he will say."

"How am I going to tell him so when I shan't see him?"

"Why, you'll be obliged to."

"I tell you I won't!" cried Singh passionately.

"There's a sneak! And you will let me go down alone and face it all."

"Oh, I say, don't talk like that," cried Singh. "Can't we get out of it somehow, old chap? Let's run away till the Colonel's gone."

"Yes, of course," cried Glyn sarcastically. "How much money have you got?"

"Oh, I don't know; half-a-crown and some shillings."

"Oh, I have got more than that. I have got half-a-sovereign. Shall we go to Plymouth, and sail for somewhere abroad?"

"Yes, anywhere, so that we don't have to meet your father."

"Ah," said Glyn, who was trying very hard to make the lock of hair he had combed over a bruise stop in its place, but it kept jumping up again and curling back to the customary position in spite of applications of cold water and pomatum.

"Well, what do you mean by 'Ah'?" grumbled Singh.

"Mean by 'Ah'?" replied Glyn slowly. "Why, it means what a stupid old chucklehead you are. Run away! Likely, isn't it?"

"Oh, too late! too late!" cried Singh, for there was another sharp tap at the door, and Wrench entered smartly, closely followed by his cat.

"Doctor's compliments, gentlemen, and you are to come down into the drawing-room directly.—And just you go back to the pantry at once," he shouted at his cat. "How many more times am I to tell you that you are not to follow me up into the young gentlemen's rooms?"

"Bah!" shouted Glyn, and he threw the hairbrush he held smartly at the footman, who caught it cleverly, as if he were fielding a ball at mid-wicket, and deposited it upon the dressing-table.

"Well caught, sir!" cried the man, eulogising his own activity. "There, never mind, gentlemen; go down and get it over. There ain't anything to be ashamed of. If I was you, Mr Severn, I should feel proud at having licked that great big disagreeable chap. I shall be glad to see his back. He's quite big enough to leave school."

"Ah!" said Glyn with a sigh. "Come on, Singhy; Wrench is right. Let's get it over; only I want to bathe my face again. It smells of old Mother

Hamton's embro— what did she call it? You may as well go on first. I won't be long."

"What!" cried Singh, looking aghast at the speaker. "Go down and see him alone? I won't! He's not my father; he's yours. You may go first, and I won't come unless I'm obliged."

"Won't you?" said Glyn, laughing softly, and he caught hold of his companion's wrist and drew it under his arm. "Open the door, Wrenchy, and make way for the hospital—two wounded men going down.—I say, Singhy, look as bad as you can. Here, I know: Wrenchy and I will carry you down in a chair."

Singh opened his mouth quickly and shut it sharply, making his white teeth close together with a snap. Then knitting his brows and drawing a deep breath, he held on tightly to his companion, and walked with him in silence downstairs into the hall. Here the pair stopped short by the drawing-room door, where Wrench slipped before them and raised his hand to show them in; but Glyn caught him by the arm.

"Wait a moment," he said, and the three stood there by the mat, forming a group, listening to the slow, heavy murmur of the Doctor's voice and the replies given in a loud, sonorous, emphatic tone.

"Now," said Glyn at last.

The door was thrown open, and they entered, to face the Doctor, who was seated back in an easy-chair with his hands before him and finger-tips joined; while right in the centre of the hearthrug, his back to the fireplace and legs striding as if he were across his charger, stood the tall grey Colonel, swarthy with sunburn and marked by the scar of a tulwar-cut which had divided his eyebrow and passed diagonally from brow to cheek.

He was gazing at the Doctor and listening politely to something he was saying in his soft, smooth voice, but turned his head sharply as the door was opened, and his ultra-long, heavy grey moustache seemed to writhe as he fixed the boys with his keen grey eyes in turn.

"Right, Doctor!" he cried, as if he were giving an order to a squadron to advance. "Disgraceful!—Well, you do look a pretty pair!"

"I'll leave you together," said the Doctor, rising slowly, and then glancing at the boys. "Yes," he said softly, "dreadfully marked; but you should have seen them, Colonel, directly after their encounter."

"Ha, yes; wounded on the field," said the Colonel drily. "Thank you. Yes, sir, I think I should like to have a few words with them alone."

For the first time since they had known him the feeling was strong upon the boys that they would have liked their preceptor to stay.

But the Doctor gave each of them a grave nod as he moved towards the door, and they both stood as if chained to the carpet till the Colonel made a stride forward, when Glyn recollected himself, ran to the door, and opened it for the Doctor to pass out.

The Colonel grunted, and then as the door was closed, he marched slowly across to his son; and as the boy faced him caught him by the shoulder with his right hand, walked him back to where Singh stood alone, grabbed him with his left, and forced them both towards the wide bay window fully into the light.

"Stand there!" he said, in commanding tones.

Then stooping stiffly to seize the Doctor's easy-chair by the back, he made the castors squeak as he swung it round and threw himself into it with his back to the window, when he crossed one leg over the other, and sat staring at them fiercely and scanning for some moments every trace of the late encounter.

Glyn drew a long, deep breath loudly enough to be heard, while Singh stood with hanging hands, opening and closing his fingers, and passing his tongue quickly over his dry lips. But the Colonel still went on staring at them and frowning heavily the while.

At last Singh could bear it no longer.

"Oh, say something, sir!" he cried passionately. "Scold us, bully us, punish us if you like; but I can't bear to be looked at like that."

It was the Colonel's turn now to draw a deep breath, as he raised himself in the chair a little, thrust one hand behind him, fumbled for his pocket, and then drew out a large soft bandana handkerchief and blew his nose with a blast like a trumpeted order to charge.

Then, as he sank back in his chair, "Ha, ha, ha! haw, haw, haw!" he literally roared. "Well, you do look a pretty pair of beauties!" he cried. "But this won't do. Here, you, Glyn, what do you mean by this, sir? Didn't I warn you against fighting, and tell you to protect and set an example to young Singh here?"

"Yes, father."

"Look at yourself in the glass. You look a pretty pattern, don't you?"

"Yes, father."

"I told you to look at yourself in the glass. Why don't you?"

"Because I know every scratch and bruise thoroughly by heart, father."

"But—" began the Colonel.

Here Singh interposed.

"It wasn't his fault, sir," cried the boy. "It was mine. He didn't want to fight, and said he wouldn't."

"Ho!" said the Colonel. "Said he wouldn't fight, did he."

"Yes, sir, and he actually let the big bully hit him."

"Ha!" said the Colonel. "And then knocked him down for it?"

"No, he didn't, sir," cried Singh, with his eyes twinkling. "He wouldn't fight even then."

"Humph!" grunted the Colonel. "And what then?"

"Well, it put me in such a rage, sir, that I couldn't bear it, and I went and hit the big fellow right in the face, and he hit me again."

"Ah, you needn't tell me that," replied the Colonel; "that's plain enough. Well, what after?"

"Well, that made Glyn take my part, and he swung me behind him; and oh, sir, he did give the big fellow such an awful thrashing!"

"Ha!" said the Colonel, taking his great grey moustache by both hands and drawing it out horizontally. "A thorough thrashing, eh?"

"Yes, sir."

"And what were you doing?"

"Oh, I was seconding him, sir."

"Oh, that was right. You were not both on him at once?"

"Oh no, sir; it was all fair."

"Then Glyn thoroughly whipped him, eh?"

"Yes, sir, thoroughly."

The Colonel turned to his son, and looked him over again; and then, after another two-handed tug at his moustache, he said slowly:

"I say, Glyn, old chap, you got it rather warmly. But tut, tut, tut, tut! This won't do. What did that old chap say: 'Let dogs delight to bark and bite'? Here, I have been talking to the Doctor, and the Doctor has been talking to me. Look here, you, Singh, military fighting, after proper discipline, and done by fighting men, is one thing; schoolboy fighting is quite another, not for gentlemen. It's low and blackguardly.—Do you hear, Glyn?" he cried turning on his son. "Blackguardly, sir—blackguardly. Look at your faces, sir, and see how you have got yourselves marked. But er—er—"

He picked his pocket-handkerchief up from where he had spread it over his knees and blew another blast. "This er—this er—big fellow that you thrashed—big disagreeable fellow—bit of a bully, eh?"

"Regular tyrant, father. We hadn't been here a month, before not a day passed without his insulting Singh or making us uncomfortable."

"Ha! insulted Singh, did he?"

"Yes, sir," cried that individual through his set teeth. "He was always calling me nigger, and mocking at me in some way."

"Humph! Brute! And so, after putting up with a good deal, and obeying my orders till he couldn't stand it any longer, Glyn took your part and thrashed the fellow, eh?"

"Yes, sir, bravely," cried Singh, with his eyes flashing. "I wish you'd been there to see."

"I wish—"

The Colonel stopped short. "No, no. Tut, tut! Nonsense! I did not want to see. Here, hold out your hands, Glyn. No, no, not like that. Double your fists. Hold them out straight. I want to look at your knuckles. Dreadful! Nice state for a gentleman's hands. Fighting's bad.—Do you hear, Singh? Very bad. But I must confess that I didn't get through school without a turn-up or two myself. Glyn took your part, then, and thrashed the fellow. Well, he won't bully either of you again. Yes, I got into my scrapes when I was a boy; but you know times were different then. Everything was rougher. This sort of thing won't do. You must be more of gentlemen now—more polished. Fighting's bad."

"But you let the sergeant, father, teach us how to use the gloves after you had got them over from England."

"Eh? What, sir—what sir?" cried the Colonel sharply. "Well, yes, I did. It was a bit of a lapse, though, and every man makes mistakes. But that, you see, was part of my old education, and through being in India so many years and away from modern civilisation, and er— Of course, I remember; it was after your poor father had been talking to me, Singh, and telling me that he looked to me to make you a thorough English gentleman, one fit to occupy his throne some day, and rule well over his people—firmly, justly, and strongly, as an Englishman would. And, of course, I thought it would be right for you both to know how to use your fists if you were unarmed and attacked by ruffians. And—er, well, well, you see I was not quite wrong. Mind, you know, I detest fighting, and only this morning I have been quite agreeing with the Doctor—fine old gentlemanly fellow, by the way, and a great scholar—agreeing with him, I say, that this fighting is rather a disgrace. At the same time, my boys, as I was about to say, I was not quite wrong about those gloves. You see, it enabled Glyn here to bring skill to bear against a bigger and a stronger man, and er—um—you see, there are other kinds of fighting that a man will have to go through in life; and then when such things do happen, mind this—I mean it metaphorically, you know—when you do have to fight with your fists, or with your tongue, thrash your adversary if you can; but if he from superior skill or strength thrashes you, why then, take it like a man, shake hands, and bear no malice against the one who wins."

The Colonel blew his nose again.

"That's not quite what I wanted to say, my boys; but I shall think this affair over a bit, and perhaps I shall have a few more words to say by-and-by."

"Oh, I say, dad—" cried Glyn.

"What do you mean by that, sir?" said the Colonel sharply.

"Finish it all now, and don't bring it up again."

"Glyn!" cried the Colonel sternly.

"Yes, father."

"Don't you dictate to me, sir. I promised the Doctor that I would talk to you both severely about this—this—well, piece of blackguardism, ungentlemanly conduct, and I must keep my word. But I will reserve the rest till after dinner."

"After dinner, father?" cried Glyn eagerly.

"Yes. I have come down to stay at Plymborough for a few days at the hotel, and I have told them there that I should have two gentlemen to dine with me to-night, of course, if the Doctor gives his consent."

"Oh, but look at us, sir!" cried Singh. "We are in the infirmary, and not fit to come."

"Infirmary!" said the Colonel scornfully. "Ha, ha! You look infirm both of you!"

"Oh, we don't feel much the matter, father," said Glyn; "but look at us."

"Look at you, sir? How can I help looking at you? Yes, you do look nice objects."

"But we can't help it now, sir," said Singh, "and we should like to come."

"Humph! Yes, of course you'd like to come, my boy, and I want to have you both to finish my lecture after I have thought it out a little more. Well, look here, my lads; you are both bruised and—er—a bit discoloured; but the world isn't obliged to know that it was done with fists. You might have been thrown off your horses or been upset in a carriage accident. Oh yes, it's no business of anybody else's. I shall ask the Doctor to let you come."

"Oh, thank you, father!" cried Glyn eagerly. "But I say, dad, you didn't shake hands with Singh when we came in."

"Well, no, boy; but—there, there, that's all right now. You see I had to listen to what the Doctor said. Why, he tells me that you fellows showed them all down here how to deal with a rowdy elephant."

"Singh did, father."

"Well done, boy! You see, that's one great advantage in learning. Nearly everything comes useful some time or other, and— There, let me see," he continued, referring to his watch. "I must be off. Visit too long as it is. Ring the bell, one of you. I want to see the Doctor again before I go."

"And you will get us leave, sir?" cried Singh, as he returned from pulling at the bell.

"Oh yes, I'll manage that. Seven o'clock, boys, military time; and now you both be off; but mind this, I am going to finish my lecture after dinner, for I am not satisfied with what I said. There, right about face! March!"

As the boys reached the door the handle was turned and the Doctor entered the room.

Chapter Fourteen
A Little Bit about the Past

"Well, boys, glad to see you! Did Dr Justinian say anything to you about coming away to-night?"

"No, father; but—Dr Justinian—who do you mean?"

"Why, your law-maker and instructor. He spoke very seriously to me about breaking his laws and rules. Well, here you are. Come along. The dining-room is this way.—I have been very busy since I saw you, Singh. I have seen the cook and given him a good talking to, and he has promised us a regular Indian dinner, with curry."

The Colonel laid his hand on Singh's shoulder, and they passed out into the hall of the hotel.

As they were crossing, Morris entered from the other side, nodded and smiled to the boys, raised his hat to the Colonel, who stared at him, and then passing on, went up to the office to speak to the manager.

"Friend of yours, boys?" said the Colonel. "Yes, father; one of our masters."

"Oh! What brings him here?"

"I don't know, father. Perhaps he thought you might ask him to dinner."

"Ho!" said the Colonel, with a snort. "Then he thought wrong. Ah—but one moment! Would you like me to ask him, my boy?"

"Oh no," cried Glyn, with a look of dismay. "We want you all to ourselves, father."

"But you, Singh; would you like him to join us?"

The boy shrugged his shoulders and shook his head.

"No," he said; "I think like Glyn does," and Singh clung in a boyish, affectionate manner to the stalwart Colonel's arm, greatly to that gentleman's satisfaction.

"Then we will have our snug little dinner all to ourselves, boys, and a good long talk about old times and the last news I have had from Dour.— Yes, all right, waiter; serve the dinner at once, and mind everything is very hot.—There you are: snug little table for three. I'll sit this side with my back to the light, and you two can sit facing it, so that I can look at you both."

"Oh, but that isn't fair, father," cried Glyn. "We ought to be with our backs to the light."

"Not at all, sir," said the Colonel, laughing. "A soldier should never be ashamed of his scars."

The seats were taken, the dinner began, and had not proceeded far before Glyn noticed that the waiter was staring very hard at his bruised face, getting so fierce a look in return that the man nearly dropped the plate he was handing, and refrained from looking at him again.

"Better bring candles, waiter," said the Colonel.—"One likes to see what one is eating, boys;" and as a few minutes later the waiter placed a tall branch with its four wax candles in the centre of the table, the Colonel nodded to Singh. "There," he said, "now we can all play fair, and you can see my scars."

"Yes," said Singh, looking at the Colonel fixedly. "There's the big one quite plain that father used to tell me about."

"Indeed!" said the Colonel sharply. "Why, what did he tell you about it, and when?"

"Oh, it was when I was quite a little fellow," replied Singh. "He said it was in a great fight when three of the rajahs had joined against him to attack him and kill him, and take all his land. He said that there was a dreadful fight, and there were so many of his enemies that he was being beaten."

"Oh—ah—yes," said the Colonel. "Your father and I had a great many fights with his enemies when the Company sent me to help him with a battery of horse artillery, and to drill his men."

"Was that, father, when you drilled and formed your regiment of cavalry?"

"Yes, boy, yes. But never mind the fighting now. That was in the old days. Go on with your dinner."

But Singh did not seem to heed his words, for he was sitting gazing straight before him at the scar on his host's forehead; and laying down his knife and fork he continued, in a rapt, dreamy way, "And he said he thought his last hour had come, for he and the few men who were retreating with him had placed their backs against a steep piece of cliff, and they were fighting for their lives, surrounded by hundreds of the enemy."

"My dear boy, you are letting your dinner get cold," said the Colonel, in a petulant way.

"Yes," continued Singh, "and it was all just like a story out of a book. I used to ask father to tell it to me, and when I did he used to smile and make me kneel down before him with my hands on his knees."

"But, my dear Singh," interposed the Colonel, who looked so annoyed and worried that Glyn kicked his schoolfellow softly under the table, and then coloured up.

"Don't!" cried Singh sharply; and then in his old dreamy tone, "When he told me I used to seem to see it all, with his fierce enemies in their steel caps with the turbans round them, and the chain rings hanging about their necks and their swords flashing in the air as they made cuts at my father's brave friends; and first one fell bleeding, and then another, till there were only about a dozen left, and my father the Maharajah was telling his men that the time had come when they must make one bold dash at their enemies, and die fighting as brave warriors should."

"Yes, yes, yes, yes!" cried the Colonel querulously. "But that curry is getting cold, my boy, and it won't be worth eating if it isn't hot."

"Yes, I'll go on directly," continued Singh in the same imperturbable manner, and he leaned his elbows now upon the table, placed his chin upon his hands, and fixed his eyes upon the Colonel's scar.

"I can see it all now so plainly," he said; and with a quick gesture his host dropped his knife sharply in his plate and clapped his hand across his forehead, while Glyn gave his schoolfellow another thrust—a soft one this time—with his foot.

But Singh paid not the slightest heed to his companion's hint. He only leaned a little more forward to look now in the Colonel's eyes; and laughing softly he continued:

"That doesn't make any difference. I can see it all just the same, and I seem to hear the roar like thunder father spoke about. He said it was the trampling of horses and the shouting of men, and it was you tearing over the plain from out of the valley, with all the men that you had drilled and made into his brave regiment. They swept over the ground with a rush, charging into the midst of the enemy and cutting right and left till they reached my father and his friends, when a terrible slaughter went on for a few minutes before the enemy turned and fled, pursued by your brave soldiers, who had left their leader wounded on the ground. Father said he had just strength enough to catch you in his arms as you fell from your horse with that terrible gash across your forehead. That was how he said you saved his life and always became his greatest friend."

The Colonel's lips had parted to check the narration again and again; but he seemed fascinated by the strange look in the boy's eyes, and for the time being it was as if the whole scene of many years before was being enacted once again; while, to Glyn's astonishment, the boy slowly rose from his seat, went round to the Colonel's side of the table, to stand behind his chair till the waiter left the room, and then laying one hand on the old warrior's shoulder, with the other he drew away that which covered the big scar, and bending over him he said softly:

"Father told me I was to try and grow up like you, who saved his life, and that I was always to think of you as my second father when he was gone."

As Singh ended he bent down gently, and softly and reverently kissed the scar, while the Colonel closed his eyes and Glyn noticed that his lips were quivering beneath the great moustache, which seemed to move strangely as if it had been touched.

For a few moments then there was a deep silence, during which Singh glided back to his seat, took up his knife and fork, and said, in quite a changed tone of voice:

"It always makes me think of that when I sit and look at you. And it comes back, sir, just like a dream. My father the Maharajah told me I was never to forget that story; and I never shall."

Just at that moment the door was opened, and the waiter entered bearing another dish, while through the opening there came a burst of music as if some band were playing a march.

"Hah!" cried the Colonel, speaking with quite a start, but with his voice sounding husky and strange, and the words seeming forced as he gave Singh a long and earnest look. "Why, surely that is not a military band?"

"No, sir," said the waiter, as he proceeded to change the plates, two of them having their contents hardly touched. "There's a wild-beast show in the town, sir, in the field at the back," and as he spoke the man looked sharply at the boys.

"Oh," said the Colonel with a forced laugh. "Why, boys, is that where your elephant came from?"

And then the dinner went on, with the Colonel forcing himself into questioning the boys about their adventure, and from that he brought up the elephants in Dour, and chatted about tiger-shooting and the dangers of the man-eaters in the jungle. But all the time Glyn kept noting that his father spoke as if he had been strangely moved, and that when he turned his eyes upon Singh his face softened and his voice sounded more gentle.

As they sat over the dessert, Singh asked him to tell them about one of the other old fights that his father and the Colonel had been in.

"Don't ask me, my boy," said the Colonel gently. "You can't understand it perhaps. When you grow as old as I am perhaps you will. But I don't know. You like Glyn after a fashion, I suppose?"

"Like him?" cried Singh half-fiercely. "Why, of course I do!"

"Ha!" said the Colonel. "And Glyn likes you, I know; and no wonder— brought up together as you were like brothers. Well, my boy, I went out to India not very much older than you two fellows are, as a cadet in the Company's service, and somehow or other, being a reckless sort of a fellow, I was sent into several of the engagements with some of the chiefs, and was picked out at last, when I pretty well understood my work, to go to your father's court as you said, my boy, with half-a-dozen six-pounders and teams of the most dashing Arab horses in the service. Then, somehow, your father got to like me, and I liked him, and then we did a lot of fighting together until he was fixed securely upon his throne, and he never would hear of my leaving him again. But there, you know all about it. He left you to me, Singh, to make a man of you with Glyn here, and I hope to live to go back with you both to Dour and see you safe in your rightful position and fight for you if the need should ever come. And some day I hope that you two boys will have grown into two strong, true-hearted men, with the same brotherly love between you as held your fathers fast. And then— Oh, hang that music! The fellows can't play a bit. Here, what do you say? Shall we walk into the field and listen to them and see the show? Your elephant too?"

"No," said Singh softly. "Let's stop here and talk about Dour and my father. We don't often see you now, sir, and I should like that best."

"To be sure, then, my dear boys, we will stop here. I want you to do what you like best.—But you, Glyn: what do you say?"

"I like to hear you talk, father, and to be with you as much as we can."

"That's good, my boy. Then, to begin with," cried the Colonel with a chuckle, "I'll just finish my lecture. I was very nearly letting it slip."

"Oh, but, father," cried Glyn, "I thought you had looked over all that."

"I have, my boy; but you know I am not good at talking. The Doctor would have given you a splendid lecture on fighting."

"He did," said Glyn drily, and the Colonel laughed.

"I suppose he would, my boys; but since I saw you this morning something occurred to me that I might have mentioned to you. How much do you boys know about Shakespeare?"

"Not much, father—neither of us, I am afraid."

"Ah, well, I dare say it will come to you by-and-by; but there are some words that Shakespeare put into the mouth of an old court official in *Hamlet*, when he was bidding his son good-bye before he went abroad. There, don't yawn, either of you. I am only trying to quote it to you because to my mind they were very good words, and just suitable for you, because they were about fighting: 'Beware of entrance to a quarrel; but being in, bear't that the opposer may beware of thee; and—' Humph! Ah, dear me, let me see; there was something else about borrowing and lending. But never mind that. It was about the fighting that I wanted to speak, and the long and short of it was, don't fight, boys, if you can possibly help it; but if you do fight, show the other fellow that you know how. There, that's enough about that. Now then, what shall we talk about next?—Yes, waiter, what is it?"

"Beg pardon, sir, but there's a person, sir, in the hall wants to know if he can see the young gentlemen."

"Eh? Who is it?" said the Colonel sharply. "Not one of the masters?"

"No, sir. It's the proprietor, sir, of the big wild-beast show, sir, in the field—Mr Ramball, sir."

"Oh, pooh! pooh!" cried the Colonel. "Tell him the young gentlemen are engaged, and don't care to visit his show to-night."

"Yes, sir. But beg pardon, sir, I don't think it's about that. He's in great trouble about something, sir. He's well-known here, sir; has a large farm two or three miles away where he keeps his wild things when he's not taking them round the country."

"Well, but—" began the Colonel.

"Said it was very particular business, sir, and he must see the young gentlemen."

"Why, it must be something about his elephant, father," cried Glyn eagerly.

"Well, but, my dear boys, you can't be at the beck and call of this man because he owns animals that he can't manage. But there, there, I don't want you two to withhold help when you can give it. We'll hear what he has to say.—We'll come out and speak to him.—I'll come, boys, because you may want to refer to me."

The little party followed the waiter out into the hall, where Ramball was standing, hat in one hand, yellow handkerchief in the other, dabbing his bald head and looking very much excited.

"Hah!" he cried. "There you are, gentlemen!" And he put his handkerchief on the top of his head and made a movement as if to thrust his hat into his pocket, but recollected himself and put the handkerchief into the hat instead. "I have been up to the school, gentlemen— Your servant, sir. I beg pardon for interrupting you; but I have been up to the school to ask for the young gentlemen there, and I saw Mr Wrench the Doctor's man, and he said that you had come on here to dinner.—Pray, pray, gentlemen, come and help me, or I am a ruined man."

"Why, what's the matter?" cried Singh and Glyn in a breath.

"Didn't you hear, gentlemen? He's got away again—pulled the iron picket out of the ground, and gone off with the chain and all chinkupping from his leg. I have got men out all over scouring the country, and as soon as they have found out where he is I'd take it kindly, gentlemen, if you'd come and bring him home."

"Come, come, my man," said the Colonel good-humouredly, "isn't this rather cool?"

"Cool, sir! It's too hot to be borne. That great beast will be the death of me before he's done. Do say a kind word for me, sir, to the young gents. They have got a power over that beast as beats miracles. I wouldn't ask, sir, but I'm about done. I should have shot him the other day if these 'ere young gents hadn't stopped me and showed me, a man of fifty, as has handled poisonous snakes and gone after lions before now when they'd got out— showed me, I say, that I didn't understand my work."

"Oh, well," said the Colonel, "I—I—"

At that moment the elephant's keeper and another man, a driver of one of the caravans, hurried excitedly into the hotel hall, dragging between them a miserable-looking object, drenched with mud and water, and trembling in every limb.

"Mr Ramball, sir!" cried the keeper.

"What, have you found him?" cried the proprietor.

"No, sir; but we've come across this chap, as has got a cock-and-bull story about something, and I think it means that he's seen him."

"Yes—what? Where? How?" cried Ramball, catching hold of the man by the shoulders and letting go again directly, to dive into his hat for his handkerchief. "Why, you are all wet and muddy!" he cried, wiping his hands. "Where did you see him?"

"The giant, sir?" said the poor fellow, shivering.

"Giant?" cried Ramball. "Well, yes, giant if you like. Where did you see him?"

"It was about a mile down the road, sir, and we was coming down the Cut Lane with a load of clover, my mate and me, which we had been to fetch for the governor's horses in the yard here. My mate was driving, and I was sitting on a heap of the clover, stacked up on the hind ladder of the cart. We'd stopped a while after loading up, being a bit tired, to give the horses a drink, and it had got dark, while as we was coming home, me sitting behind as I told you, and my mate driving in front, all of a suddent, and just as I was half-asleep and smoking my pipe, a great big giant loomed up on t'other side of the hedge, and before I knew where I was he reaches down, slips his arm round me, and lifts me right out of the cart."

The man wiped his face with his muddy hand and uttered a low groan.

"Well, go on," cried Ramball. "What next?"

"Don't hurry me, master, please," said the man piteously. "I'm shook all to pieces, and feel that freckened that I could sit down and cry. I was too much staggered to call out for help, and when I tried to look round, my mate and the cart was gone, and this 'ere great thing was carrying me away right across Snow's field, and all I could think of was that he was hungry and had made me his prey."

"Humph! An ogre, I suppose," said the Colonel to the boys.

"No, sir," said the man; "it was one of them there great giants as you read of in books; and no matter how I tried to get away, he only hugged me the tighter."

"Well, well," said the Colonel; "but you did escape."

"No, sir; I didn't, sir. He carried me right across the field and dropped me into the big horse-pond in the corner. I was half-drowned, I was; and when I struggled to the side my legs stuck in the mud right up to my knees. And then I found that I had come out, half-blind with mud and water, just where he was standing with his back to me, and then I daren't move. But he took no more notice of me, and walked right off, so that I saved my life. Next thing was I come upon your two men, Mr Ramball, sir, and they got asking me questions; but I was too skeart to understand what they meant, and so they brought me here.—You don't know, I suppose," he continued, speaking to one of the waiters who had come into the hall, "whether my mate came home safely with the clover cart?"

"Bah!" cried Ramball. "With your giant indeed! Which way did he go?"

"I dunno, sir; it was too dark. But it were a giant. I could swear to him if I saw him again. I should know him by his trowges."

"Know him by what?" cried the Colonel, laughing heartily.

"By his trowges, sir. I was down in the mud close behind him, and I could see right up his great legs to his waist. I couldn't see any farther, he was so big. Awful giant, he was. You may take my word, sir, for that."

"Bah!" roared the proprietor. "Here, my lads, he's frightened this poor lad nearly into fits, and we are wasting time. Off with you, and follow his track from the spot where you found the man. Run him down, and then don't do anything more to scare him or make him turn nasty; but one of you stop and watch, and t'other come back here and tell me where he is."

The two keepers obeyed promptly, and hurried away, while one of the waiters sent the scared carter out into the kitchen.

"That's 'im, sir," said Ramball; "and if the young gents would just give me a hand to make things easy—"

"Yes, yes," said the Colonel; "but from what I know of elephants, that great brute may go wandering about through the country for half the night. You'd better go after your men and track him. He'll be most likely in some turnip-field having a gorge, and if you can't get him quietly back come to me again and I'll see what I can do."

"Beg pardon, sir," said Ramball quietly, "I am ready for anything now, cunning as I used to think myself. But does your honour understand elephants?"

"Does he understand elephants, Glyn!" cried Singh.—"Why, Mr Ramball, my friend's father has trapped scores out in the Terai."

"Of course he has, sir," said Ramball.—"Thank you kindly, then, sir. I'll have my pony put to and go after him at once."

Ramball hurried out of the hall, and the Colonel with his young guests was about to return to the dining-room when they found that Morris and Professor Barclay were standing close behind them.

"Quite a succession of adventures, Mr Singh," said Morris.

"Yes," said the Professor, "and most interesting your knowledge of the habits of those great beasts."

"Yes, exactly," said the Colonel drily. "They are rather difficult to deal with.—Come boys," and he led the way into the dining-room. "There, sit down for a bit," he said, resuming his old seat. "Are both those your masters, Glyn, my boy?"

"No, father; only one. The other's a friend of his, I think."

"What, that rather shady-looking individual?"

"No, father, the Professor—Professor Barclay. He dined at the Doctor's the other night."

"Oh," said the Colonel. "Well, I don't wish to be too exclusive; but somehow I never care for strangers who are so very eager to make friends."

"But oughtn't we to have gone to help find the elephant, father?" said Glyn.

"No, my boy, I think not. You are my guests to-night, and we don't often meet. If they find him, and there is any real necessity, perhaps we will go; but we shall see."

They did not see; for a quiet chat was enjoyed for another half-hour, and then the Colonel walked with them to the Doctor's gates and said goodnight.

Chapter Fifteen
The Rajah's Morning Call

"Singh!"

There was no answer. "Singh! Oh, what a sleepy old mongoose it is! Singhy! What's that row out in the playground?"

It was early dawn. The first faint rays of day were peering in on both sides of the drawn blind, the speaker was Glyn, and the words were uttered in consequence of a peculiar clanking noise heard out in the play-yard.

Now, the most common-sense way of finding out the meaning of the noise which had awakened the boy from a deep sleep would have been to jump out of bed, draw up the blind, and throw up the window, letting in the fresh, cool morning air, as the head was thrust out and eyes brought to bear upon the dimly seen shadowy space below. But Glyn felt very drowsy, exceedingly comfortable, and not in the slightest degree disposed to stir. Consequently he called across the little room to the other bed, and, as before said, there was no reply.

"Oh, you are a sleepy one!" muttered the boy, and reaching up his hands he turned them into a catapult, seizing the pillow by both ends, and drawing it upwards from beneath his head, when without rising he hurled it across at Singh, striking him with a pretty good whop.

"Great cowardly bully; that's what you are," muttered the boy. "Oh, I wish I was ten times as strong! Take that, and that, and that!"

The commands were accompanied by a heavy panting, and the sound of blows.

"Why, what's he doing?" said Glyn to himself, growing more wakeful, and beginning to chuckle as he grasped the situation. "Oh, what a game!" he said softly. "He's lying on his back, and got the nightmare, only it's a morning mare; and he's dreaming he's fighting with old Slegge again, and punching my pillow, thinking it's his head. I only wish it had been as soft, and then I shouldn't have had so much skin off my knuckles.—There! There it goes again! It must be the workpeople come to open a drain or something. They must be cross at having to get up so early, or else they wouldn't be banging their tools down like that! Hi! Singhy!"

"Cowardly brute!"

"Singhy!"

"Eh? What's the matter? Time to get up? I haven't heard the bell."

"There it goes again," cried Glyn, as the jangling rattle rose to his ears once more.

"Glyn, what's that?"

"Oh, what an old stupid it is! Here have I been shouting ever so long to make you get up and see. Go and open the window and look out."

"Heigh-ho-hum!" yawned Singh. "I was dreaming that old Slegge hit me in the face again."

"Yes, I know you were."

"Why, you couldn't know I dreamt it."

"But I tell you I did know."

"How could you know, when I was dreaming and you weren't?"

"Why, you were shouting it at me, and pitching into my pillow, thinking it was old Slegge's head."

"Get out! I wasn't. I— Here, how is it I have got two pillows here? Why, you wretch, you must have thrown one at me to wake me!"

There was a sharp rustling, an expiration of breath, and the soft head-rest was hurled back again, just as the jangling noise was repeated more loudly.

"There! Hear that?" cried Glyn.

"I am not deaf, stupid."

"Then jump up and go and see what it is."

"Shan't! It's quite dark yet, and I am as tired as can be."

"Well, only get up and see what that noise is, and then you can go to sleep again."

"Shan't, I tell you. I am not your coolie. What lazy people you English are!"

There was a fresh jangling from below, exciting Glyn's curiosity almost to the highest pitch.

"Look here, Singhy, if you don't get up directly and see what that noise is, I'll come and make you."

"You do if you dare!"

Glyn threw the clothes back, sprang out of bed, and the next moment the coverings of his companion were stripped off on to the floor.

"Oh, you—" snapped Singh. "I'll pay you out for all this!"

"Come on, then."

Glyn did not wait to see whether his companion did come on, but stepped to the window, pulled up the blind, and raised up the window to look out.

"Here, Singh!" he cried, turning to look back. "Come here, quick!"

"Shan't! And if you don't bring those clothes back I'll—I'll— Oh, I say, Glyn, don't be an old stupid. Throw my things over me again and shut that window. Ugh! It is cold!"

"Will you come here and look? Here's the old elephant again."

"Gammon!" cried Singh, whose many years' association with Glyn had made him almost as English in his expressions. "Think you are going to cheat me out of my morning's snooze by such a cock-and-bull story as that?"

Oddly enough at that moment there rang out from one of the neighbouring premises the shrill clarion of a bantam-cock.

"Ha, ha!" laughed Glyn merrily. "It's a cock and elephant!"

"Don't believe you."

But as the rattling noise was continued, Singh sat up in bed.

"I say," he continued, "what's the good of talking such stuff?"

"Stuff, eh? You come and see. Here's that great elephant right in the middle of the playground."

"Tell you I don't believe you, and I shan't get up."

"Ugh! What an old heretic you are! Didn't he get away last night and go no one knows where? Well, he's here."

"I say, though, is he really?"

Clinkitty, clank! clinkitty, clank!

"Hear that?" cried Glyn. "Now you will believe. He's got in here somehow, and he's dragging that chain and the big iron peg all about the playground. Here, I know, Singhy," continued Glyn in a high state of excitement, "he's come after you."

"Rubbish!" shouted Singh; and, springing out of bed, he rushed to the window, where in the gradually broadening dawn, half-across the playground, looking grey and transparent in the morning mist, the huge bulk of the elephant loomed up and looked double its natural size.

"There, then," cried Glyn, "will you believe me now?"

Singh uttered an exclamation aloud in Hindustani, and in an instant there was a shrill snort and a repetition of the clinking of the great chain, as the huge beast shuffled slowly across till it stood close up to the hedge which divided the garden from the playground; and there, muttering softly as if to itself, it began to sway its head from side to side, lifting up first one pillar-like leg and foot and then the other, to plant them back again in the same spot from which they had been raised.

"Well, this is a pretty game," continued Glyn. "Here, you had better say something to him, or shall I?"

"What shall I say?" answered Singh.

"Tell him to kneel down, or lie down and go to sleep before he comes through that hedge and begins walking all over the Doctor's flower-beds."

Seeing the necessity for immediate action, Singh uttered a sharp, short order, and the elephant knelt at once.

"Ah, that's better," cried Glyn.

"What shall I do now?" asked Singh, rather excitedly.

"Do? Why, you had better dress as quickly as you can, and go down to him."

"But it's so early," said Singh. "I haven't finished my sleep."

"And you won't either; and you had better look sharp before he rams that great head of his against the door and comes upstairs to fetch you."

"Bother the elephant!" cried Singh irritably, for this early waking from a comfortable sleep had soured his temper.

"All right; bother him, then," replied Glyn, who was wonderfully wakeful now; "but it seems to me that he's going to bother us. I say, Singhy, the Doctor said he wouldn't let Slegge keep that fox-terrier dog he bought a month ago."

"Well, I know; but what's that got to do with the elephant coming here?"

"Oh, I only meant that the Doctor won't let you keep him as a pet," said Glyn with a chuckle.

"Such rubbish!" snapped out Singh in a rage, as he stood on one leg, thrust one foot through his trousers, and then raising the other he lost his balance somehow, got himself tangled up, and went down with a bang.

"Oh, bother the old trousers!" he cried angrily, as he scrambled up. "Here, I don't know what we are going to do."

"Don't you? Well, I do. It's plain enough that the great brute has been wandering about till he found his way here."

"But how did he get in?" cried Singh jumpily and with a good deal of catching of the breath, for in his haste he kept on getting into difficulties with his buttons and the holes through which they ought to have passed.

"Well, I don't know," said Glyn; "but I should say he tramped along yonder under the wall till he came to where the hedge had been mended up, and then walked through."

"Well, suppose he did," said Singh angrily. "What difference does that make? You see what a mess we are in. You are always pretending to give me good advice; now one is in regular trouble you don't say a word."

"Yes, I did," cried Glyn, who was also hastily dressing. "Not give you advice! Why, didn't I just now tell you I was quite sure the Doctor would not let you keep him for a pet?"

"Look here," snarled Singh, "you'll make me angry directly," and he glanced viciously at his water-jug.

"Can't," cried Glyn. "You're so cross now I couldn't make you any worse. But, I say, what are you going to do?"

"I don't know," replied Singh. "Take it home, I suppose. I came here to England to be educated and made into an English gentleman, not to be turned into a low-caste mahout."

"Oh, what's the good of being so waxy? Look at the fun of the thing! Here, I know; let's finish dressing, and then send old Wrench to tell Mr Ramball that we have found his elephant, or that he has found us."

"But he won't be up till it's time to ring the six o'clock bell. What time is it now?"

"I don't know. About half-past one, I should think," cried Glyn, laughing merrily.

"There you go again! You know it must be much later than that. Yet you will keep on saying things to make me wild. Are you going to help me get out of this dreadful scrape?"

"It isn't your scrape. It's only an accident. You talked to the beast in the old language, and it came after you again, just like a dog after its own master."

"Look here," said Singh, "do you know where Wrench sleeps?"

"Yes."

"Where?" cried Singh eagerly.

"In his bed."

"Oh!" roared Singh passionately; and hearing his loud voice the elephant grunted and began to rise slowly.

"There, I knew you would do it," cried Glyn, who was bubbling over with fun. "He's coming upstairs."

"Oh!" cried Singh again, with an ejaculation of dismay, as he hurried to the window, thrust out his head, and shouted something that sounded like "Gangarroo rubble dubble."

But whatever it meant, it stopped the elephant from crashing through a piece of palisading, and made it kneel again with its head over a flowerbed, and begin picking all the blossoms within its reach.

"Oh dear, just look at him!" cried Singh piteously. "And here you are laughing as if it were the best fun you have ever seen!"

"Well, so it is," cried Glyn—"a regular game!"

"Game! Why, I feel as if I could run away to guardian at the hotel, and never show my face here again."

"Here, don't be such a jolly old stupid, making *Kunchinjingas* out of pimples. Here, I know what I'll do. Of course we couldn't get to old Wrench's place. He sleeps in a turn-up bed in his pantry, I believe. I'd soon turn him down, if I could," cried Glyn, as he poured the contents of his jug into the basin.

"But you had an idea," said Singh.

Bubble, bubble, bubble, bubble, came from the basin as the boy thrust in his face.

Singh uttered a sound like a snarl.

"Wait till I get my towel," gasped Glyn as he raised his face for a moment, and directly after—sounding half-smothered in huckaback, and coming in spasmodic jerks—the boy panted out, "I guess it's about four o'clock now. I'll—I'll go down and make—believe it's six, and ring the big bell. That'll make old Wrench come tumbling out in a fright."

"Ah, to be sure; now you are talking sense. Capital! Make haste."

"Well, I am making haste."

"Oh, Glyn, old chap," cried Singh piteously, "don't, pray don't, begin making fun of it all again. I feel just as if I am to blame for all the mischief that great beast has done and is going to do. He'll obey me, and as soon as I am dressed I am going down to talk to him and try and keep him quiet while you rouse up Wrench."

"Rouse up Wrench!" said Glyn laughing. "Why, it'll rouse up the whole school. Only that I know that the fellows won't be in any hurry to get up, I should be afraid that they would come scrambling out into the playground, and we should have the great monster picking the little ones up one at a time and taking them like pills."

"Oh, there you go again," cried Singh piteously.

"Oh, all right, old chap. That was a slip. But I say, I suppose I'd better not stop to take my hair out of the curl-papers."

"Glyn!"

"There, all right. Dry now. Must put a comb through my hair. I look so fierce the elephant would take me for an enemy. There we are," he continued, talking away as he busied himself. "Is the parting straight? There, come along. Well, you are a fellow! I am ready first."

They hurried down the stairs and made for the door, to find to their great dismay that it was locked, bolted, and chained, and so dark at the end of the passage that it was hard work to find the fastenings; and while Glyn was fumbling about in utter ignorance of how the chain was secured there came, faintly heard, from outside a shrill trumpeting sound.

"Oh," gasped Singh, "he has missed us, and thinks we are gone."

"Run up to the window again and order him to lie down," cried Glyn, speaking earnestly now. "I'll get the door open somehow, or a window, and go out to him and make-believe to mount, till you come down. That'll keep him quiet."

"Yes, yes," panted Singh; "only do make haste."

The boy hurried back along the passage, and in the darkness kicked against a mat and went down with a bang.

"Don't stop to pick up the pieces," cried Glyn, and there was a sound came out of the darkness as if Singh had snapped his teeth together.

Then for nearly five minutes Glyn went on fumbling over the fastenings, and succeeded at last in throwing open the door, to see a few golden fleck-like clouds softly bright high overhead, and away to his right the great animal that had roused him from his peaceful sleep.

He went straight to it without hesitation, and as he got close up, the huge beast began to mutter and grumble, and raised its trunk, while the boy felt it creep round his waist like a serpent and hold him tightly.

"What's he going to do next?" thought Glyn. "He must know I'm not Singh. Why doesn't he come? Hasn't hurt himself, has he?"

Just then Singh appeared at their bedroom window, and called to the intruder softly, with the result that the trunk was uncurled, raised in the air, and used like a trumpet, while a shuffling movement suggested that the animal was about to rise.

"Kneel!" cried Singh, and the animal crouched once more.

"Now you get on his neck, and sit there till I come down."

"It's all very well," grumbled Glyn; "but I don't much like the job while you are away."

All the same, the boy did not hesitate, but took hold of the crouching beast's ear, planted the edge of his shoe in one of the wrinkles of the trunk, and climbed into the mahout's place, his steed raising and lowering its ears and muttering and grumbling impatiently as if waiting to be told to rise.

Meanwhile Singh had disappeared from the window, and after what seemed a very long time made his appearance through the door.

"Oh, what a while you have been!" cried Glyn. "Now then, you had better come here and sit on him to hold him down while I go and ring the bell. Here, I say, though, it won't make him think breakfast's ready, will it, and send him scrambling off after buns?"

"No, no, no! Nonsense!" cried Singh.

"Oh, well, if you don't mind, I don't, because I shall be over there. But, all the same, I shouldn't like to see him kick up behind and throw you over his head."

Singh uttered an impatient ejaculation, and began to climb on to the animal's neck.

"No, no," cried Glyn. "I'm going to get off now."

"No; you must wait till I am up there behind you, and then as you get down I'll slide into your place."

"But you will have to tell him to lift up his ears, for he's nipping my legs hard, and they feel as if they were going to hold me down."

"It will be all right," said Singh impatiently, and throwing his right leg over, he came down upon the elephant's neck; while before the boys could grasp what was about to happen, the animal rose and began to turn round, slinging the massive iron peg over the palisade; and then, as he began to move off and the chain tightened, he drew with him eight or ten feet of the ornamental woodwork.

"Oh, what will the Doctor say?" cried Singh piteously.

"That he'll stop your pocket-allowance to pay for it. Here, I say, old chap, do, do something to steer him."

"But I haven't got a—"

"Here, try a pin," cried Glyn, making-believe to pull one out of the bottom corner of his waistcoat.

"But that won't go through his skin."

"No, I suppose not. He'll think you are tickling him. Here, shall I try my knife?"

"No, no, no! It will make him mad."

"But we must do something," cried Glyn, who couldn't sit still for laughing. "Can't you turn his head? We are mowing and harrowing all these flower-beds with this wood-stack he's dragging at his heels. Ah, that's better!" continued Glyn, as, finding the impediment rather unpleasant, the animal turned off at right angles and reached out with its trunk to remove the obstacles attached to its leg.

"Why, we are anchored! Oh, now he's off again. Why, where's he going?"

"I think he's going to make for the hedge where he came through first, in the cricket-field."

"But we couldn't get through there with all this garden-fence. It would catch in the hedge, and we should be dragging that too all through the town."

"Oh, I don't know," cried Singh.

"Let's scramble down and try to stop him. If you take hold of one leg I'll hang on by his tail if I can reach it.—Ah, that's better!"

For the elephant suddenly came to a standstill about a third of the way across the playground.

"Here, he's stopping for something. I wish we were near a baker's shop."

But the elephant had not stopped for nothing but only to balance itself upon three legs while it kicked out with the fourth, making a loud crashing and jangling noise, which was repeated till the length of wooden palisade was broken into splinters. But the chain and picket-peg were as firmly attached as ever, and were dragged steadily across the remaining portion of the playground right for the hedge, which now stood before the boys, displaying not only the demolished reparations, but a good-sized gap as well.

It seemed as if their steed meant to pass straight through, and he did so. The great iron peg got across a couple of tough old stumps of the hawthorn bushes and drew him up short, but only for a few moments; the huge beast putting forth its strength and dragging them out by the roots, after which it turned off to the left, to go on straight through the still sleeping town, making its way in the calmest manner for the show-field at the back of the principal hotel. Here it stopped at last close to the loosened earth from which it had originally wrenched the picket; and then, raising its trunk, blew such a blast that it produced a chaotic burst of sounds from the quadrangle of cages and dens, each creature after its kind joining in the chorus, and rousing and bringing every keeper and labourer attached to the menagerie upon the scene, the last to arrive, eager and smiling, but before anything was done, being the proprietor himself, who came up cheering and waving hat and handkerchief in the air.

"Think of that now!" he cried. "I say, young gentlemen, it all points to it, you see, and you needn't tell me; the old Rajah saw what was right. He only went to fetch you, and you've come to stay."

Chapter Sixteen
"Halt! Right face!"

The yellow silk handkerchief was brought a great deal into use by Mr Ramball to dab his head; and once Glyn nudged his schoolfellow's elbow and suggested that the proprietor was going to cry with disappointment from being told that he was labouring under a very grave mistake.

Soon after the two boys slipped away so as to make for the school and excuse themselves for being out of bounds and going out unseen so early in the morning.

They "slipped away" at Ramball's request. "Just walk up and down with me a few times," he said, "till we get on the other side of the caravans. No, not yet," he said. "I have sent one of the men for a big basket of carrots. They are nice and sweet, and his highness likes them. Once get him busy on them and he won't notice you going."

A big two-handled basket made its appearance a few minutes later, piled up with the orange-red vegetables, and carried by a couple of Ramball's men.

"Just give him two or three yourselves, gentlemen," said the proprietor, "and start him on them. Then get behind him and walk right away straight from his tail. You may do anything of that sort, as I dare say you know, without his seeing. Elephants are very stupid beasts about what goes on behind their backs."

The two boys did as requested, and as soon as the elephant was busy they strolled off with its owner, who was very eager to shake hands with them again and beg of them to come to his place.

"Here, I have had enough of this," cried Glyn as soon as they were out of the great field, "and I never thought of it before. What time is it?"

"I don't know," said Singh. "I have left my watch on the dressing-table."

Just then the striking of the church clock fell upon their ears, and Singh began to count aloud, while Glyn expressed his belief that it must be seven.

"Why, all the chaps will be out when we get back," he said.

"Eight!" said Singh loudly.

"Nonsense! You have muddled it," cried Glyn.

"Nine!" cried Singh.

"Rubbish!"

"It is. Look at the shops all open, and the people about."

"Well; but the time couldn't have gone like that," cried Glyn. "Here, what are we going to say? If you are right—why, breakfast's over ever so long ago, and the fellows are all going in to class. But you can't be right."

"Well, there's the clock," said Singh contemptuously. "Look for yourself."

The hands and Roman numerals of the great church clock had only lately been re-gilded, and they seemed to twinkle and blink and point derisively in the bright morning sunshine.

"Oh, I say," cried Glyn, "who could have thought it! Bother old Ramball and his beasts! Feeding his elephant! I wish somebody would feed me! Why, we shall get no breakfast."

"Oh yes, we shall," cried Singh confidently. "Why, you forget we are in the infirmary still, and Mrs Hamton won't let us go without our breakfast. But come along; let's trot back round by the shortest way."

They started the military double directly, and were about half-way back to the school when, as they turned a corner to get into the main road, a sharp military voice shouted:

"Halt! Right face!"

"Father!" cried Glyn.

"Morning," cried the Colonel, as he shook hands warmly with both. "You two invalids having your constitutional? Well, you ought to be taken off the sick-list now. I have just been having my walk before breakfast. I came past the Doctor's, but could not see anything of either of you."

"Going in to breakfast, father?" said Glyn.

"Yes, my boy. You had yours at eight o'clock, I suppose. What time were you up? Seven o'clock, I suppose."

"No, father," said Glyn, laughing. "It must have been about four."

"Four o'clock! What made you get up so soon as that?" cried the Colonel, as he looked from one to the other.

"We were called, father, and obliged to get up." And between them the boys narrated their early morning adventure.

"Tut, tut, tut, tut!" ejaculated the Colonel. "Then you have had no breakfast at all?"

Singh shook his head.

"Come along with me, then," cried the Colonel. "I'll soon put that right."

"Can't, father. We haven't got leave. We shall be punished for breaking out of school."

"Nonsense!" cried his father. "You didn't break out of school. You were carried off. Here, I'll put that right with the Doctor; but there must be no more of this. You lads don't want elephants till you go back to Dour, and that won't be for years to come."

Very shortly afterwards the boys were once more seated at the Colonel's table, to partake of a leisurely breakfast, before he, as he termed it, marched them back like a couple of deserters to the Doctor's establishment.

Wrench looked at them at first wonderingly, and then shook his head as he announced that the boys were all in their classes, and that the Doctor was going round the grounds with the gardener to see what damage was done by the second visit of the elephant; when the Colonel proposed that they should follow and give the boys' version of their adventure.

They came upon him they sought almost directly after, for he had inspected the damaged hedge, and was gazing very ruefully at the broken-down palisade and the torn and trampled flower-beds.

He was busy pointing out the mischief to his companion, for Morris was with him, looking very sympathetic, as he borrowed the Doctor's walking-cane and carried his mathematical studies into daily life and utility by bending down and taking the dimensions of the elephant's great circular foot-prints.

The Doctor frowned as he turned and saw who were approaching; but explanations followed as he rather ponderously led the way into his study, where everything connected with the discipline of his school was always discussed.

"Oh, of course, Colonel Severn," he said, as his visitor took leave. "I hold your ward and son perfectly blameless, and have nothing to say about their absence from my establishment this morning.—But I hope, young gentlemen, that this is the last of these adventures; and I am glad, Colonel, that you met them and made them your guests."

"Unintentionally, my dear sir—unintentionally," said the Colonel stiffly. "I did mean to ask your permission for them to dine with me once more; but after this morning's meeting I shall not do so. We mustn't interfere with the discipline of the school boys," he said. "To-morrow morning I return to town, and probably I shall not see you again for a couple of months. Good-morning, Doctor; good-morning.—You will see me to the door, boys?"

The Doctor smiled and bowed, and the two lads walked past Wrench and then down with the Colonel to the Doctor's gate, where he stood for a few minutes talking.

"That fellow civil and attentive?" he said, giving his Malacca cane a wave in the direction of Wrench.

"Yes, father; very nice and obliging."

"Give him that," said the Colonel, slipping a crown-piece into his son's hand; "and, let's see; you get your month's allowance regularly. Not overrunning the constable, I hope—not getting into debt?"

The boys shook their heads, and after a few words more the Colonel marched off, erect and soldierly, while the boys rather slowly and unwillingly returned to their room to give a finishing touch or two to their rather hasty morning toilet.

Chapter Seventeen
The Professor makes a Request

Morris, being off duty, as he termed it, walked down the road to clear his head a little of mathematical calculations, as well as to devise an examination paper intended for the improvement of his pupils; not that he looked upon it in that light, for as soon as he had mentally got it into shape, ready for committing to paper, he laughed to himself and rubbed his white hands over and over again in his intense satisfaction.

"That will puzzle their brains," he said maliciously. "That will give some of them a headache;" and as he spoke, on his way back, he suddenly awakened to the fact that he was just coming to the damaged hedge, where a couple of men were for the second time, by Ramball's orders, restaking, half-cutting through, and bending down for interlacing purposes sturdy old growths of hawthorn.

The next moment he was conscious of the fact that Professor Barclay, who looked particularly neat, refined, and clean, was coming up to him with a most friendly smile and with extended hand.

The Professor was clean-shaven, wore his hair cut very short, and from his hat to his boots he was spotless; but somehow or other there was a suggestion that the profession of Sanskrit did not result in the possession of wealth, for the Professor's hat was not so new as it had been once, one of his well-polished boots had a smile in its upper leather just where the little toe pressed outwards, there was a suggestion about his very stiff shirt-collar of the growth of saw-like teeth that might be very unpleasant if they came in contact with his ears, while his tightly buttoned-up frock-coat, which looked very nice in front, had grown extremely shiny in two places at the back where the wearer's blade-bones were prominent.

Morris took the extended hand and shook it, but not half so affectionately as the Professor shook his, while agreeing very simply that the day was remarkably fine; and then, oddly enough, Morris, though the Professor gave him no reason for his thoughts in words, began thinking of a quiet little place in the town where modest dinners were provided, one of which Morris did not require in the least, inasmuch as a repast would be provided for him gratuitously in the Doctor's establishment. Item, he began thinking, too, of half-crowns. But his thoughts were turned in another direction by the Professor.

"So this is the spot," he said, "where the elephant broke through?"

"Yes," said Morris eagerly; "great mischievous beast! It will be a good thing when it's out of the town."

"Exactly," said the Professor, "unless the proprietor had some one to manage it who understood its ways. Is it true, as I have heard, that the young Prince and his friend and fellow-pupil controlled the huge beast by giving it orders in Hindustani?"

"Oh yes," said Morris, smiling now, as he ridded himself of thoughts of cheap dinners and half-crowns.

"Well, I am not surprised," continued the Professor; "but it was a pity I was not there."

"Pity you were not there?" said Morris, making a suggestion with his hand preparatory to saying "good-bye—can't stop," and then telling something very much like a fib; for it was in his mind to say, "So glad to have met you."

"Yes," said the Professor nonchalantly, "you see, I know Hindustani thoroughly; and though I suppose my pronunciation would be faulty in the ears of a native, I could very well make myself understood."

"Ah, yes," said Morris hastily; "so I should suppose; but—er—you will excuse me?" And he glanced at his watch. "I am afraid I must be back at the college. It is close upon dinner-time."

The Professor sighed and inadvertently sniffed as poor boys sniff who are passing cookshops.

"In a moment, my dear friend. I will not detain you; but I will walk with you as far as the college. It will be in my way. You see, just when one wants them most, important letters—important pecuniary letters—have such a bad habit of being delayed."

Morris coughed.

"Now, nothing could have happened better for me than that I should have met you, a brother-student; though we follow divergent lines, you for the attainment of mathematical precision, I for the diffusion of Eastern lore, you of all men seem to have extended towards me a kindly interest."

"Oh, well, that was perfectly natural," said Morris feebly, as, inadvertently he thrust his right hand into his pocket, started, coloured, and withdrew it quickly.

"Now," continued the Professor, "I want you to give me your advice about seeing the Doctor again."

Morris shook his head.

"Ah, I see what you are thinking; but that was for a permanent post. Now, don't you think he might accept my services, say, for a non-resident and three days a week?"

"No," said Morris, "I am sure he wouldn't. Your coming made Rampson dreadfully jealous, and he told me afterwards that the Doctor assured him that he should make no change."

"Well, say one day a week."

Morris shook his head again and looked down the road, as if hoping that some one would come and rescue him from his position.

"Don't speak in haste," said the Professor, taking him with finger and thumb by the plaited guard of silk, as if he had intentions upon the watch—not to know the time.

"I am obliged to speak in haste," replied Morris. "You see, it is so near—"

"Exactly—dinner-time. But for Sanskrit, a lesson a week—"

"The Doctor declared he should not introduce Sanskrit in the curriculum of study."

"Dear, dear! And with that young Eastern Prince in the establishment, and his companion the son of that magnificent old Colonel with the wondrous moustache!" And as he spoke the Professor passed his hand over his closely shaven upper lip. "Well, well, the Doctor knows his own business best; but I must confess that I am disappointed, my dear friend."

"I am very, very sorry," said Morris, drawing back a little; and as the guard tightened, and the watch began to rise out of his pocket, he gave way again and the watch sank down.

So did its owner's spirits, for the Professor continued:

"Don't you think I might go back with you to the college and call upon the Doctor once more?"

"No, that I don't," said Morris hastily; "for almost directly he will be going into the dining-hall."

"Well, what would that matter? Country hospitality and—you understand. But there, if you think the time adverse, I certainly would not presume. But, by the way, would you believe it, that letter has not come this morning?"

"Yes," said Morris faintly. "You said so just now."

"And it puts me to the greatest inconvenience. I am almost ashamed to ask you."

"Would that you were quite!" thought Morris.

"But would you mind—say a couple of half-crowns—a mere trifle, and the moment the letter comes—really, I think it must be stuck in the post-office somewhere from wrong direction. Is there another Plymborough in England?"

"Oh no; this is the only one."

"Yes, two half-crowns, and the moment the letter arrives I shall hurry to you to repay you with many thanks, your kindly interest in my welfare."

"And the other two?"

"Oh, of course," said the Professor. "The-ank you. Some day, my dear Morris, I hope and believe— But, by the way, that young Prince: I could not help taking the greatest interest in what he told me. It came naturally as the result of questions and in conversation upon the beauty of Eastern costume. I remember saying to him, 'Why are not you, a young Eastern potentate, robed in the resplendent garments of your country, wearing a picturesque helmet, plumed, and decked with gorgeous jewels? I remember,' I said, 'a visit paid by the Nawab of Puttyputty when I was one of the masters at the college at Longbourne. He was magnificently dressed, a most picturesque figure amongst the gentlemen, who in their sombre black looked like so many waiters. I remember he wore a resplendent belt, the clasps of which were formed of gigantic emeralds engraved with Eastern characters— Sanskrit, I believe, though I never had them in my hand.' And the boy proudly told me that he possessed just such a one, though he never wore it, because it would not be suitable with modern English costume. All a boy's romance, I suppose—recollections of the *Arabian Nights*."

"Oh no," said Morris; "it is quite true."

"Dear me," said the Professor, "what an opportunity! Why, I would give worlds to see it," he added with a laugh. "It has been one of the regrets of my life that I did not ask the Nawab's permission to inspect those clasps. To my thinking, the inscriptions must have been of that so-called talismanic kind in which these weak heathen believe. Now, do you think it possible that you could prevail upon your young friend—"

"Oh no, I am sure I couldn't," said Morris, trying hard to read the distant church clock.

"But say you convey to him my invitation, and ask him to bring the belt to my rooms one afternoon."

"Oh, really I—"

"Oh, such a simple thing—educational, and—I beg your pardon, you must go? Of course. I am afraid I have been prolix; but my dear Morris, bear that in mind. A little discussion upon those inscriptions would be beneficial to the boy—I could tell him things he would be proud to know—and it would enable me to send a profitable description to the newspapers.—Yes, good-bye till we meet again."

They separated, and the Professor walked slowly away, with his attention equally balanced between recollections of the Nawab's clasps and the last little dinner he had eaten at the country refreshment-house at Morris's expense, what time he played a pleasant little game of raising one half-crown from where it lay upon its fellow at the bottom of his pocket and letting it fall again with an agreeable chink.

Chapter Eighteen
"Where's my Practice-Bat?"

The Doctor was quite facetious one morning, for, in addressing the masters, his words being meant for the whole school, he said jocularly that if Severn and Singh had formed any intention of devoting their pocket-allowance to ordering a castle from London they were too late. He looked very hard at Morris as he spoke, and waited for him to reply.

"A castle, sir?" said the master. "I don't quite apprehend your meaning."

"Oh, it was only this, Mr Morris. My mind does not serve me as to what these things are called in India; but I think, and I dare say Mr Rampson will set me right if I am wrong, that in the old classic days in the Punic or Carthaginian wars what were termed castles were fitted on to the backs of elephants, from which archers, slingers, and javelin-throwers dealt out destruction among their foes."

"Yes, sir. Quite correct, sir," said Rampson, "for Pliny states—"

"Oh, I don't think we will disturb Pliny to-day, Mr Rampson," said the Doctor, smiling, "unless your pupils particularly wish it," and he glanced round the school.

"No, sir!"

"No, sir!"

"No, sir!" came in chorus.

"Very well, gentlemen; then Pliny shall be left at rest. It occurred to me that if there was to be much more of the pursuit of elephant-riding as displayed by Messrs Severn and Singh, a castle, such, I presume, as is kept in record by a celebrated hostelry somewhere in the south of London, where, upon one occasion, I stepped into one of those popular modes of conveyance called omnibuses, would be much more suitable for a mode of progression than the animal's neck. A very slight study of the human anatomy would satisfy the most exacting that nature never intended youths of fifteen or sixteen to strain their muscles after the fashion of acrobats, so as to enable them to bestride an elephant's spine."

There was a low titter at this, and every eye was turned upon Glyn and Singh, the latter turning very red.

"By the way, Mr Singh," continued the Doctor, "you have a colloquial term for the form of castle used in India, have you not?"

The word colloquial seemed to puzzle Singh, who remained silent, and Glyn spoke up.

"Howdah, sir!" he shouted.

"How dare you, sir!" cried the Doctor, with mock indignation; and then he looked smilingly round for appreciation of his pun, which was not seen till Morris expounded it.

Then there was a roar. While he waited patiently enough, the Doctor took off his gold-rimmed spectacles, drew a neatly folded white handkerchief from his pocket, shook it out, breathed upon the glasses, and polished them, kept on holding them to the light to make sure that there was not the symptom of a blur, and as soon as the laughter had died out he exclaimed, "Because—"

There was a dead silence, the boys large and small glancing at one another in a questioning way as if asking whether this was the beginning of another mild joke or a bit of facetiae that ought to be laughed at as it stood.

"Because—" said the Doctor again, more loudly than before, and he seemed, as he glanced round, to direct his words at every boy in turn.

"Because, gentlemen—" This time the Doctor looked hard at the masters, and then continued loudly, "it seems as if I am to be allowed to possess my boarders in peace, the quickset hedge is not to be torn-up any more, the split oak palings on the farther side are to remain untouched. To be brief, I am informed upon the best authority that the visit of Ramball's menagerie is at an end. So now, Mr Singh, you may close up your repertoire of Hindustani words, and condescend to plain English with an occasional garnish from the classic writers of old. We will now resume our studies."

All traces of excitement seemed to give way now to the humdrum routine of school-life. This, however, was diversified with plenty of cricket, Slegge posing in every match as the chief batsman and captain of the eleven.

But he had to work hard to keep up his position in his own particular speciality, which was that of slogging batsman, for he was a bad bowler, too cowardly to keep a wicket, and too big, heavy, and lazy to field.

At the same time he was too jealous and vain to let others step in and help themselves to some of his laurels, notably the two young Indians, as he called them, for none of the older lads, his fellow-pupils for years past, ever dreamed of disputing his position. But both Glyn and Singh, untroubled by a thought of giving way to the older boy, proved themselves a splendid addition to the eleven that was picked from time to time to combat the town players or some other school.

To Slegge's annoyance, he very soon found that if the prestige of the school was to be kept up Glyn and Singh must be in the eleven, for the former in a very short time was acknowledged to be the sharpest bowler in the school, while, from long practice together, Singh was an admirable wicket-keeper—one who laughed at gloves and pads, was utterly without fear, and had, as Wrench said—he being a great admirer of a game in which he never had a chance to play—"a nye like a nork."

"But they can't beat me at batting," Slegge said to himself grimly, and he worked at his practice like a slave. But as a slave he made others slave— to wit, all the small unfortunates who took his fancy.

"You needn't grumble, you lazy little beggars," he used to say. "Nasty, ungrateful little beasts! See what bowlers I'm making of you, and what fielders!"

And in his manufacture of cricketers he would have out five or six at a time, with three or four cricket-balls, to keep on bowling to him while he went on slogging and hitting the balls in all directions, utterly reckless of the poor little fellows' exhaustion and of the risks they ran, as he drove or cut the balls right at them or far away over the field.

The natural result was that in regular play Slegge's score always mounted up when he was not opposed to Glyn and Singh, when there was generally what the delighted younger boys denominated a "swodge of rows;" while Slegge himself, always ready to pick a quarrel, never now attempted to settle it with fists, but he fought pretty hard with his tongue, and always declared that there was "a beastly conspiracy."

Possibly there was; but it was only between the two friends, who strove their best to put him out, the one by a clean ball which sent stumps and bails flying, the other by laying his wicket low with a sharp movement when Slegge's long legs had, in his excitement carried him off his ground.

One morning there was a little meeting held under the elms by twelve of the very junior juniors, for they had found out a malicious act on the part of their tyrant, or rather he had openly boasted of it himself, and not only showed the little fellows visually what he had done to his practice-bat, as he called it, but also awakened them thoroughly to his play.

"'Tisn't fair," said one of them. "I vote we lay it all before Burney and Severn and Hot Pickles."

"No," said another, "it isn't fair. He couldn't do it off Glyn Severn's bowling; not that we chaps bowl badly. Severn calls some of us toppers, and last week and several times since he put me up to giving the balls a twist. You know; you saw—those long-pitched balls that drop in as quiet as a mouse, and look as if they are going wide, but curl in round the end of a fellow's bat, just tap a stump, and down go the bails before he knows where he is."

"Yes; but I don't see much good in that," said another. "You didn't take much out of it yesterday when you put old Shanks's wicket down, and he gave you a lick on the head for it."

"I don't care if he'd given me a dozen," said the little fellow with a grin. "I took old Bully Bounce's wicket. Oh, didn't it make him wild!"

"Yes; but it isn't fair, as I said before," cried the first speaker. "He could do what he liked with our bowling before, but now we have got to run nearly off our legs to fetch up fivers. I say it isn't fair. He must have got half-a-pound of lead let into the end of his bat. Took it down to the carpenter's, he did, and made old Gluepot bore three holes in the bottom with a centre-bit, pour in a lot of melted lead, and then plug the bottom up again with wood."

"Here, I know," said one; "let's watch for our chance, and get Wrench— he'll keep it a secret; he hates Longshanks—let's ask him to make a fire under the wash-house copper, and one of us could do it I'll volunteer. I'll smuggle out Slegge's bat, and it wouldn't take long. Just hold it on the fire where it's hottest, and the lead would all melt and run out."

"And what about the end of the bat?" said another.

"Well, it would be all light again, just the same as it was before."

"Light?" cried the objector. "Why, it would be all black. The wood would all burn away before the fire got to the lead."

"Would it?" said the inventor of the scheme thoughtfully. "Well, I suppose it would. But we must do something."

This was agreed to *nem con*, and, after a long meeting for boys, their faces indicated a satisfactory termination of their debate.

That something had been done was proved two days later, for the intervening day had been wet; and as usual, on the second day, when it was time to turn out in the grounds, Slegge ordered up his little band of slaves and marched them to the cricket-shed for the necessary implements. Half-a-dozen balls were got out of one locker, the stumps and bails from another, and from his own particular lock-up, flap-topped receptacle, Slegge proceeded to take out the special bat with which he practised hitting—two more, his club-bat and his match-bat, lying there in their cases of green flannel.

Taking his key, one of a bunch, from his pocket, Slegge proceeded to unlock the flap-topped cupboard; but somehow the key would not go in, and he withdrew it, and under the impression that he had made a wrong selection he passed another along the ring and tried that. This was worse, and he tried a third, before withdrawing it, blowing into the pipe, and making it whistle, and then tapping it and bringing forth a few grains of sand.

"Here, what game's this?" shouted the big fellow in what his enemies called a bubble-and-squeak voice, due to the fact that in the change that was taking place his tones were an awkward mingling of treble and bass; and as he spoke he seized the boy nearest to him by the ear.

"Oh, please don't, sir! Please don't! Please don't! I haven't done nothing!"

"Done nothing, you little vermin!" shouted Slegge. "Who said you had? But you've done something. Now, don't deny it, for I'll half-skin you. You can't deceive me. You have been blowing this lock full of sand and gravel with a pea-shooter."

"I haven't, sir; I haven't indeed!" cried the boy.

"Then tell me who has?" cried Slegge; and, seizing the boy's fingers, he held his hand, palm downwards, on the top of the locker, and then began to torture him by sawing the knuckles of his own doubled fist across the back.

The boy squealed and yelped, but bore the inquisition-like torture bravely enough.

Nothing was got out of him, however; and, getting between the boys and the door of the shed, Slegge tortured one after the other, but could not find a traitor to impeach the rest. And at last, in a fit of rage, he stepped back and with a furious kick sent the lid of the locker flying upwards; while, tearful though some of the eyes of the lookers-on were, they were full of a strange kind of exultation as they glanced at one another and waited for the *dénouement* that was to come.

As Slegge saw the result of his kick to the heavy lid, he stepped quickly forward and thrust in his right hand to withdraw the bat; but he uttered a yell, for the great cover rebounded and came down with a bang, sending one of the little fellows skimming out of the shed to get round to the back so that his laughter should not be seen.

"That's one for you, Burton, when I get hold of you again," cried Slegge. "I shan't forget it. And—here, what's the meaning of this? Where's my practice-bat?"

There was a dead silence in the shady, wooden room, and three or four of the boys stood looking as if they were going to have apoplectic fits, for their eyes started and their teeth were clenched together, and they seemed as if they were trying to swallow something.

But there was no danger. It was only bottled-up mirth that they were striving hard to suppress.

"Ugh–h–h–ugh!" snarled Slegge, making a rush at the boys, who scattered at once, dashed out of the door before any of them were seized, and ran as if for their lives, to begin shrieking with laughter as soon as they were out of reach.

In his rage at what he looked upon as a theft, Slegge chased first one and then another; but he was too big, heavy, and clumsy to catch the delighted imps, who, as active as monkeys, dodged him at every turn, till at last he stood panting.

"All right," he said. "I am not going to make myself hot with running after you; but the Doctor's going to know that he has got thieves in the school. I am not going to be robbed for nothing, and if my practice-bat is not back in its place before night I shall go and tell Bewley that he's got blackguards and fellows who use false keys in his school. So you'd better look sharp and bring that bat back. And here, mind this; the carpenter will charge six or seven shillings for putting on a new lock here, so you have got to find sixpence apiece before Saturday night and hand it over to me."

But in spite of threats the bat was not brought back nor its purloiner or annexer betrayed. The bat was gone, and its owner's practice was modified, for he did not care to improve the driving power of his first-class bats by having them bored and weighted with lead.

Chapter Nineteen
Wrench is Confidential

The Doctor was very fond of lecturing the boys on the beneficial qualities of water.

"Gentlemen," he said, "I pass no stern edicts or objections to the use of beer, and for those who like to drink it there is the ale of my table, which is of a nature that will do harm to no one"—which was perfectly true—"but I maintain that water—good, pure, clear, bright, sparkling spring water—is the natural drink of man. And being the natural drink of man, ergo—or, as our great national poet Shakespeare puts the word in the mouth of one of his clowns, *argal*—it is the natural drink of boys."

As he spoke, the Doctor poured out from a ground-glass decanter-like bottle a tumblerful of clear cold water, which he treated as if it were beer, making it bubble and foam for a moment before it subsided in the glass.

The Doctor said good, pure, sparkling water, and the supply of the school possessed these qualities, for it came from a deep draw-well that went right down, cased in brick, for about forty feet, while for sixty feet more it was cut through the solid stone.

The Doctor was very particular about this well, which was furnished with a mechanical arrangement of winch and barrel, which sent down one big, heavy bucket as the winder worked and brought up another full; and it was Wrench's special task to draw the drinking-water from this well for the whole of the school, that used for domestic purposes coming from two different sources—one an ordinary well, and the other a gigantic soft-water tank.

One morning early, after Singh and Glyn descended from their dormitory, and were strolling down towards the Doctor's neatly-kept garden by a way which led them past the well-house, they stopped to listen to a clear musical pipe that was accompanied by the creaking of a wheel and the splash of water.

The pipe proved to be only Wrench the footman's whistle, and its effect was that of a well-played piccolo flute, as it kept on giving the boys the benefit of a popular air with variations, which stopped suddenly as the big full bucket reached the surface and was drawn sideways on to a ledge by the man, while a hollow musical dripping and tinkling went on as a portion of the superfluous water fell splashing back into the depths.

As Wrench uttered a grunt and proceeded to fill the water-can he had brought and a couple of jugs, he turned slightly and saw that the shadow cast into the cool, moist-smelling interior was that of the two boys.

"Morning, gentlemen," he said. "What do you think of this for weather?"

"Lovely," cried Glyn. "Why, Wrench, you beat the blackbirds."

"Oh, nonsense, sir! I have often tried; but I can't get their nice soft, sweet notes."

"No; but your whistle is of a different kind.—It's beautiful; isn't it, Singh?"

"Yes; it's just like those minas that we have got at home.—Give me a glass of water."

"Haven't got a glass, sir, only a mug. Here, I'll run and fetch you one."

"No, no," cried Singh, and taking up the mug he held it to be filled and then drank heartily, Glyn following his example.

"Beautiful clear water, young gentlemen, isn't it?" said the man. "The Doctor says it will make you strong, and there's iron enough in it to do any man good. I should like to have a well like that in my place when I start for myself. I should put out bills about it and call it mineral water, same as the Doctor says this is."

"How deep is the well really?"

"Just a hundred foot, sir."

"How do you know? You haven't measured it."

"Well, I measured the rope, sir. When the Doctor bought a new one for it, just a year ago, he let me fit it on instead of getting the workpeople in. That cost nothing, and the men would have made a regular job of it."

"But I meant the water. How deep is the water itself?"

"Oh, the water, sir. That gets to be about twenty or thirty feet in the winter-time; but in the summer it gets very low—in the dry time, you know. I don't suppose there's above six or eight feet in now."

"But I say," cried Glyn, "set up for yourself? Why, you're not going to start a school?"

"School, sir?" said the man, laughing. "'Tain't likely! No, sir; me and somebody—never you mind who—is going to be married one of these days, when we have saved up enough, and we are going to take a house at the seaside and let lodgings to visitors who come down for their health. Why, a well of water like that would be the making of us."

"Oh!" cried Glyn, with his eyes twinkling. "You with your somebody and your never mind who! Why, I have found you out, Wrenchy. I know who the lady is."

"Lady she is, sir," said the man sharply, "and right you are, though she's only poor and belongs to my station of life. But, begging your pardon, with all your Latin and Greek and study, you haven't found that out."

"That I have," cried Glyn. "It's the cook."

The man turned scarlet and stood gazing at the boy with his mouth a little way open.

"Why, who told you, sir?" he stammered at last.

"She did," said Glyn quietly.

"What! My Emily told you that?" cried the man. "In them same words?"

"No; she never spoke to me in my life," replied Glyn. "Singh and I were going down the garden one day, down one path, and she'd been to get some parsley, while you were carrying in one of the garden chairs, and she looked at you. That was enough, and we two laughed about it afterwards. So you see we know."

"Well, I always did say as you was two sharp uns, sir," said the man. And then confidentially, "Yes, sir, that's right. We have been thinking about it for the last five years, and we'd like it to come off at any time. For, you see, it's just the same with us, sir, as it is with rich people—I mean, well-to-do people. It don't do to get married until you see your way."

"Till you can see your way?" said Singh, frowning. "What does he mean by that?"

"Oh, I'll soon tell you, sir. Money enough to make a fair start. There's plenty of hard work to do here with the Doctor and such a large family of you young gentlemen as he's got; but he's a very good master, kind-hearted and just, and if any of us is unwell there's everything he could want, and plenty of rest. And one don't like to give up a comfortable home and start one that's worse. It's money that's in the way, sir. We have both been saving ever since we were engaged; but it takes a long time to make your saving much when you can only put away a few pounds apiece every year."

"Oh, well, look here," cried Glyn; "if you'll promise not to get married while we are here at the school, I'll give you—let's see, what shall I say?— five pounds. I dare say father will give it to me.—Now, Singh, what will you do?"

"Just the same," replied Singh.

"Thank you, gentlemen," cried Wrench. "Come, I call that handsome; but you know," he added laughingly, "I shouldn't like to make any promises, for I don't know what a certain lady would say. Thank you all the same, both of you. You've both been very pleasant gentlemen and very nice ever since you have been here. You neither of you ever called me a lazy beast and shied your boots at me because they wasn't black enough, or called me a fool for not making your water hotter so as you could shave."

"Why, who did then?" cried Glyn.

"Oh, I am not going to tell tales, gentlemen. Some young gents are born with tempers and some ain't, while there are some again that come here as nice and amiable as can be, after a year or two get old and sour and ready to quarrel with everything. I don't know; but I think sometimes it's them Greek classics, as they call them. You see, it's such unchristian-like looking stuff. I have looked at them sometimes in the Doctor's study. Such heathen-looking letters; not a bit like a decent alphabet. But there, I must be off, gentlemen. I have all my work waiting, and I am going away—only think of it!—ten pounds richer than when I first began to turn that there handle this morning, if—if I stop here—I mean, if we stop here till you young gents have done schooling."

Wrench finished filling his cans of water and stooped to pick them up, but set them down again, to look at them both thoughtfully.

"My word, gentlemen, you would both begin to wonder at the times and times I have laid awake of a night trying to hit a bright—I mean, think of some idea by which I could make a lot of money all at once: find some buried in a garden, or bring up a bag of gold in the bottom of one of those two water-buckets, or have somebody leave me a lot, or pick it up in the street and find afterwards it belonged to nobody. I wouldn't care how I got it."

"So long as it was honest, Wrenchy?" said Glyn, laughing.

"Oh, of course, sir—of course. You see, a man's got a character to lose, and when a man loses his character I suppose it's very hard to find it again; so I have been told. But I never lost mine. But I do want to get hold of a nice handy lump of money somehow, and when I do, and if I do—"

"Well, what would you do then?" cried Singh.

"Well, sir, I shouldn't stop here till you two gents had done schooling."

Then, picking up his two water-cans once more, the Doctor's footman trudged off towards the house.

"That must have been old Slegge who threw his boots at him," said Singh thoughtfully. "What a disagreeable fellow he is!"

"Yes," said Glyn. "I wish I had been there to stop it. He's been knocking some of the little fellows about shamefully because he says that they have hidden his bat."

"You wish you had been there?" said Singh. "Why, I thought you said that you wouldn't fight any more."

"To be sure; so I did. Well, then, I don't wish I had been there. But I say," continued Glyn, laughing merrily, "what a lot of Greek he must know!"

"But he doesn't," cried Singh. "He doesn't know much more than I do, for he came to me to help him with something the other day."

"Well, then, as Wrenchy says, how what he does know must have disagreed with him!"

"Yes," said Singh thoughtfully, as he laid his hand on his companion's shoulder and they strolled down the garden together, waiting for the breakfast-bell to ring. "Poor old fellow! Poor old fellow! Poor old fellow!"

"Well, you are a queer chap, Singh! You say you want to be thoroughly English, and you talk like that."

"Well, I do want to be English," cried Singh, "and I try very hard to do as you do, because I know what guardian says is right."

"Well, you never heard me pity Slegge and call him poor old fellow."

"I didn't. I meant poor Wrenchy, who wants money so badly. It must be very queer to want money very badly and not be able to get it."

"I suppose so," replied Glyn. "I seem to have always had enough, while as for you, you're as rich as rich; quite a king you'll be some day, with servants and a little army, and everything you want. I say, what do you mean to do with all your money?"

"I don't know," said Singh, laughing, and then knitting his brows, "but I should like to give Wrench some. He's such a good, hard-working fellow, and always does everything you tell him with such a pleasant smile. I wonder how he will get all he wants. Do you think he will find it some day in a garden or in the street?"

"Or have a big lump of it tumble out of the moon, or find that it's been raining gold all over the Doctor's lawn some morning when he gets up? No, I don't—not a bit; and there goes the breakfast-bell, so come along."

Chapter Twenty
A Squabble

"Anybody seen anything of Singh?" cried Glyn one day as he went out into the cricket-field, where Slegge was batting to the bowling of some of his little slaves and several of the older boys were looking on.

"Baa! Baa! Baa!" cried Slegge, imitating a sheep, and stopping to rest upon his bat. "Hark at the great lamb calling after its black shepherd! Go on, some of you, and help me," and in answer to his appeal a chorus of bleating arose, in which, in obedience to a gesture made with the bat, the little bowlers and fielders were forced to join.

"Well, if I were a quarrelsome chap," said Glyn to himself, "I should just go up to Master Slegge and put my fist up against his nose. Great, stupid, malicious hobbledehoy! But it's very plain Singhy hasn't been here. Now, where can he be? Gone down the town perhaps to buy something—cakes or fruit I suppose. How fond he is of something nice to eat? But there, he always gives a lot away to the little fellows. Well, so do I, if you come to that; but I don't think it's because I give them buns and suckers that they all like me as they do. Well, I suppose that's where Singh's gone; but he might have told me and asked me to go with him."

The boy strolled back with the intention of going into the class-room, now empty, to sit down and have a good long read; but as he drew near the house he came upon the page, who, wonderful to relate, displayed a face without a vestige of blacking.

"Hi, Sam!" cried Glyn. "Seen anything of Mr Singh?"

"Yes, sir; I see him down the town—saw him down the town, sir, I mean," said the boy hastily, recalling the fact that he had been corrected several times about his use of the verb "To see."

"Saw him down the town," he muttered to himself. "See, saw; see, saw. Wish I could recollect all that."

"Which way was he going?" said Glyn.

"Straight down, sir, towards the church, along of Mr Morris, sir."

"Humph! Gone for a walk, I suppose," said Glyn thoughtfully.

"Yes, sir, they were walking, sir. Shall I tell him you want him, sir, when he comes back?"

"Oh no, I don't think you need. I dare say he'll come to me," replied Glyn, and he strolled into the big class-room, unlocked his desk, got out a book of travels, opened it at one particular spot which he had reached a day or two before, and then began to read, growing so interested that a couple of hours glided away like half of one.

Then, closing the book with a sigh, as the dial on the wall insisted upon the fact that time was passing, he replaced the work and went up to his room to prepare for the evening meal.

"What a pity it is," he said, "that half-holidays will go so quickly. Classic afternoons always seem three times as long, and so do Mr Morris's lessons. I wish I were not so stupid over mathematics."

On reaching the door of his room he thrust it open quietly, and found Singh kneeling down before his Indian bullock-trunk, lifting out some of its contents ready to make place for something else.

"Why, hallo! There you are, then!" Singh started as sharply as if he had received a slap on the shoulder, scrambled up something long tied up in brown paper that lay by his side, thrust it into the trunk, and began to cover it quickly with some of the articles that had been taken out.

'I'm going to see what you have got there.'

"Ha, ha! Caught you!" cried Glyn. "What have you got there? Cakes or a box of sweets?"

"Neither," said Singh rather slowly.

"Oh, all right, I don't want to know," cried Glyn good-humouredly. "But I know: you mean a surprise—a tuck-out to-night when we come to bed. Who are you going to ask?"

"No one," said Singh shortly.

"Oh, I would. Ask Burney and Miller. They're good chaps, only Slegge keeps them under his thumb so. They'd give anything to break away, I know."

Singh was silent.

"Here, I say," cried Glyn, "I tell you what would be a rare good bit of fun, and if the Doctor knew he wouldn't notice it. Let's get about a dozen of the little chaps some night, Burton and Robson, the small juniors, and give them a regular good feed quite late. They would enjoy it. What do you say?"

"Yes," said Singh; "to be sure we will."

"I say," said Glyn, "I'd have come with you if you had asked me this afternoon. What a close old chap you are! Where have you been? Here, I'm going to see what you have got there."

"No, no!" cried Singh excitedly, as Glyn stepped forward, only meaning it as a feint; and the boy threw himself across the open box, to begin scrambling the dislodged things over the something that was loosely covered with brown paper, and in his hurry and excitement, instead of hiding it thoroughly, exposing one small corner. But it was quite big enough to let Glyn see what it was; and, laughing aloud, he cried:

"Why, what a coward you are! I was only pretending."

Singh hurriedly closed the lid of the trunk.

"Where have you been?"

Singh was silent for a moment, for a struggle was going on in his mind.

"I have been out for a walk with Mr Morris," he said.

"Well, there's no harm in that," said Glyn. "Where did you go? Across the park, or down by the river?"

Singh was silent for a moment or two once more, and then in a hurried way he seemed to master his reserve, and said:

"We didn't go regularly for a walk. We went to see Professor Barclay."

"Mr Morris took you to see Professor Barclay?" said Glyn.

"Yes, yes; but I wish you wouldn't keep on questioning me so."

"Well, I want to know," said Glyn quietly. "You don't speak out and tell me, so I am obliged to ask."

"Well," said Singh gloomily, "I want to be open and tell you; but you are such a queer fellow."

"Yes, I am," said Glyn, looking hard at his companion.

"Well, so you are," said Singh half-angrily; "and you are so fond of finding fault with me and not liking what I do."

"I don't know that I should have minded your going to see Professor Barclay," said Glyn slowly, "especially if you went with Mr Morris."

"No, you oughtn't to," cried Singh hastily. "Mr Morris said that it would be a kindness to go and see the poor gentleman, for he is a gentleman and a great scholar."

"So I suppose," said Glyn, "in Sanskrit."

"Yes; and he's very poor, and can't get an engagement, clever as he is; and it seems very shocking for a gentleman to be so poor that he can't pay his way, and we are so rich."

"Oh, I'm not," said Glyn, laughing.

"Yes, you are, while that poor fellow can hardly pay the rent of his room, and he confessed to me—I didn't ask him—but he was so anxious to tell me why he had not paid me that money back that—"

"Why, you haven't been lending him money, have you?" cried Glyn.

"Well—yes, a trifle. He called it lending; but when I heard from Mr Morris how badly the poor fellow was off, of course I meant it as a gift; but I couldn't tell a gentleman that it was to be so."

"Then you have been there before?"

"Yes, two or three times. Mr Morris said that it would be a kindness, for the Professor sent me messages, begging me to go and see him, as he has led such a lonely life among strangers, and he wanted to communicate to me some very interesting discoveries he had made in the Hindustani language."

"Oh," said Glyn slowly; "and did he ask you to lend him money each time you went?"

"Well, not quite. He somehow let it out how poor he was, and I felt quite hot and red to think of him being in such a condition; and Mr Morris, too, gave me a sort of hint that a trifle would be acceptable to him. And there, that's all. Why do you want to keep on bothering about it?"

"Mr Morris took you there, and talked to you like that?"

"Yes, yes, yes," cried Singh petulantly. "I told you so."

"And did he say something to you about Hindustani and Sanskrit?"

"Yes. But there, let's talk about something else."

"Directly," said Glyn. "And did he read the letters on the emeralds?"

Singh looked up at him sharply. "What made you ask that?" he said.

"I asked you," said Glyn, "because I see you took the belt with you this afternoon."

"How did you know that?" snapped out the boy.

"Why, a baby would have known it. It was plain enough when you were in such a hurry to scramble it out of sight, and were so clumsy that you showed me what it was."

"Oh!" ejaculated the boy sharply; and he stood biting his lip. "I—I—"

"There, don't stammer about it," said Glyn.

"But I felt that you would find fault with me and object."

"That's quite right," said Glyn, frowning. "I should have done so, for you promised me not to begin showing that thing about to anybody. Why will you be so weak and proud of what, after all, is only a toy?"

"It isn't a toy," cried the boy indignantly. "It is something very great and noble to possess such a—such a—"

"Showy thing," said Glyn grimly.

"You can't see it correctly," said Singh; "and I only took it that Mr Barclay, who is a great student, might read—decipher, he called it—the words engraved on the stones; and he was very grateful because I let him read them, and thanked me very much."

"But you might have remembered what I said to you about it."

"I did remember, Glynny," cried the boy warmly. "I thought of you all the time, and I even offended him at last by not doing what he wished."

"What did he wish? To get you to lend him more money?"

"No," cried Singh. "He wanted me to leave the belt with him, so that he might sit up all night and copy the inscription."

"He did?"

"Yes; and I wouldn't, because I thought you wouldn't like it, and that it wouldn't be right. But you don't know how hard it was to do. Mr Morris said, though, that I was quite right, and he told me so twice after we came away."

"But why was it hard?" asked Glyn.

"Because Mr Barclay said it would be nothing to me, and it meant so much to him. But it worried me very much, because it seemed as if I, who am so rich, would not help one who was so poor."

"I don't care," cried Glyn angrily. "You did quite right, and this Mr Barclay can't be a gentleman. If he were, he would not have pressed you so hard. It isn't as if it were a book. If that were lost, you could buy another one."

"But he said that he'd take the greatest care of it, and never let it go out of his hands till he had brought it back and delivered it to me."

"I don't care," cried Glyn. "He oughtn't to have asked you, for that belt belonged to your father, and now it belongs to you, and some day it will have to go to your successors."

"Then you think I have done quite right, Glynny?"

"Well, not quite; if you had you would have told me that you were going to take it there for the Professor to see."

"Oh, don't begin again about that," replied Singh piteously. "I told you I didn't mention it because I thought you would find fault."

"Yes, you did," said Glyn rather importantly, "and that shows that you felt you were not doing right. There, I am not going to say any more about it. I am only your companion. It isn't as if I were your guardian and had authority over you; but I am very glad that Mr Morris thought you did quite right in not leaving the belt. I wish you hadn't got it, and the old thing was safe back with all the rest of your treasures. You'd no business to want to bring it. A schoolboy doesn't want such things as that."

"Don't say any more about it, please," cried Singh piteously.

"Lock it up then, quite at the bottom of your box, and never do such a thing again. It would serve you jolly well right if you lost it."

"Oh, I say!" cried Singh.

"And promise me that if that man asks you to let him have it again you will come and tell me and go with me to the Doctor. I am sure he wouldn't like this gentleman—I suppose he is a gentleman—"

"Oh yes," said Singh thoughtfully; "he's a professional gentleman."

"Well, whatever he is," said Glyn, "I am sure the Doctor wouldn't like it."

"Look here," cried Singh eagerly, "I'll promise you, if you like, for I am getting to hate the old thing. I am tired of it, and I shall be ashamed to wear it now after all you have said, and feel as if I were dressed up for a show. You take it now, and lock it up in your drawers. You'd take more care of it than I could; add then you wouldn't bully me any more."

The boy made for his bullock-trunk; but Glyn caught him by the arm and stopped him.

"That'll do," he said.

"What do you mean?" cried Singh. "You will take care of it for me?"

"That I won't," cried Glyn, "and you ought to be ashamed to ask me to."

"Ashamed?" cried Singh, flushing. "Ashamed to put full trust in you?"

"No; but you ought to be ashamed not to be able to trust yourself. It's like saying to me, 'I am such a weak-minded noodle that I've no confidence in myself.'"

"Oh," cried Singh passionately, "there never was such a disagreeable fellow as you are. You are always bullying me about something, and you make me feel sometimes as if I quite hate you."

"Don't believe you," said Glyn, with a half-laugh.

"Well, you may then, for it's true." Then, changing his tone and drawing himself up, Singh continued, "Why, it's like telling me that I am a liar. How dare you, sir! Please have the goodness to remember who I am!"

"Don't want any remembrance for that," said Glyn coolly. "Why, who are you? My schoolfellow in the same class."

"I am the Maharajah of Dour, sir," said the boy haughtily.

"Not while you are here. You're only a schoolboy like myself, learning to be an English gentleman."

"Do you want me to strike you?" cried Singh fiercely.

"No," said Glyn coolly. "I shouldn't like you to do that."

"Then, you do remember who I am," cried Singh, swelling up metaphorically and beginning to pace the room.

"I shouldn't remember it a bit," said Glyn coolly. "But I should punch your head the same as I should any other fellow's—the same as I often have before."

"Yes, in a most cowardly way, because you were stronger and had learned more how to use those nasty old boxing-gloves, you coward!"

"Ah, well, I can't help that, you know," said Glyn coolly. "I have always felt squirmy when I have had to fight some chap for bullying you. I felt so shrinky when I had that set-to with old Slegge, till he hurt me, and then I forgot all about it. Yes, I suppose I am a bit of a coward."

Singh walked up and down the chamber with his eyes flashing and his lips twitching every now and then, while his hands opened and shut.

"Yes," he cried passionately, "you forget yourself, and you are taking advantage of me now I am over here in this nasty cold country, where it's nearly always raining, and right away from my own people, instead of being the friend that my guardian wished. But there's going to be an end of it, for I shall ask the Doctor to let me have a room to myself, and I'll go my way and you may go yours. Yes, and if it were not degrading myself I should strike you the same as I did that great bully Slegge."

"Well, do if you like. I won't go crying to the Doctor and saying, 'Please, sir, Singh hit me.'"

"It would be lowering myself, or else I would. I, as a prince, can't stoop to fight with one of my own servants."

"Well, look here," cried Glyn, "I don't want you to fight. Come on now and punch my head. I promise you that I won't hit back."

Singh advanced to him immediately with doubled fists, and Glyn stood up laughing in his face and put his hands behind him.

"No," cried Singh. "Come down the cricket-field behind the trees, and we will take two of the fellows with us and have it out, for I am sick of it, and I'll put up with no more."

"All right," said Glyn coolly. "But lock that belt up first at the bottom of your box or where it's safest."

"Not I," cried Singh loftily. "I can't stop to think of a few rubbishing gems when my honour's at stake like this."

"Well," said Glyn, "if you won't, I must;" and, crossing to the trunk, he opened it, saw that the belt-case was right down in one corner below some clothes, banged down the lid, locked it up, and offered Singh the keys.

"Bah!" ejaculated the boy, and he turned away.

"Let's see," said Glyn, in the most imperturbable, good-humoured way; "we'll have Burney and one of the other big chaps. I'll have Burney. What do you say to Slegge?"

Singh made no reply, but stood scowling out of the window.

"But I say, the first thing will be that they will ask what the row's about. What were we quarrelling for, Singhy?"

There was no reply.

"Oh, I remember," continued Glyn. "Because I bullied you about showing off with that belt. Well, we can't say anything about that. What shall we say? Look here, how would it be to go down the field together and fall out all at once, and you hit me, and I'll hit you back, and then we will rush at one another, calling names, and the fellows will come up to see what's the matter, and then we will fight."

"Ur–r–r–r–r–ur!" growled Singh, rushing at him with clenched fists; but as he saw the good-humoured twinkle in his companion's eyes, the boy stopped short, and his clenched fists dropped to his sides. "You are laughing at me," he said; "laughing in your nasty, cold-blooded English way."

"Well, isn't it enough to make a fellow laugh? Here are you trying to get up a quarrel about nothing, and threatening to break with me, when you know you don't mean it all the time."

"I do mean it!" raged out the boy. "For you have insulted me cruelly."

"Ah, that's what you say now, Singhy; but before you go to bed to-night you will be as vexed with yourself as can be, and wish you had not said what you have. You will feel then that I have only spoken to you just as the dad would if he had been here. And then what would you have done? Looked at him for a minute like a tiger with its claws all spread out, and the next minute you would have done what you always did do."

"What was that?" cried the boy fiercely.

"Held out your hand and said, 'I am sorry. I was wrong.'"

Singh turned away and walked to the window, to stand looking out for a few minutes before turning back; and then he walked up to Glyn and said: "Come down into the cricket-field."

"To have it out?" said Glyn quietly.

"Oh, Glynny!" cried the boy, and he held out his hand.

Chapter Twenty One
Singh finds Flannel too hot, and—

There was a game going on in the cricket-field, a sort of French and English affair, which necessitated a good deal of running, and proved to be very hot work; and in an interval of rest, when the boys were gathered together under the elms, Singh threw himself down, panting and half-exhausted, crying: "Oh, I wish to goodness I had something else on but this hot flannel! Here, I know. I'll go and change it for my silk."

He left the group of companions, walked slowly along under the row of elms, and came suddenly upon Glyn, who was playing on the opposing side.

"Hallo!" cried the latter anxiously. "What a face! Aren't you well?"

"Oh yes, quite; only what you call pumped out."

"What, are you going in?"

"Yes; I shall be all right directly. I had no business to play in this hot jacket. I am only going in to change it."

"You're sure you are not done up?" said Glyn anxiously.

"Done up? Nonsense! I only want a bit of rest, and then I shall get back to my side and we can beat you."

"Jacket?" said Glyn, still looking at him in doubt. "Here, let me fetch it for you. I haven't had so much running."

"Do! There's a good chap," cried Singh eagerly, and thrusting his hand into his pocket he brought out his keys.

"In the bottom drawer, isn't it?" said Glyn.

"Yes, I think so. If it isn't, it's in the bullock-trunk."

"All right," cried Glyn, catching the keys that were pitched to him; and he trotted off, while Singh picked out a shady spot and threw himself upon the turf.

Just about the same time, book in hand, Morris, apparently deep in study, after walking all round the field, came up to the group that Singh had just left, and closed his book, retaining the place with his thumb. He glanced round amongst the resting little party.

"Why, where is Singh?" he said quietly, addressing Burton. "I thought he was playing on your side."

"Yes, sir; he is, sir," cried the little fellow eagerly. "He's just gone up to his dormitory, sir, to get his thin cricketing-jacket."

"Oh," said the master softly. "Nice day for your sports, boys. Don't let the other side win."

"No, sir!"

"No sir!" came in chorus. "We won't."

But the book of Morris was open once more, and he seemed to be poring over a mathematical problem as he walked slowly away.

Meanwhile Glyn had reached the door of the lecture-room, hurried in, mounted the stairs, entered the room he shared with Singh, and selecting the key of the drawers, opened the one at the bottom, to find flannel trousers, Eton suit, and a carelessly folded overcoat.

"It is not here," he said. "What an untidy chap he is with his togs, and how he gets them mixed! Don't want to brag; but I believe I could get anything out of my drawers with my eyes shut. Well, I suppose it was because of dad. He always used to say that a soldier's traps should be neatly packed together in the smallest space. Perhaps it's in the next drawer," he continued, as he thrust in and locked the one at the bottom. "No; he said it would be in the trunk," and changing the key, he went to the corner of the little room, knelt down, thrust the key into the lock, and threw open the lid.

"Why, it isn't here at the top," he said to himself. "Oh, I am not going to turn over all his things."

An ejaculation behind him made him spring to his feet, to find himself face to face with Morris, book in hand, the pair sharing the astonishment due to the sudden encounter.

"You here, Severn!" cried Morris, flushing up with anger, Glyn felt, for it was out of hours for being in the dormitory.

"Yes, sir. I was getting something from his box for Singh."

"Oh," said Morris, recovering himself. "Young Burton told me he was here in his room."

"He was coming, sir; but I came for him," cried Glyn, into whose brain now flashed a memory of a late conversation and dispute with his companion.

"I suppose you know," said Morris coldly, "that one of the Doctor's rules is that the pupils should only retire to their dormitories at certain times."

"Yes, sir, but—"

"That will do," said Morris, turning to go; and his cold, stern manner stung the boy, whose mind was now flooded with the recollection of all that Singh had told him, and a feeling of resentment sprang up within his breast.

"I shouldn't have come, sir, if Singh had not asked me."

"That will do, sir," said Morris, affecting the Doctor's sternest manner. "You know you have no business to be here, and I shall feel it my duty to report the matter to the Principal."

Glyn was silent for a few moments, and then he started, for he saw that Morris was evidently waiting for him to leave the room; so, going down on one knee quickly, he locked up the trunk, with a feeling of resentment growing stronger within him, and as he rose and faced the master again his mind was made up. His father had told him more than once that he looked to him to use his common-sense and do the best he could in any emergency on behalf of Singh, and for the moment, as he stood facing Morris, he asked himself whether he ought not to write to his father. The next moment he was speaking. "I beg your pardon, sir."

"That will do, Mr Severn," said Morris coldly. "I am not in the humour to hear any excuses."

"I was not going to make excuses, sir," said the lad, "but to say a word or two about Singh, who is to me as a brother."

"What do you mean, sir?" said Morris sternly. "I mean, sir, that knowing how good and generous he is, and ready to do anything charitable, still I do not think that he ought to be imposed upon and induced again and again to lend money to a stranger."

Morris stared at him wildly.

"And above all, sir, there is that belt of his, which it has always been understood between us should be kept perfectly private on account of its value. It ought not to have been taken to Professor Barclay's lodgings."

"Mr Severn—" began Morris, and then he stopped, unable for a few moments to utter a word. Then, in quite an agitated tone, he exclaimed: "Singh has told you of all this?"

"Of course, sir. We never keep anything from each other, though I didn't know he was going to take it till afterwards; and I feel quite sure that the Doctor will be very angry when he knows."

"When he knows!" cried Morris. "Mr Severn, you are never going to tell him this?"

"What do you think, sir? Singh is in my charge—by my father's orders."

"But, Mr Severn," cried Morris, "I—I am very sorry that I had occasion to speak so angrily to you; but I—I felt it my duty, and—yes, under the circumstances, I must confess that it was a mistake on my part to take your schoolfellow there. And those emerald clasps—yes, I see perfectly clearly now that it ought not to have been done. I should never have dreamt of such a thing had not the Professor, who has been a most unfortunate man, felt so deeply interested in the inscription."

"Yes, sir; I know all about that," said Glyn coldly; "and Singh told me that this Professor Barclay wanted the belt left with him."

"Yes," cried Morris; "but it was not done, and I strongly commended Singh for his firmness in refusing."

"Yes, sir, I know that too," said Glyn; "and Singh must not go to this man's apartments again."

"My dear young friend," cried Morris, whose brow was damp with perspiration, "I quite agree with you there. It was rather thoughtless on my part—a slip such as we are all liable to make. I was led away by the literary part of the question, and I somehow thought that it would be to the advantage of our young fellow—student if he learned from a good authority a little more about the inscription upon those stones."

"Yes, sir; there was no harm in that," said Glyn quietly.

"No, Severn, not the slightest, and as soon as I found the Professor making such a request—one that he certainly ought not to have made—I repented very bitterly of that which I felt to be a gross error on my part. There," he continued, with a half-laugh, "you see I can speak frankly when I have made a mistake. I hope you will always do the same. But, of course, you do not think it in the slightest degree necessary that you should make any report about this to the Doctor?"

"What do you think, sir?" said Glyn coldly.

Morris uttered a gasp, and, looking wildly in the young speaker's eyes, he felt behind him till one hand touched a chair-back, and then he sank down speechless, to seek for his pocket-handkerchief and wipe his wet brow.

"What do I think?" he said, at last, with a groan. "I think it means ruin for me. Mr Severn, I have apologised for speaking so sharply to you, and now I must humble myself to you. If you report this to the Doctor only one thing can follow. I shall have lost his confidence for ever, and he will tell me at once to send in my resignation. Mr Severn, you and your young companion don't know what it is to be poor. The loss of my post here under such circumstances, due to a weak desire to help a fellow-master in distress, would be quite sufficient to injure me dreadfully. If I have sinned I am bitterly punished for what I have done. This is a humiliation, a cruel humiliation, such as you can hardly realise."

"Please don't say any more, sir," said Glyn quickly. "This hurts me almost as much as it does you. What I have said was on behalf of Singh, and I shall certainly not say a word to the Doctor, for I know that now you will help me in watching over my father's ward."

"Mr Severn," began Morris, "I—I— Oh, I cannot speak. Try and realise what I feel. But tell me once more, so that I may go away at rest: this is to be a private matter between us two?"

"Yes, sir, of course," cried Glyn earnestly, and they separated.

"Well, where is it?" said Singh, a few minutes later.

"I couldn't find it," was Glyn's reply. "Here you had better take your keys."

Chapter Twenty Two
The Professor's Gratitude

There was a great talk at the Doctor's establishment about the event of the season, an event that filled the boys' brains, seniors and juniors, for weeks before it took place, and brought forth a rebuke from the Doctor one morning at breakfast, for the masters were reporting that the papers sent in by the boys were very much wanting in merit. There was a report, too, going about that Monsieur Brohanne had been seen walking up and down the class-room tearing his hair—a most serious matter in his case, for it was exceedingly short.

Matters had come to such a pitch that the Doctor sternly gave quite a little lecture upon the duty of every pupil to do his very best, whether at work or play, saying that a boy who could not give his mind to working could not devote it to playing well. And if in future, he said, his pupils did not work hard, he should be obliged to make them suffer the contumely of sending in word that they would not be able to meet Strongley School in the annual cricket-match.

"I regret it very much, young gentlemen," said the Doctor; "but if you will disgrace your *alma mater* by idleness, I have no other alternative. Duty and pleasure must go hand in hand."

The boys groaned that morning, and broke up into little knots after breakfast to discuss the matter. Little jealousies were forgotten, and Slegge declared it was too bad of the Doctor, who seemed to be blaming them, the seniors, for the failings of those lazy little beggars the juniors, just when their picked eleven had arrived at such perfection, through his batting, Glyn's bowling, and the Nigger's wicket-keeping, that success was certain.

There was gloom in every face save one, and that appertained to Morris, who watched his opportunity, button-holed Glyn and Singh, and led them off into the solitude of the lecture-hall.

"Good news!" he said. "Splendid news! Gentlemen, this is entirely a private matter between us three, and I know you will be ready to rejoice."

"What, have you got some fine appointment, Mr Morris?" cried Glyn, who had grown to be on quite friendly terms with the master in a very short time of late, Morris making a point of treating him always with genuine respect, and aiding him in every way possible—coaching him, in fact, with his mathematics, in which, truth to tell, Glyn did not shine.

"No," cried Morris, in answer to the lad's question; "it is better than that. Somebody else has."

"You mean Professor Barclay?" said Singh.

"Yes, sir; I mean Professor Barclay. I have had a letter from him this morning telling me of his success, and that he leaves for India directly, to take up some post in connection with the Sanskrit college."

"I am very glad," said Singh, "for he must have been dreadfully poor."

"Sadly so," said Morris.

"I am glad too," said Glyn; "very."

"You don't know what a relief it is to me," continued Morris confidentially.

"Is he coming down to see you before he goes?" said Glyn.

"Oh no. He writes word that he is staying at apartments in London in the neighbourhood of the East India Docks until the great Indiaman sails, and desires his most respectful compliments to you both, and above all he begs me to tell you, Mr Singh, that the feelings of gratitude within his breast will never expire. While, as now he is entering upon a career of prosperity, many weeks will not elapse before he sends something, upon receipt of which he hopes you will return to him certain little memoranda that you hold, signed by his name."

"Ha, ha!" laughed Singh, "he'll wait a long time. Why, I burned them all directly after he gave them to me. Are you going to write to him, Mr Morris?"

"Yes; I must reply to his letter."

"Then, please tell him from me that I wish him all success in my beautiful country, and that he is never to trouble himself any more about the memoranda."

"For you have burned them?" said Morris.

"Yes, of course."

Chapter Twenty Three
Somebody is Untrustworthy

The boys did their best to worthily earn their cricket-match, and it came off some weeks after in due time.

The morning broke gloriously; four wagonettes came round to the door after a very early breakfast, and the masters followed in an open carriage with the Doctor, Wrench closing the door of each vehicle, and confiding to each party as it started that he wished it had been his luck to go as well; but he was going to enjoy himself that day by having a regular good polish at the Doctor's plate.

Strongley was reached in good time, the wickets were pitched, and the enemy, as the boys called them, made such a poor score in their innings that they had to follow on to another failure, the result being that the Doctor's pupils beat them in one innings, and drove back to Plymborough cheering madly.

As it happened, during the return, Glyn and Singh were separated; Glyn being in the first wagonette and reaching Plymborough a good half-hour before the last one, in which Singh rode.

Hurrying up to his room for a good wash and change, to get it over before Singh returned, the first thing that caught the boy's eyes was Singh's little bunch of keys hanging from the lock of the bullock-trunk in the corner.

Glyn was in such high spirits that the sight of the bunch set him laughing.

"Well, of all the untrustworthy fellows I ever knew," he said, "poor old Singh's about the worst."

Crossing to the trunk, he raised the lid, which yielded easily to his hand, banged it down again, turned the key, and put the bunch in the pocket of his flannel trousers ready to transfer to his ordinary garments when he dressed.

He had just finished when a burst of cheering and the rattle of wheels announced the coming of the last wagonette; and soon after, tired and hungry, Singh came up, to help fill the corridor with a chorus of chattering, and then hurriedly went on for his change of dress.

Then followed the supper the Doctor gave them, and, later on, the bell for prayers and rest.

"Hope you haven't lost your keys," said Glyn, as they began to undress, utterly wearied out.

"Lost my keys! Why should I lose my keys?" said Singh with a yawn. "Here they are! No, they are not! I left them in my flannels."

"Nice fellow you are to take care of your things!" said Glyn, as his companion limped across the room to where he had thrown his dusty and green-marked cricketing suit—anyhow—upon a chair.

"Oh, murder!" he said. "I am so stiff. I can hardly move, and my right hand feels all bruised and strained; but I say, Glynny, I hardly missed a ball; and didn't I play old gooseberry with some of their stumps?"

"Yes, we must have rather astonished them," cried Glyn. "They haven't had such a licking as that for a long time."

"Here, I say," cried Singh, "you have been up to some games," and he fumbled in vain in his flannels-pockets. "I say, you shouldn't do this, Glynny. The key of my India trunk is one of the bunch, and you know I don't like any games played with that."

"I haven't played any games," said Glyn quietly.

"Now, no nonsense," cried Singh pettishly. "You have got my keys."

"Oh yes, I have got them," cried Glyn. "Here they are. Catch!"

The bunch went flying through the air, and with one quick snap of the hand Singh caught them and laid them down sharply on the dressing-table with a bang.

"I don't like it," he said angrily, for he was very tired. "You shouldn't take my keys."

"Yes, I should," said Glyn quietly.

"I tell you you shouldn't."

"Then you oughtn't to leave them stuck in your box, as if to invite all the servants to come and have a rummage, when you go out to a cricket-match."

"I say, I didn't do that, did I? I had them in my pocket just before I started."

"If you did, how could I have them in mine when you came back?"

"Why, I—I am certain—" began Singh; and then, "Oh!"

"'Oh,' indeed!" cried Glyn. "But how did it happen?"

"I was just getting in the wagonette, when I thought it would be good fun to have one of those red Indian silk handkerchiefs to tie to a stump and use as a flag."

"Yes; as you did."

"Well, there were six of them in my big box, and I ran up to get one."

"And then left the keys in the box?"

"Well, I suppose I did, in the hurry and confusion. Oh, Glynny, what a beast I am! I wish I hadn't such a brute of a temper. It makes me flare up all at once and say such nasty things; and you are always as cool as a gourd, and get the best of me."

"Well, you should be more careful," said Glyn. "I wish, too, that you hadn't such a temper. You ought to master it."

"I can't," said the lad sadly. "It always masters me. It's through being born in such a hot climate, I suppose. Oh, I do hate to have to be always begging your pardon."

"Then I suppose that's why you don't do it now?"

"Oh, you know, old chap! I do beg it heartily. You don't want me to go down on my knees like a coolie?"

"Not I; only, somehow or other, I seem to be always ruffling up your coat about something."

"Well, go on; I do deserve it," cried Singh. "I shall be such a good boy some day, thanks to Professor Severn. No, no; don't lecture me any more."

"Not going to, only to say one word or two that the dad used to say to me when I had been flying out with some of the servants over yonder."

"Let's have it then, and done with it," said Singh with a sigh.

"'A man who cannot govern himself,'" said Glyn slowly, "'is not fit to govern other people.'"

"Oh, but I shall be a splendid governor by the time you have finished me off; and you will always be there to put me straight when I am going crooked; and I say, don't go and spoil a jolly day by a fuss over such a little matter as a bunch of keys."

"No, I won't," said Glyn. "But, you know, somebody might—"

"Bother somebody! And if he, she, or it had, I should have said that it was all your fault."

"My fault? Why?"

"Because you wouldn't take charge of you know what."

Chapter Twenty Four
The Doctor's Opinions on the Belt

Time glided on, with the friendly feeling between Morris and the boys increasing, for the mathematical master, with all his weakness and vanity, felt at heart somewhat touched by the respect and deference paid to him by Glyn.

"A thorough gentleman at heart," he said to himself. "Why, some boys would have gloried in the feeling that they had got me under their thumbs. And that Singh—what a splendid man he'll make!"

He was one of the first to display his genuine delight when the Strongley School lads came over to play a return match at Plymborough to avenge the beating, coming strengthened in their eleven by four old pupils of their school, two of them almost men.

But it was in vain, for Glyn's bowling played havoc with their wickets, and Singh stumped out all four of them in their two innings, three in the first and one in the second; while, when the Plymborough lads went to the wickets, Slegge playing his slogging game as soon as he got well in, and then after Burney had had a very fair innings, Slegge was joined by Glyn, and these two, amidst burst after burst of cheers, kept piling up the score till, with one unlucky cut, Slegge sent the ball up like a rocket, to travel far away, and then be cleverly caught out by long-field-off.

After that the game went on, with Glyn seeming to do what he liked with the enemy's bowling, all the rest of his eleven playing a good steady game, Singh getting the most modest score; for, much as he shone as a wicket-keeper, he was not specially handy with his bat. Still, he added his modicum, till all had fallen. And Singh, who was standing with Morris, enthusiastically joined the master in the applause and cheers that welcomed Glyn as he carried out his bat.

"Splendid!" cried Morris. "Grand! The finest bit of batting I have seen in schoolboy life. I am proud of you, my lad. Oh, if you would only shine like this over your algebra!"

It was all genuine.

So the result was that the Strongley boys went back after a second bad beating, in spite of the four old members of their eleven, one of whom had actually begun to shave.

And then the school-life went on, with its ups and downs, pleasures and pains, as school-life will, till one morning—the morning following a pillow-chat in bed between the two boys who play the principal parts in this story, when their discourse had been about the length of time that had elapsed since the Colonel had visited Plymborough—Wrench came to the class-room to announce that the Doctor desired the presence of Mr Severn and Mr Singh.

There was a whispered word or two as the pair rose from their seats wondering what it meant, and there were plenty of malicious grins, Slegge's containing the most venom, as he whispered to Burney loud enough for Singh to hear, "Cane!" while Burney's merry little face grew distorted as he caught Glyn's glance, and then began to rub his knuckles in his eyes, as if suggesting what his big friend would be doing when he came back from seeing the Doctor.

"I say, is anything the matter?" said Singh nervously.

"No. Nonsense!" replied Glyn. "I am sure we have both been doing our best."

This was as they got outside the class-room and were following Wrench into the hall.

"Hurrah! I know!" whispered Glyn. "I believe it's the dad come down at last."

"Oh!" cried Singh joyously. "Then he'll want us to come and dine with him. How jolly!"

For it was long indeed since the Colonel had been down; and though he wrote pretty regularly, first to one and then to the other, excusing himself on the ground that he had been very busy of late over Indian business connected with the late Maharajah's affairs, letters did not mean a day's holiday ending with a pleasant dinner and a long talk about old days in Dour.

So the boys fully expected to find the fierce-looking old Colonel chatting with the Doctor and waiting to greet them in his hearty manner. But they were disappointed, for as they entered the study the Doctor laid down his pen, nodded gravely to both, and picked up a letter.

"I have just heard from Colonel Severn inquiring after your welfare, though he says that one of you proves to be a very fair correspondent."

The Doctor turned over the letter and read a scrap here and there, almost muttering, as if to himself, and then aloud:

"Ah, here it is," he said: "I hope Singh is taking care of his belt, and that he is not foolish enough to wear it at any time."

The Doctor looked up from one to the other.

"I must confess to feeling a little puzzled here," he continued. "'Foolish enough to wear it at any time.' Now, as a boy, I have a very vivid recollection of regularly wearing a belt, especially when cricketing or running. We had a tradition amongst us that a belt was a very valuable support; and then we have antiquity on our side, the *cestus*, for instance, and allusions in the old writers regarding the gladiatorial sports, and the use of the belt by strong men. Does the Colonel mean the reverse of what he says, and is this a hint that I should give you a word of warning, Mr Singh, not to neglect its use?"

The Doctor directed a glance at Glyn, and then said sternly: "Have I said anything, Mr Severn, to excite your risible muscles?" For he had detected the exchange of a glance between the boys and a faint smile upon Glyn's lips.

"No, sir. I beg your pardon, sir. It is only the remark about the belt."

"Well, sir, I was not aware that in my remark about the belt I had said anything facetious. Perhaps, Mr Singh, you can explain Colonel Severn's allusion without turning my words into a subject for buffoonery."

Singh looked questioningly at Glyn.

"I am speaking to you, Mr Singh," continued the Doctor angrily. "Have the goodness to reply yourself. You can do so without Mr Severn's aid."

"Yes, sir," said Singh hastily; "but Glyn Severn gave me strict orders not to speak about the belt to anybody."

"Dear me!" said the Doctor, looking from one to the other. "And by what authority?"

"My guardian's, I suppose, sir."

"Dear me!" said the Doctor again. "The Colonel says he hopes that you are not so foolish as to wear the belt at any time. Your schoolfellow forbids you to speak about it to any one. Well, there, I do not wish to ask impertinent questions. That will do, gentlemen. I merely sent to you for enlightenment. You need say no more."

"I beg your pardon, sir; I think I ought to," said Glyn. "I did tell Singh not to talk about it, and to keep it safely locked up in his box, for it is very valuable, and I believe it is the one that his father the Maharajah used to wear."

"Oh," said the Doctor, "now I begin to understand. But a belt, you say?"

"Yes, sir," said Glyn, "an ornamental belt with a large clasp formed of three emeralds engraved with words in Sanskrit."

"Then it is quite an article of ornamentation?" said the Doctor.

"Yes, sir."

"And valuable, I suppose?"

"I suppose so, sir, very valuable, besides being a family relic that has been worn by the different chiefs for many years past."

"A family heirloom, then," said the Doctor in a tone which showed his interest. "Now I understand," and he smiled pleasantly. "I hope that 'he is not foolish enough to wear it at any time.'—Of course; hardly an article of ornament for a young scholar to wear, Mr Singh."

"No, sir," replied the boy. "That's what Glyn said."

"And very properly," continued the Doctor, giving the lad in question a friendly nod.

"And that I was not to show it to anybody, sir."

"Quite right, Mr Singh, and I am very glad to hear that your schoolfellow displays a wisdom beyond his years. You see, the world is far from perfection; and weak, wicked, foolish people might have their cupidity excited by the sight of such an object, with results that would be extremely painful to every one here. May I ask, then—by the way—is this belt attractive-looking?"

"Yes, sir, very handsome," said Glyn. "It is meant to bear a jewelled sword."

"Dear me!" cried the Doctor. "I hope that Mr Singh has no lethal weapon of that kind in his room."

"Oh no, sir," said Singh hastily.

"I am glad to hear it," said the Doctor, smiling; and he took up and raised his quill-pen, giving it a gentle flourish in the air. "Remember, my dear boy, what one of our writers has said: that the pen is mightier than the sword. And where may this handsome belt be?"

"Locked up in the bottom of my trunk that I brought from India, sir."

"In your room, then?" said the Doctor.

"Yes, sir."

"But securely locked up, you say?"

"Yes, sir," replied Singh, colouring a little, as he directed a sharp glance at Glyn, who added to his confusion by making a grimace.

"Ah," said the Doctor thoughtfully, "that is quite right. Emeralds," he continued thoughtfully, "engraved with Sanskrit letters. An ancient Indian relic, of course. And very curious, no doubt. It is quite an old custom that of engraving gems, Mr Severn. The Greeks and Romans really excelled in the extremely difficult art, and I have seen in museums very beautifully engraved heads of Grecian monarchs and Roman emperors and empresses, and also signet-rings and other ornaments. Dear me," he continued, with a smile from one to the other, "I am much surprised to find that such a specimen of the engraver's work has been lying here in my establishment, and my curiosity is greatly excited. But really, from what you say, such a thing as this ought not to be kept in a schoolboy's box, but in an iron safe along with plate, or lying at a banker's. Mr Singh, really I should like to see this—er—article of—er—er—this ornamental belt. Will you show it to me?"

"I can't, sir," said the boy half-spitefully, and he flashed a look at Glyn. "Severn said, sir, that I was not to talk about it or show it to anybody."

"As I have before said," continued the Doctor, "I quite approve of your friend's anxiety respecting your position. It was very wise, and I will not press to see it, feeling as I do that no parade should be made of such an object as this. Why, every pupil in the establishment would be wanting to see it, and— There, it is much better not."

"But I didn't mean, sir," said Glyn, "that Singh should refuse to show it to you. It was only to guard against such a thing as you have suggested.— Go and fetch it, Singh, at once."

Singh hurried eagerly out of the room; and as soon as he was gone Glyn said, "Singh is getting more and more English, sir, every day; but he used to be very fond of talking about being an Indian prince, and was weak enough to be proud of that belt and ready to show it to any one who asked."

"Not to his fellow-pupils, I hope?" said the Doctor.

"No, sir," replied Glyn, who began to feel that he was treading upon dangerous ground, and he hastened to add, "that's why I gave him such strict orders, sir."

"Quite right, Mr Severn; quite right," said the Doctor. "I highly approve of what you have done. But between ourselves—I say it because you are a very sensible lad, and I trust that you will see that it is something not to be repeated, for I speak with the best intentions—I am a little surprised that your father the Colonel, Mr Singh's guardian, should have placed at a mere boy's disposal what I presume to be a very valuable and unique portion of an Indian regalia."

"Well, sir, it was like this," said Glyn, flushing and speaking hastily. "Like a child who, longing for a toy, Singh was always bothering my father to let him have it to wear. You see, sir, Indian princes dress up so very much, to look big before their people, and they have such numbers of jewels and ornaments that one more or less does not seem of much consequence. Singh has got hundreds of things belonging to him that he will have some day to do what he pleases with, and my father, I suppose, thought that it didn't much matter about letting him have one."

"No doubt, Mr Severn, the Colonel had perfectly correct views upon the subject, living as he has done nearly all his life at an Indian court, and I am only looking at the matter with the eyes of an ordinary Englishman who never wears so much as a ring. Oh, here he comes. Let me see. I have a large magnifying-glass here in my table-drawer that may be useful to help to decipher the intaglio writing. Ah, we ought to have had here that poor friend of Mr Morris's who applied to me for an engagement; but I hear that he has left the town."

The Doctor was searching in his drawer so that he did not see the change in Glyn's countenance; and as he looked up it was not at his pupil, but at the door, which was suddenly thrown open, and Singh rushed in, looking wild and staring, as he literally shouted: "It's gone! It's gone!"

Chapter Twenty Five
Singh's Announcement

"Gone!" said the Doctor, letting the reading-glass fall upon his blotting-pad. "What has gone?"

"My father's belt!" cried the boy passionately. "It has been stolen. It is not in the box."

"Stop, stop, stop!" said the Doctor firmly. "You are speaking excitedly. My dear boy, be calm."

"But it's gone, sir!" cried Singh, with his eyes flashing now, as he looked from one to the other. "I tell you it's been stolen.—Oh, Glyn, what will your father say? What shall I do?"

"Be calm," repeated the Doctor slowly. "My dear boy, recollect that I stand to you, as we say in Latin, *in loco parentis*; and in the place of your guardian I must tell you that in your excitement you are making a very rash and cruel charge."

"But, sir—" began Singh, with an imperious stamp of the foot.

"Stop!" cried the Doctor. "At my time of life I have learned a good deal of the weakness of human nature, and how prone we are to judge wrongfully, especially in a case like this. On several occasions I have known people to be suspected and charged with theft through the weakness of the accuser. Nothing is easier or more common than for money or a missing jewel or a book to be hastily looked upon as stolen when the one has been spent and forgotten, the others in the same way been placed elsewhere for security."

"Yes, sir," cried Glyn excitedly, "and I don't want to go against Singh here; but I have known him do stupid things like that.—Look here, Singhy," he continued hotly, "did you properly search the box?"

"Yes," cried Singh. "When I found the case wasn't there where I put it, I turned it upside down, and the contents are lying all over the floor."

"And what about your drawers? Did you look in them?"

"You know I never kept it in my drawers," cried Singh.

"Yes, but you might have put it in one of them."

"Shouldn't I have remembered that I did?" snapped out the boy.

"You might," replied Glyn quietly; "but I have put away things sometimes and forgotten where, and when I found them afterwards I have wondered how they got there."

"Ex—actly, Mr Severn," said the Doctor; "and so have I, especially in the case of books."

"I am sure it's been stolen," cried Singh passionately.

"Well, I am sure you're wrong," said Glyn, "for there's nobody here who could do such a thing, though you always were very stupid about your keys."

"What's that?" said the Doctor sharply.

"Oh, I have found his keys left in his box or drawers, sir, more than once."

"Well," cried Singh, in the same excited tone, and he literally glared at his companion, "suppose, when I was busy, sir, or in a hurry, I did leave them in the lock! Was I to think that some thief was waiting to go in and take that case away? Why, when my father was alive, if one of his people had done such a thing as steal anything he would have been given over to the guards, killed at once, and his body thrown into the river."

"Ah, yes," said the Doctor quietly. "But that was in India, my young friend, and matters are different here. Now, if you please," he went on gravely, as he replaced the reading-glass in the drawer, "you will be good enough to smooth your countenance and hold your tongue. Have you told any one else of this?"

"No, sir," cried the boy. "I ran down directly to come and tell you."

"Here! What are you going to do?" said the Doctor, as Singh moved quickly towards the fireplace.

"Ring for the police to be fetched," cried Singh.

"Stop!" said the Doctor sternly. "And please recollect that I am master here."

"But—"

"Silence, sir! Now come with me and Mr Severn up into your dormitory; and, until I give you leave, neither you nor Mr Severn will say a word to a soul."

"But—"

"Did you hear me tell you, sir, to be silent?" cried the Doctor, in his deepest and most commanding tones. "If there has been a theft committed, which I greatly doubt, this jewel or jewels must be recovered. Such an ornament, if taken by a thief, could not easily be disposed of, and we must first have a calm and quiet investigation of what will in all probability prove to be a mistake.—What do you think, Mr Severn?"

"I think it is a mistake, sir."

"Then come with me up into your room, and I desire that you both treat the matter in a calm and thoughtful way. I cannot have a matter of this kind made into a piece of gossiping scandal.—Mr Severn, will you be kind enough to open the door?"

Glyn sprang to the handle, and the Doctor walked slowly out, followed by the boys, while Glyn gripped his companion by the wrist and said hastily. "Come quietly, and if we meet anybody don't make them see that something is wrong by wearing a face like that."

Singh looked at him fiercely, and then followed in silence, passing nobody, as they made for the corridor and entered the door of their dormitory, which Singh in his haste had left open.

The Doctor stepped in and made way for the two boys to pass, himself closing the door after them, and then turning, raising his eyebrows a little as he saw the state of the floor, where the carpet was scattered with different garments and odds and ends, while the bullock-trunk lay upside down.

The Doctor glanced at Glyn, who read his wish in his eyes.

"Where are your keys, Singh?" he cried.

"I don't know. What do you want with them?"

"Why, to search your drawers, of course."

"I can do that myself," said the boy haughtily.

"I know that; but I am going to do it," said Glyn firmly. And brushing by his companion, he went to the overturned trunk, turned it back into position, and drew the keys from the lock.

Singh made no attempt to check him, but drew himself up and stood with folded arms, scowling angrily as Glyn unlocked and carefully emptied drawer after drawer in turn, replacing the contents as he went on.

"Was the belt or girdle lying loose, Mr Singh?" said the Doctor calmly, as the search went on.

"No, sir," and the boy, more himself now, described the colour and shape of the missing case.

Then there was silence, which was only broken by the rustling noise that Glyn was making as he went on with the search till he had finished, closed the last drawer, locked it, and taken out the key. Then, with sinking heart, he said quietly, "I am afraid he's right, sir. It's gone."

"Is there any other receptacle," said the Doctor, "in which it could have been placed?"

"No, sir," said Singh bitterly; "there is nowhere else."

"I am thinking," said the Doctor, "that it has not been stolen. If it had been, the person who took it would have been content with rolling up the girdle, as you say it was of soft leather, placing it in his pocket, reclosing the case, and leaving it behind—for two reasons: one, that it would be noticeable if carried about; another, that it might lie shut up in your box for any length of time, with the change that had taken place unsuspected. For, going to your box again and again and seeing the case there, the chances are that you would not have opened it to note that the contents were safe."

The Doctor was silent for a minute or two. Then—"So there is no other receptacle in the room where the belt could have been placed?"

"No, sir," said Singh, with a scarcely perceptible sneer in his tones. "There is nowhere else, sir, unless Glyn has put it away in his own drawers so as to keep it safe."

"Oh!" cried Glyn, starting round angrily.

"Be silent, my boy," said the Doctor, laying his white hand upon the boy's shoulder. "Such a thing is quite possible, as I have previously explained. I was about to ask you to open the drawers yonder."

"But, oh, sir," cried Glyn, "you don't think—"

"My dear boy, no," replied the Doctor, with a look which made Glyn eagerly take out his keys, rapidly unlock every drawer, and then turn to Singh with a keen, angry look upon his countenance, which was now growing hard; and as he pointed towards the drawers he uttered hoarsely the one word, "Look."

"No," said the Doctor gravely. "Examine the drawers yourself, Severn. You feel now that it is impossible that you can have done this thing. Possibly, perhaps, after coming into the room alone and finding that your companion had left his own keys in his box—"

"I did find them like that, sir, twice."

"Ah," said the Doctor, "and changed the *locale* of the missing belt."

"No, sir," said Glyn. "I only took the keys out after seeing that the trunk was locked, and gave them to Singh."

"Each time?" said the Doctor. "Tax your memory. Are you sure of that?"

"Quite, sir. Certain. I wouldn't have taken the thing out. I hated his having it here."

"But tell me this," said the Doctor; "the last time you found the keys hanging in the lock, did you look in to see if the case was there?"

Glyn shook his head.

"Ah," said the Doctor, and he stood looking on while Glyn deftly emptied and restored each drawer in turn, the task being facilitated by the orderly state of the contents.

"Nothing," said the Doctor, as that task was ended. "Now, Mr Singh, it will be as well to replace those scattered objects of attire in your box."

"Oh," cried Singh angrily, "I can't think now of such trifles as those."

"Replace them in the box," said the Doctor sternly.—"Mr Severn, have the goodness to help your friend."

As the Doctor spoke he gravely sank into one of the little bedroom chairs, and sat thinking with wrinkled brow, and watching the proceedings of the two boys till they had ended.

"Now," he said, "can you think out any clue to help us to find the missing case?"

"No, sir," came almost simultaneously from the boys' lips.

"No," said the Doctor. "The mystery, for so I must call it, is at present dark and impenetrable. I am not going to send for the police to make a clumsy and painful investigation at once, because I still cling to the belief that something will occur to you two boys that will help us to pierce what now looks very black and impenetrable. You will kindly do as I tell you: go on with your daily avocations as if nothing had happened, and leave any expose of what may or may not be a painful matter to come gradually and from me."

Both boys responded by a sharp nod of the head.

"If you have not thought about the matter," continued the Doctor, "let me tell you this—though you, Severn, must have felt it only a short time back. Every person who is questioned or examined about this missing belt is bound to feel a pang of indignation at what he looks upon as being treated as a thief. We are approaching to fourscore personages in this establishment;

and if the belt has been stolen, the probability is that seventy-nine are innocent and only one guilty. Now, you see, to find the one guilty we must spare the seventy-nine innocent. Do you apprehend my meaning?"

"Yes, sir, of course," cried Glyn, while Singh was silent.

"Then I shall proceed as I think best; but I tell you this: I shall be perfectly firm and just, and shall leave no stone unturned to find out the author of this scandal."

The Doctor turned and left the room, leaving the two boys alone.

Chapter Twenty Six
Down the School Grounds

Later on in life, when Dr Bewley's pupils had grown up to manhood, they used to think that in spite of school-troubles and a great deal of hard work, with the natural accompaniments of temporary fits of ill-health (which matured reason taught them had generally been due to some bit of boyish folly not unconnected with pocket-money, extra home-tips, and visits to the highly popular tuck-shop), the sun had always seemed to shine brightly at Dr Bewley's establishment.

There was only one boy there who wore spectacles, not because he had bad eyes, for they were very bright and good, but because nature had formed the lenses of a more than usually rounded shape, with the consequence that their owner was short-sighted and needed a pair of concave glasses to deal with the rays of light and lengthen the focus of the natural lenses. But, metaphorically and poetically, as somebody once wrote, every boy wore glasses of the *couleur-de-rose* type—those which make everything that is happily beautiful seem ten times more so, and in later days have made many a man say to himself, "Oh, if I could see life now as I saw it then!"

There were cloudy and rainy days, of course, at Plymborough; and when the former were recalled it was generally in connection with the loss of Singh's belt.

It was on one of these cloudy days, when paradoxically the sun was shining brilliantly in the pure blue south-western sky, that Glyn and Singh were strolling down the grounds together, looking straight before them, with the full intention of driving the school-troubles out of their minds for the time being.

"What's the good of worrying about it, Singhy?" Glyn had said. "I know it's a horrible nuisance, with the suspicion and unpleasantry, and it was a very beautiful thing, which I am very, very sorry has been lost; but let's try and forget it."

"Oh, who can forget it?" cried Singh impatiently.

"Well, I know it's hard work, and it all seems like a nasty little bit of grit in the school machine. I can't get on with a single lesson without your wretched belt getting into it."

"My wretched belt!" cried Singh hotly.

"Now, don't get into a passion, old chap. That isn't being English. You must learn not to put so much pepper in one's daily curry."

"Oh, I am not cold-blooded like you. You English are so horribly tame."

"Oh no, we are not," said Glyn. "We have got plenty of pepper in us when we want it; but that's where education comes in. I don't mean Dr Bewley's stuff and all we learn of the masters; but, as my dad says, the cultivation that makes a fellow an English gentleman. And do you know what that means?"

"Oh, bother! No."

"Then I'll tell you, Singhy. It's learning to be able to keep the stopper in the cruet till it's really wanted. Do you understand?"

"No; and I wish you'd talk in plain English and say what you mean, and not build up a rigmarole all round it. Our people at home never do so."

"Oh, come, I like that!" cried Glyn, laughing. "Why, people out in the East are always, when they want to teach anything, turning it into a fable."

"Bother fables! Bother the belt! It's made the whole place seem miserable."

"Then don't think about it any more."

"I can't help it, I tell you. Why, you owned just now that you were as bad."

"Not so bad as you are, Singhy. I do try to throw it all aside. You don't."

"Ah, it's very well for you to talk. You haven't lost something that's worth nobody knows how much."

"Well, but never mind; you can afford it. See what a jolly old Croesus you are going to be when you grow up!"

"Bah! How do I know that I am going to be rich?"

"Don't be a humbug. Why, father has been looking after your revenues for years, and I heard him say once that money was accumulating tremendously during your minority. After all, what's a belt with some bright stones in it? You could have a dozen more made if you wanted them. But you don't! Who wants to look pretty like some great girl? The greatest thing in life is to be a man. Father says so, and you know he's always right."

"Yes," said Singh thoughtfully; "he's always right; but did he say that?"

"Well, not quite," said Glyn, laughing; and Singh looked at him suspiciously. "What he said was that the grandest thing in life was to be a boy."

"Ah," cried Singh argumentatively, "but that is very different. A man can do what he likes, but a boy can't."

"Oh, but a boy's a young man, or is going to be. I mean to be always glad that I am a boy, for father says that when I grow up to be a man I shall be often wishing that I was young again. Now, don't let's go on worrying about this and the old belt. You never wore it, and if it hadn't been lost I don't believe you ever would have used it. You see, after living in England you'll have learned that great English people never dress up except on some grand day when Parliament's going to be opened or somebody's going to be crowned; and then noblemen, I suppose, put on robes and wear their coronets. You'd never have wanted the belt."

"Well, I don't know about that," said Singh. "Of course I shall always dress like an Englishman; but I suppose sometimes, by-and-by, I shall have to dress up to show myself to my people."

"Oh yes, just once in a way, and when you are going to meet the other chiefs; but I'll bet sixpence you will soon be glad enough to take the things off again."

"But I say," cried Singh, "look here. What about soldiers and officers? They dress up pretty grandly."

"Well, yes," said Glyn laughingly; "we are obliged to make them look nice, or they wouldn't care about going shooting people and cutting off heads. Now, promise me you won't worry any more about the belt."

"Well, I will try," cried Singh, "and I shouldn't have bothered about it so much now, only every fellow in the school looks at me as if he were thinking about it all the time."

"Don't believe it," said Glyn. "You fancy he does. There now, let it go. Here, come and have a turn at something."

"What?"

"I don't know. Let's go across the field there and get under the elms. There are a whole lot of the fellows there. They have got some game on. There's Slegge yonder."

"Oh, I don't want to go where Slegge is."

"But you should want to go where Slegge is. I know he's a nasty, disagreeable fellow; but you needn't notice that. If he's civil—well, that will be right enough. If he isn't, treat him with good-humoured contempt. You aren't afraid of him, are you?"

"I! Afraid of him!" cried Singh indignantly, and he emitted quite a puff of angry breath.—"What did you do that for?" he continued angrily, for, as if by accident, Glyn, with a quick gesture, had knocked off his cap, and then stooping quickly snatched it from off the grass and put it carefully on again. "You did that on purpose," cried Singh angrily.

"Oh, it's all right. It was the stopper came off, and I put it on again."

"Bah!" cried Singh with a snort; but he walked quietly on, gradually calming down as his companion half-guided him towards the group of boys who were idling about under the elm-trees, pretty close to where the new piece of fence marked the place where the elephant went through.

Yielding to Glyn, Singh would have walked quietly up with him and been ready enough under his friend's guidance to embark on any sport or game that was going on; but as Glyn afterwards said when he was laughing it over, "old Slegge" made the pepper-stopper shoot out at once, for, after evidently seeing who were approaching, he slowly edged himself round till his back was to the companions, and began talking aloud, measuring the time by means of his ears till he came to the conclusion that Singh was near enough to catch everything he said, and even Glyn winced as he heard the lad say:

"Oh, by the way, you fellows, I suppose you have done it for a lark, and you mean to put it back in my box; but I have missed my turban, the one with the big pearl in it that fastens the plume of feathers."

The boys were silent, staring at the speaker, for they did not catch the point of the remark; and Slegge continued:

"You see, I set great store by that turban. It was an old one of my father's, and of course it was very valuable. You see, in Bungly Horror a turban like that—some fellows call them puggamarees, but that's only because they are ignorant beggars—but as I was saying, turbans like that come down from father to son. I don't know how old this one was, and nobody notices that they are old, because they always go so regularly to the wash; and you know the more muslin's washed the whiter it gets, while as for the holes, of course, they are the beauty of it, because it gets to look more and more like splendid old lace."

Slegge's remarks remained problematical for a few moments, and then the meaning came with a flash to Burton, who had suddenly caught sight of Singh and Glyn.

He burst into a merry guffaw at once, and thus set off the rest, while Slegge waited till they had done before going on with the by no means poor imitation of Singh's manner of speaking and a rather peculiar utterance of the consonant r.

"I don't know what you fellows are laughing at," he said, with a look of supreme innocency; "but I suppose you don't know any better. It's your ignorance of the value of family relics like that; and because you never see me bouncing about the schoolyard with my turban on, you think I haven't got one in my box—I mean, had one; so now no more nonsense. Whoever took it for a lark had better put it back before I get my monkey up—Indian monkey, I mean—for if I do there's going to be head-punching, and no mistake."

"Come on, Singh," said Glyn quietly, as he slipped his arm through his companion's and tried to lead him away. "Don't take any notice of the malicious brute."

But Singh's feet seemed to be shod with something magnetic which made them cling to the ground, and he stood fast.

"Come on, I say," cried Glyn. "No nonsense! Do you hear?"

Singh turned upon him quickly with an angry flash in his eyes, and he was about to burst out with some fierce retort; but in those brief moments it seemed to him that it was not Glyn's but the Colonel's masterful eyes that were gazing down into his, as, truth to tell, they had more than once looked down upon his father in some special crisis when in the cause of right the brave English officer had with a few words mastered the untutored Indian chief, and maintained his position as adviser as well as friend.

The next minute Singh was walking quietly away by his companion's side; but his arm kept giving a sharp jerk as Slegge went on speaking more and more loudly, uttering words so that the friends might hear.

"I don't care," said Slegge; "you fellows can do what you like, but I am not going to believe it. It's all a got-up thing. I don't believe there ever was any precious belt, or, if there was, it was only a green glass sham. Emeralds set in gold, indeed! Whoever heard of a fellow coming to school with a thing like that in his box? Bah! Yah! It isn't likely that even a nigger would do it." And as the companions passed out of earshot, Slegge continued, "It doesn't matter to me; my time's nearly up at school, thank goodness! and I shall finish with the next half. But I do pity you poor beggars who have got to stay. I don't know what the place is coming to. It seems to me that old Bewley's head's getting soft, unless he's getting so hard-up that he's glad to take anybody's money to keep the old mathematical musical-box going, or else he wouldn't have taken a nigger to be put in the same rank with English gentlemen."

"Here, you had better mind," said Burney.

"Why?" snapped out Slegge.

"Because you will have old Glyn hear you."

"Pooh! What do I care for Glyn?"

"Ever so much," said Burney. "I don't suppose you want another licking."

"Look here, Burney, none of your cheek, please, or else somebody else will get a licking. None of that. You were always a sneak, and trying to curry favour with the Indian nigger."

"Curry, eh?" said Burney with a half-laugh. "Well, suppose I did. I like Indian curry."

"Do you. But you won't like my curry," snorted out Slegge, "for I'll give you such a curry-combing down as will make you sore for a week, my fine fellow.—Look here, boys, all of you; I am not ashamed to own I was licked that day, for I was weak and ill, and in one of the first rounds I nearly put my elbow out of joint. Something was put out of joint, but it snapped back."

"He means his nose," whispered little Burton. "It has been ever since Severn came. I never heard it snap back; did you?"

"I saw him blow it several times," said the companion to whom he spoke, "and I saw his pocket-hanky after, and, oh my!"

"What are you two boys plotting there?" snarled Slegge. "My ears are sharper than you think, and if you don't want yours pulled you had better drop it."

Little Burton dropped upon his knees, crouching down all of a heap and seeming to subside into the worn brown earth as he laid his forehead upon the ground, while Slegge seized the opportunity and rushed at him as if he were a football, delivering a heavy kick that sent the poor little fellow over.

"Serve you right!" cried Slegge, as the boy uttered a sharp cry of pain. "Now, go and yelp somewhere else. Let's have none of your howlings here."

But only a faint sob followed, while the little fellow rose with his teeth closely set and lips compressed, as he tried to stifle the cries that were struggling to escape, and then stood leaning against his nearest companion without uttering a sound.

"Look here, Burton," sneered Slegge, "go and tell Severn, and ask him to come and lick me again. I am ready, and I'll let him see.—Yes, you may look, Mr Burney, Esquire. I saw that letter yesterday you had from home. Esquire indeed! It's sickening!—I am ready to have it out with him whenever he likes, and take the nigger after him when he's had his gruel. Go and tell him if you like. It's been dull enough in the place ever since that miserable imposture about the lost belt. You want something to rouse you up, and I'll give it you if you can bring those two fellows up to the scratch; but that you can't do. Look at them sneaking off like a street cur and an Indian jackal. Contemptible beasts! I only wish they would come back. I feel just in the humour now to give them what for. Yah!—Well, any of you going to fetch them back?"

"I'm not," said Burney, shrugging his shoulders. And he turned half-away as if to go and lean against the fence, but really to hide his face as he muttered to himself, "Oh, shouldn't I like to see you licked again!"

"Well, who's going?" cried Slegge haughtily.—"No one?—Here, you, you snivelling little wretch," he continued, turning to little Burton, "go, and tell that big bully Severn that I am waiting here to give him his dose, and that he's to bring the nigger with him to have his lot when I have done with number one.—Yes, boys, I feel just in the humour for it, and I am going to cut both their combs.—Do you hear, Burton?"

The little fellow drew a long, deep breath, but he did not move.

"Do you hear what I say?" roared Slegge.

"Yes," said the little fellow sturdily.

"Well, be off, then, at once, before you get another kick."

"Shan't!" cried the little fellow, through his set teeth; and a sharp jerk seemed to run through his body as he clenched his fists.

"Oh, that's it, is it?" cried Slegge, making a stride towards him.

"Run, Burton, run!" cried two or three voices.

"Shan't!" came again.

"No," cried Slegge. "He'd better! I'd run him! Here, I don't want to hurt you, young un. You go and tell them both what I say."

"Shan't!" cried the little fellow fiercely, and he looked his persecutor full in the face.

"Hark at him! Hark at the little bantam!" cried Slegge, with a forced laugh. "And look at them, boys. Look at the two slinking off like the curs they are, with their tails between their legs. There, you will be disappointed; there's no fight in them."

The big school-hero was quite right certainly as far as one of the pair was concerned, for just then Singh was saying, "Oh, it's cowardly of you. I can't bear it. I will go back and have a go at him myself."

"No, you won't," said Glyn sturdily, and he locked Singh's arm well within his own.

"How dare he insult me like that! I don't care if he half-kills me; but I won't bear it."

"Yes, you will," said Glyn, "like a man."

"Like a coward, you mean."

"No, I don't. I am not going to have you knocked about just because a low bully abuses you."

"Well, will you go and thrash him yourself?"

"No. I have whipped the cur once, and I am not going to lower myself by fighting again because in his spite he turned and barked at us. I could do it again, and I feel just in the humour; but what does it mean? Black eyes and bruises, and the skin off one's knuckles, and a nasty feeling that one has degraded one's self into fighting a blackguard, for that's what he is, or he wouldn't have insulted you as he did just now.—Come away."

"Oh, I didn't think you were such a coward, Glyn."

"And you don't think so now," replied Glyn coolly. "You are in a regular rage, and that's just the difference between you Indian fellows and an Englishman. You begin going off like a firework."

"Yes, and you go off as if you had had cold water poured on you."

"Very likely," replied Glyn. "There, we are both hot now. Let's try and cool down. I don't care whether it seems cowardly or whether it doesn't; but I am not going to get up a fight and make an exhibition of myself for the other fellows to see. Once was quite enough; and perhaps after all it's harder work to bear a thing like this than to go over yonder and punch old Slegge's head and have it out."

"I don't care whether it is or not," said Singh fiercely. "Let's go, and if you won't fight, I will."

"Look here, Singhy; you and I have had lots of wrestles, haven't we?"

"Yes; but what's that got to do with it?"

"Why, this. I am not bragging; but I have more muscle in my arms than you have, and if I like I can put you on your back at any time."

"Ur–r–r–r–ur!" growled Singh.

"That means you own it. Well now, look here; if you try to get away from me I'll put you down on your back and sit upon you till you grow cool."

"Do if you dare!" cried Singh.

Glyn closed with him on the instant. There was a short struggle. The young Indian prince was laid neatly upon his back almost without an effort on the part of Glyn, who the next moment was seated calmly astride his companion's chest, fortunately well out of sight of the group beneath the elms. Then for a few minutes Singh heaved and struggled, glaring the while into his companion's eyes, until, as if he had caught the contagion of the good-humoured smile in Glyn's frank young face, a change came over Singh's, and the fierce heaving gave way to a movement that was certainly the beginning of a laugh, followed by a good-humoured appeal.

"Let me get up, Glyn. I am quite quiet now," said the boy.

"No games?"

"No; honour bright. It's all over now, and I don't want to fight."

The next minute the two lads were walking away as if nothing had happened.

Chapter Twenty Seven
A Little Victim

That same evening Singh went down the town to relieve his feelings and the heaviness of one of his pockets, for the day before both he and Glyn had received letters from the Colonel with their monthly allowance. Glyn had refused to join his companion, to Singh's great annoyance, for the occurrences of the day had left him touchy and ready to take offence at anything.

"I wouldn't have refused to go with you," he said. "It's precious disagreeable, and you might come."

"Can't," said Glyn firmly. "I can't come, and you know why."

"Oh yes, I know why; all out of disagreeableness. You haven't got any other reason."

"Yes, I have. You haven't written to father, have you, to thank him for what you got?"

"No; I am going to write to-morrow."

"And then when to-morrow comes you'll say the same, and the same next day. There never was such a fellow for putting off things."

"Well, you needn't talk," cried Singh. "You haven't written to the Colonel to say you have got yours."

"No," said Glyn firmly; "but I am going to write this evening."

"No, you are not. Come on down town with me. I want to go to the old shop. Do come, there's a good chap! I hate going alone."

"Why?"

"Because if I go alone I always see so many things I want to buy, and then I go on buying, and my allowance doesn't last out till next time."

"Nonsense! What difference would it make if I came with you? You'd be just as bad," cried Glyn.

"Oh no, I shouldn't. When you are with me you always keep on interfering and stopping me; and then the money lasts out twice as well."

"Well, look here," said Glyn; "wait till I have written my letter, and I will make it a short one this time, and go with you afterwards."

"Oh, you are a disagreeable one! There won't be time then, and it will be too late for going out. There, you see if I ask you to go again."

Uttering these words in his snappiest way, Singh whisked himself round and stalked off.

"Can't help it," said Glyn to himself. "I will get it done, and then go and meet him. He'll soon cool down, and there will be time enough to go to the shop and get back before supper."

But, all the same, Glyn uttered a low sigh as he thrust his hands into his pockets, to jingle in one the four keys that made his bunch, and in the other several coins which formed the half of the Colonel's previous day's cheque.

The keys felt light in his right hand and the coins very heavy, and there was a something about him that seemed to suggest that they ought to be spent; but the boy turned his face rigorously towards the door of the theatre, when his attention was taken by Wrench's tom-cat. He was crouching upon the sill of one of the lower windows, which was raised a little way, and evidently intently watching something within.

"What's he after?" said Glyn to himself. "Some bird got inside, I suppose, and flying about among the rafters."

Walking quietly up to see if his surmise were true, the cat did not hear him till he was quite close, when it bounded off the sill and made for the Doctor's garden, to disappear among the shrubs.

"I thought he was after no good," said Glyn to himself; and, before making for the door, he peered in at the window in expectation of seeing a robin flitting about—a favourite habit these birds had of frequenting the long room and flying from beam to beam.

But there was no bird, Glyn seeing instead the back of little Burton, seated at his desk with the flap open resting against his head, as he seemed to be peering in; and just then the little fellow uttered a low sob.

"Poor little chap!" thought Glyn. "Why, that brute of a cat must have had one of his white mice, and he's crying about it."

Glyn went in at once and crept on tip-toe in the direction of his own desk, where he was about to write his letter; but he contrived to pass behind Burton unheard, and stopped short, to find that he was right, for the little fellow was bending low into his desk crying silently, save when a faint sob escaped him, while his outstretched hands were playing with three white mice. The door of their little cage was wide open, and they kept going in and out, to run fearlessly about their master's fingers, the cuffs of his jacket forming splendid hiding-places into which they darted from time to time, to disappear before coming out again to nestle in the boy's hands.

Glyn watched him for a few minutes, amused and pleased by the little scene and the affection that seemed to exist between the owner and the tame pets he kept within his desk.

"Why, the cat hasn't got one," he said; "he's only got three, and they are all there."

"Why, what's the matter, youngster?"

Just then there was a heavier sob than usual, and Glyn sympathetically laid his hand upon Burton's shoulder.

The little fellow gave a violent start, and the mice darted into their cage, as their owner turned guiltily round to gaze with wet and swollen eyes in his interrupter's face.

"Why, what's the matter, youngster?" said Glyn, bestriding the form and sitting down by Burton to take his hand.

"Oh, nothing, nothing," said Burton hurriedly, trying to withdraw his hand; but it was held too tightly, and he had to use the other to drag out his handkerchief from his jacket-pocket and wipe his eyes.

"You don't cry at nothing," said Glyn gently. "You are too plucky a little chap. I saw Wrench's cat watching you, and I was afraid he had got one of your mice."

"No, no; the poor little things are all right. But you oughtn't to have watched me, Severn."

"I didn't. I was coming to my desk to write a letter to my father, only I heard you sob."

"Oh!" ejaculated the boy.

"Come: out with it. You know you can trust me."

"Oh yes," said the little fellow earnestly. "I know that, Severn. You always are such a good chap."

"Well then, why don't you tell me what's the matter?"

"Because I was ashamed," said the other, nearly in a whisper.

"Ashamed! You! What of?"

"Because it hurts so, and I couldn't help crying," faltered the boy; "and I came in here so as no one should see me. Don't laugh at me, please!"

"Laugh at you because you are in trouble and something hurts you! You don't think I should be such a brute?"

"Oh, I didn't mean that, Severn," cried the boy earnestly, as he now clung to his sympathiser's hand. "I was afraid that you would laugh at me for being such a girl as to cry."

"But tell me," said Glyn.

"And I came in here to play with my mice, and it didn't seem to hurt me so much then, because it kept me from thinking."

"Come, what was it?" said Glyn. "You are keeping something back."

The little fellow tried to speak, but it was some minutes before he could command his voice. Then out came the story of the brutal kick he had received, and of how hard he had struggled to conceal the pain.

"A beast!" exclaimed Glyn. And then half-unconsciously, as if to himself, "I shall be obliged to give him another licking after all."

"Oh, do, please, Severn!" cried the little fellow joyously. "I'd give anything to be as big and strong as you, and able to stick up for myself; for, you see, I am such a little one."

"Oh, you will get big and strong some day," said Glyn. "Only wait."

"Yes, I'll wait," said the boy; "but it will be a long time first, and old Slegge is going away at the end of this half, so that I can't fight him myself. But I say, you will give him another licking, please?"

"Well, we'll see," said Glyn. "I dare say he'll make me before I have done."

"That's right," cried little Burton joyously; and he began to busy himself in putting his mice together, as he called it, and hooking the wire fastening before shutting up and closing the lid of his desk, while it was quite a different face that looked up into Glyn's, as the boy cried: "There, it doesn't hurt half as much now."

"If I were you I'd go and wash my face," said Glyn.

"What; is it dirty?"

"Oh, it's all knuckled and rubbed. You must have been crying ever so long; your eyes are quite swelled. There, be off. I want to write my letter."

While Glyn had been earnestly engaged comforting Burton and before he started his letter, he had not observed the return of Singh with his pockets looking bulgy and his face wearing a good-tempered smile.

"Done?" he said, as Burton took his departure.

"What, you back again?" cried Glyn. "I thought I should have been in time enough to come and meet you. If you had been another quarter of an hour I should."

"What; did you mean to come?" cried Singh joyously.

"Of course."

"Oh, you are a good chap! Here, come on up to our room. Look here."

He slapped his pockets as he spoke, and half-held open that of his jacket, the thought of the succulent treasures contained therein having completely swept away all his past ill-humour.

"Oh, I don't know that I want anything to-night," said Glyn.—"Yes, I do. I want to find little Burton. After we had gone away to-day Slegge kicked him brutally."

"What for?" cried Singh indignantly.

"Because he wouldn't bring an insulting message to fetch us back."

"Oh!" cried Singh. "And you wouldn't stop and lick him! He'll get worse and worse. Poor little chap! I like Burton."

"So do I," said Glyn rather coldly.

"What makes you speak like that?" asked Singh.

"I was thinking about what I ought to do."

"To do? What do you mean?"

"About giving him such a hiding as he deserves—that is, if I can."

"Oh, you can," cried Singh joyously; "and you will now, won't you?"

"Well, I wasn't going to because he was insolent to me; but now he's been such a brute to that poor little chap I feel as if I ought to—and I will."

But somehow that encounter did not come off, and possibly the recollection of the active little white quadrupeds that were closely caged-up in the desk may have suggested the idea enunciated by the Scotch poet who said:

> The best-laid schemes of mice and men
> Gang aft a-gley.

So do those of boys; for something happened ere many weeks had elapsed, and before Glyn Severn had found a suitable opportunity for administering the punishment that he thought it was his bounden duty to inflict.

In fact, the thoughts of Dr Bewley's pupils were greatly exercised about the trouble that hung like a cloud over the school; and in its dissipation Glyn Severn and Singh had a good deal to do, while, oddly enough, Wrench's cat played his part.

Chapter Twenty Eight
Mr Morris prepares

Examination-Day was rather a frequent periodical affair at Dr Bewley's. One month Monsieur Brohanne would have all the fun, as Glyn called it, an afternoon being devoted by the boys to the answering of questions, set by the French master, neatly printed upon a sheet of foolscap paper at the local printing-office, and carefully arranged upon a rough pad consisting of so many sheets of perfectly new blotting-paper upon each pupil's desk.

At another time it would be the Doctor's day, and his examination-papers would be distributed. By the same rule, in due time in the periodicity, Mr Rampson would revel in Latin puzzles; and Mr Morris would request the young gentlemen to build up curious constructions with perpendiculars, "slanting-diculars," and other varieties of the diagonal, in company with polygons and other forms of bodies with their many angles and curves, as set forth originally by a certain antique brain-puzzler of the name of Euclid, for the first part of the examination, the second portion consisting of that peculiar form of sport in which, instead of ordinary figures, the various letters of the alphabet were shuffled up and used for calculations, plused, minused, squared, and cubed up to any number of degrees, under the name of equations.

It was one afternoon prior to Morris's day, which was to begin at ten o'clock the next morning, and when the young gentlemen were all out in the play-field fallowing their brains for the next day's work, so that they might begin rested and refreshed, this being the Doctor's invariable plan, that Mr Morris was the only person in the establishment who was busy. He had received the foolscap sheets from the printer, carried them to his desk, upon which lay quite a pile of new thick white blotting-paper, and taking his seat, sat quite alone, chuckling with delight as he skimmed over his series of mathematical questions, one and all extracted from those which had been used at Cambridge.

"Ha, ha!" he chuckled. "This will puzzle some of them! This will make some of them screw up their foreheads! The stiffest paper I ever set. Eh? What's that?"

He started up, looking round, for there had been a sound like a soft thump; but he could see nothing on account of intervening desks. But, all the same, Wrench's tom-cat had leaped gently down to the floor, and from there he bounded on to one of the lines of desks, along which he stole very carefully, pausing to sniff at each keyhole as he leaned over, fully aware as he was that several of these desks were used as menageries, in addition to a very favourite one where he had paused more than once on account of the delicious black-beetly odour stealing up through the cracks, and which denoted white mice.

In one desk silkworms began as eggs upon a sheet of paper, ate, and grew themselves into fine, fat, transparent straw-coloured larvae which afterwards spun cocoons. In another there were a couple of beautiful little green lizards; while one boy had his desk divided into two portions by means of a piece of board cut to a cardboard-plan by the Plymborough carpenter at a price. In one portion of the desk there were books and sundry tops and balls; the other was the home of a baby hedgehog, which lived upon bread and milk, and had a bad habit of sitting in its saucer.

In the next row of desks there was rather an odorous creature which puzzled Tom a good deal; so much so that when the theatre was empty he made that desk a special spot for study in a very uncomfortable position, crouching as he did upon the slope with his head hanging over the edge and his nose close to the keyhole.

That desk required much thought, for he was convinced by gliding sounds that there was a live occupant therein, and his impression was that it was good to eat; but he had never seen inside, and was not aware that it contained an ordinary grass-snake.

Tom was convinced too, though he had never seen it, and was not aware of the differences in tails, that the inhabitant of another desk—enlightened as he was by sundry scratchings and gnawings—was a rat, though it was only Fatty Brown's young squirrel, which was destroying the imprisoning wood in a way that was alarming to the owner of the desk.

There were several other desks in the big theatre which gave forth sounds and excited Tom's curiosity, for Dr Bewley's young gentlemen affected zoology even as far as young birds, though not to any very great extent, as, not being nightingales, they did not nourish in the dark.

But enough has been said to account for the cat's love of study when the theatre was vacated by the pupils, and upon this particular occasion, taking little heed of Mr Morris, Tom went on investigating with his nose till he had reached the end of one series of desks, and, bounding across the intervening space, he came down with a thump upon the next, making Mr Morris look up sharply, snatch up a pocket lexicon, and send it flying, in company with the words, "Tsh! Cat!"

The next moment he was alone; and, in perfect satisfaction with the stiffness of his papers, he descended from his place and proceeded to lay neatly along the rows before him a carefully doubled set of half-a-dozen sheets of white blotting-paper, till one stood out clear and clean upon every pupil's desk.

This done, he proceeded to work his way back by placing a blue printed sheet of foolscap upon each improvised blotting-pad. It was all carefully and neatly done, for Mr Morris's mathematical brain led him to square the paper parallelograms, as he would have termed them, with the greatest exactitude, before going away to his own desk to gaze back over the blue and white patchwork before him, and give utterance once more to his thoughts regarding the puzzledom which would exist the next morning when the boys took their places.

"A magnificent mental exercise," he said proudly, before marching slowly down the big room like a mathematical general surveying the field where he was to do battle next day with the enemy in the shape of sloth and ignorance.

So wrapped up was he in self that he passed out without noticing that he was watched by one who waited till he was out of sight, and then, though the door was open, preferred to enter by the window, leap on to a desk, and then slowly proceed from one to the other; not in a bold open way, but in a slinking, snaky, crawling fashion, as if about to spring upon some object of prey.

The peculiarity of this was that it necessitated great extension of person; and as, after the fashion of all cats save those that belong to the Isle of Man, Tom carried his tail behind him, he went on in ignorance of the fact that more than once the furry end touched lightly in a more than usually well-filled ink-well, the result being an inky trail, which, however, dried rapidly in the warm theatre, and was not likely to excite notice upon unpainted desk-lids which were dotted with the blots and smudges made by hundreds of boys.

But sometimes great discoveries come from very small things, and Wrench's Tom played his part in one of the little comedies of life, those of Terence and Plautus not being intended here.

Chapter Twenty Nine
Something Unpleasant

The examination-days were not looked forward to with joy by Dr Bewley's pupils; and, sad to say, Morris's days were liked least. In fact, his was the only joyous countenance upon the morning after he had prepared the theatre, when he glanced round at the heavy expressions that pervaded the breakfast-tables. But possibly the most severe face in the room that morning was the Doctor's, as he paid his customary visit, and he took it with him afterwards into the theatre, which he entered punctually at ten o'clock, when the boys were all assembled in their places, while the masters were all at their desks, ready under Morris's leadership to sit out the examination, using their eyes, and making perfectly certain that no pupil whispered a question, furtively passed a piece of paper to another, or dipped down into his desk in search of a so-called helping "crib."

To use the schoolboy phrase popular at Plymborough—"What was up?"

The Doctor rose deliberately upon his throne-like place at the end of the theatre, coughed sonorously, settled his plump chin in his very stiff white cravat, and then gazed frowningly through his spectacles at the assembled pupils.

There was silence for quite a couple of minutes, and every boy present felt that the Doctor was singling him out and was about to speak to him about the committal of some fault, while internally he asked himself what it could be.

At last the great brain-ruler put an end to the suspense by addressing his pupils collectively; and every individual but one drew a breath of relief.

"Young gentlemen," he said, "in my long career of tuition of the boys who have been entrusted to my charge it has been my great desire to inculcate honour."

The three masters glanced at each other, making suggestive grimaces as if questioning what was to come, and at the same time expressing ignorance.

"Now, I regret very much to have to tell you that this morning I have been made aware of a most dishonourable act committed by one of my pupils. I have received by post what I can only term a very degrading letter, which I am sorry to say I fully believe to have been written by some one present. Who that is I do not know, and I tell you all that I would rather not know until the culprit allows his better feelings to obtain the mastery, and comes to me privately and says, 'Dr Bewley, I was guilty of that act of folly; but now I bitterly repent, and am here humbly to ask your forgiveness and at the same time that of my fellow-pupil whom I have maligned.' Now, young gentlemen, it gives me pain to address you all for one boy's sin, and I have only this to say, that you whose consciences are clear can let it pass away like a cloud; to him who has this black speck upon his conscience I only say I am waiting; come to me when the examination is done.—Mr Morris, it is ten minutes past ten. At one o'clock your examination is over, and the studies are at an end for the day.—Now, my dear boys, I wish you all success, and I trust that you will show Mr Morris that his mathematical efforts on your behalf have not been in vain."

There was an end to the painful silence half a minute later, as the Doctor closed the door after him, not loudly, but it seemed to echo among the great beams of the building, while it was long before his slow, heavy step died away upon the gravel path outside.

"Now, young gentlemen," said Morris sharply, "our Principal's address is not to interfere with my examination. You have your papers. Pro—"

There was a pause.

"—Ceed!" shouted Mr Morris.

There was the scratching of pens upon papers, but upon very few; most of the boys taking their pens and putting them down again, to rest their elbows on the desks and their chins upon their thumbs, as they fixed their eyes upon the column-like pile of questions printed quite close to the left side of the sheets of foolscap, while the three masters at the two ends and in the middle of the theatre seated themselves, book in hand, ready to hold up high before their faces so that they could conveniently peer over the top and make certain that there were not any more culprits than one within reach of their piercing eyes.

Mr Morris, to pass his three hours gently and pleasantly, opened a very old copy, by Blankborough, upon logarithms; Monsieur Brohanne had armed himself with a heavy tome of *La Grande Encyclopédie*, with a bookmark therein at the page dealing with the ancient *langue d'oc*; while Mr Rampson, also linguistical, opened a sickly-looking vellum volume, horribly mildewy and stained, and made as if to read a very brown page of

Greek whose characters looked like so many tiny creases and shrinkings in a piece of dry skin.

Only one boy spoke, and that was Glyn Severn, and he to himself; but at the same time he had caught Singh's eye as he sat some distance from him, and, placing his sheet of foolscap by his side, he raised his blotting-pad so that his companion could see a great blotch of ink thereon which seemed as if it had been roughly made by a brush that had been dipped in ink.

This done, he laid the pad back in its place, twisted the fold towards him, and taking a bright, new two-bladed knife that had been purchased with the proceeds of the Colonel's cheque, he opened the large blade and carefully passed it along the fold, setting free one half-sheet of the absorbent paper. This he folded and put in his pocket; but the ink had gone through to the next half-sheet, and this he also separated, treating it as he did the first. This left two half-sheets, with the possibility of their slipping about and away from the rest. So, after pocketing his knife, he opened the remainder where they were folded, and refolded the pad inside out, so as to leave the two cut half-sheets in the middle.

"That nasty nuisance of a cat!" he muttered to himself. "It must have come along smelling after poor little Burton's white mice, and smudged my paper like this. Ah," he continued, to himself, "I have promised the poor little chap that I'll lick Master Slegge, and— Hullo! What's this? What does old Morris mean by giving me half-used paper, and the other fellows new?"

His hands had been busy redoubling and smoothing the fold over the now prisoned half-sheets, and he was about to hold up his hand as a sign to the nearest master that he wanted to speak; but he let it fall again upon the desk, and sat gazing down at some indistinctly seen lines upon the blotting-paper, which looked as if a letter had been inserted wet within the pad and hastily blotted.

He could barely read a word, but somehow his curiosity was aroused, and he turned the leaf over, to find that the newly written letter had been placed in contact with the other side, the lines looking far blacker there, but seen like a page of printing type the reverse way on, so that he could not read a word.

Glyn closed the leaf again and tried to read once more, but with very little success; but for some reason or another his interest was more deeply excited, and he doubled two more leaves over so as to hide the writing, drew forward the foolscap paper to place it once more on the blotting-pad, and then began to read hard at the first section, trying the while to forget all about the freshly blotted letter, but in vain.

For two questions very different from Mr Morris's kept on appealing to him, neither of them algebraic or dealing with Euclid. One was, "How came that letter to be blotted on my pad?" and, "Who was it that wrote it?"

There was no answer; but the boy felt that he knew enough about one of Mr Morris's questions to begin to write the answer, and over this he had been busy for about ten minutes when another question flashed across his brain: "Was this the letter of which the Doctor spoke?"

Chapter Thirty
Brought to Book

Not until late that same evening did Glyn have an opportunity of investigating the mystery, for he had purposely refrained from making a confidant of Singh; so that it was after the latter was asleep that Glyn, rising softly, went over to the dressing-table and there lighted the chamber candle, which stood at the side of the looking-glass.

"Will it be too blurred?" he thought, and he held up in front of the mirror a piece of blotting-paper, and then started, for the occupant of the other bed stirred slightly, causing Glyn to step cautiously to the side of the sleeper.

"He won't wake," muttered Glyn, and he went back to the table and recommenced his task, to find that with the aid of reflection the written words on the spongy surface of the blotting-paper stood out fairly plain, though there was a break here and there. And this is what he read:

"*it was g— —ern oo thev the princes—*"

Then there was a blurred line where the ink had run, with only a letter or two distinct at intervals. Then half a blank line, and then, very much blurred and obscure, more resembling a row of blots than so much writing:

"*e as idden —sum whare —for sertane.*"

Another line all blotted and indistinct; then:

"*umble Suvvent, —Wun oo nose.*"

Then a line in which so obscure and run were the letters that minutes had elapsed before the reader could make out what they meant:

"*toe the doktor.*"

Glyn drew back from the glass as if stung, and then the question which came to him was who had written this abominable, ill-spelt accusation, evidently pointed at himself?

"That was the letter, then, that the Doctor mentioned," he said to himself, and he tried to read the words again, instinctively filling up some of the blanks so as to make the letter fit himself; and it seemed to him that there could only have been one person who was capable of writing such a thing.

He examined the lettering once again—a back-slanting hand, disguised.

"And I have only one enemy—Slegge," he thought to himself, as he softly blew out the candle and crept back into bed; but it was long ere sleep came, for the writing, run by the blotting-paper but still vivid, seemed to dance before his eyes, and as he now mentally read it: "It was Glyn Severn who stole the Prince's belt."

And it was with this to form the subject of his dreams that he fell fast asleep.

On the following morning Glyn entered the class-room early and proceeded to Slegge's desk.

"Just as I thought," he said, and he took up one of the writing folio books which lay with other volumes on the desk-cover.

There was no one else in the theatre at that early hour, and Glyn had time to compare as he wished certain of the letters and capitals in Slegge's handwriting with the wording on the blotting-paper.

"It was he; there can be no doubt," he exclaimed, and he went out of the room, making for the playground, intending to find his detractor; but he was not to be seen.

Fortune, however, favoured him as he was making his way back to the schoolhouse, for near the boys' gardens he suddenly caught sight of the object of his search.

"I say, Slegge," he said, approaching the lad, "I want to talk to you."

It did not seem to be quite the same self-confident bully of the day previous who responded, "Eh? You do, Severn? What's up?"

"Come into the class-room," said Severn. "I want you."

"What!" began Slegge. "What do you mean? Why are you trying to order me about?"

"Because I have something to tell you."

"Ha, ha, Cocky Severn! It's time you had that thrashing."

"Is it?" said Glyn. "Well, I don't think I should care to fight with a fellow who writes anonymous letters."

"What do you mean by that?" cried the other.

"I will show you what I mean if you come with me. I don't suppose you want the other fellows to hear it."

"I don't care," said Slegge. "Some cock-and-bull story you are hatching, Severn."

"You wrote that letter," said Glyn abruptly, and his voice sounded husky with the emotion and rage that were gathering in his breast.

"Letter? Letter? What do you mean? Has one come for me by the post?"

"You know what letter I mean," burst out Severn.

"Here, I say," cried Slegge, with a most perfect assumption of innocence; and he looked round as if speaking to a whole gathering of their schoolfellows, "what's he talking about? I don't know. Isn't going off his head, is he?"

"That letter the Doctor was talking about yesterday morning," cried Glyn, with the passion within beginning to master him.

"Here, I don't know what you mean," cried Slegge. "You seem to have got out of bed upside down, or else you haven't woke up yet. What do you mean by your letters?"

"You miserable shuffler!" cried Glyn, in a voice almost inaudible from rage. "The Doctor only talked about a letter; but I've found you out."

"No, you haven't," cried Slegge truculently; "you have found me in—in here by the gardens, and if you have come down here to have it out once more before breakfast, come along down to the elms. I am your man."

"That's just what I should like to do," panted Severn, whose hands kept opening and shutting as they hung by his sides; and there was something in the boy's looks that made Slegge change colour slightly, and he glanced quickly to right and left as if in search of the support of his fellows; but there was no one within sight.

"But," continued Glyn, "if you think I am going to lower myself by fighting a dirty, cowardly hound who has struck at me behind the back like the dishonourable cur that the Doctor said he was waiting to see come and confess what he had done, you are mistaken."

"There, I knew it!" cried Slegge. "You are afraid. Put up your hands, or I will give you the coward's blow."

To the bully's utter astonishment, one of Glyn's hands only rose quick as lightning and had him by the throat.

"You dare!" he cried. "Strike me if you dare! Yes, it would be a coward's blow. But if you do I won't answer for what will happen, for I shall forget what you have done, and—and—"

"Here, Severn! Severn! What's the matter with you?" gasped Slegge excitedly. "I haven't done anything. Are you going mad?"

"You have, you blackguard!" cried Glyn, forcing the fellow back till he had him up against the garden-fence. "You have always hated me ever since I licked you, and like the coward you are you stooped to write that dirty, ill-spelt, abominable letter to make the Doctor think I had stolen Singh's belt."

"Oh, I don't know what you mean," whined Slegge. "Let go, will you?"

"No!" cried Glyn, raising his other hand to catch Slegge by the wrist. "Not till I've made you do what the Doctor asked for—taken you to his room and made you confess."

"Confess? I haven't got anything to confess. You are mad, and I don't know what you mean," cried Slegge, whose face was now white. "Let go, or I'll call for help."

"Do," cried Glyn, "and I'll expose you before everybody. You coward! Why, a baby could have seen through your miserable sham, ill-spelt letter, with the words all slanting the wrong way."

"I don't know what letter you mean. Has the Doctor been showing you the letter he was talking about?"

"No," said Glyn mockingly, as he read in the troubled face before him that he was quite right. "But I have read it all the same, on the piece of blotting-paper that you used to dry what you had written—the sheet of blotting-paper that was put ready on my desk so that if it were found it might seem that I was the writer."

"That I wrote?" said Slegge, with a forced laugh. "That you wrote, you mean, before you sent it. I don't know what for, unless you wanted people to think that it was done by some one who didn't like you. What do you mean by accusing me?"

"Because you are not so clever as you thought. Come on here to the class-room. I have been there this morning, and laid the blotting-paper by the side of one of your exercises on your desk; and, clever as you thought yourself, the Doctor will see at a glance that some of the letters, in spite of the way you wrote them, could only have been written by you." And here he took a piece of paper out—a piece that he had torn from Slegge's exercise-book—and laid beside it the unfolded blotting-paper.

Slegge made a dash at them, but Glyn was too quick. Throwing one hand behind his back, he pressed Slegge with the other fiercely against the fence.

"There!" he cried triumphantly. "That's like confessing it. Come on to the Doctor. There's Mr Morris yonder.—Mr—"

"No, no, don't! Pray don't call!"

"Hah!" cried Glyn triumphantly. "Then you did write it?"

"I—I—"

"Speak! You did write it, you coward! Now confess!"

"Well, I—I was in a passion, and I only thought it would be a lark."

"You were in a passion, and you thought it would be a lark!" cried Glyn scornfully. "You muddle-headed idiot, you did it to injure me, for you must have had some idea in your stupid thick brain that it would do me harm. But come on. You have confessed it, and you shan't go alone to the Doctor to say that you repent and that you are sorry for it all, for you shall come with me. Quick! Now, at once, before the breakfast-bell rings; and we will see what the Doctor says. Perhaps he will understand it better than I do, for I hardly know what you meant."

"No, no, don't! Pray don't, Severn! Haven't I owned up? What more do you want?" And the big lad spoke with his lips quivering and a curious twitching appearing about the corners of his mouth; but Glyn seemed as hard as iron.

"What more do I want? I want the Doctor to know what a miserable coward and bully he has in the school."

"No, no," gasped Slegge, in a low, husky voice, and with his face now all of a quiver. "I can't—I won't! I tell you I can't come!"

"And I tell you you shall come," cried Glyn, dragging him along a step or two.

"Don't, I tell you! You will have Morris see," gasped Slegge.

"I want him to see, and all the fellows to see what a coward we have got amongst us. So come along."

Slegge caught him by the lapel of his jacket, and with his voice changing into a piteous whisper, "Pray, pray don't, Severn!" he panted. "Do you know what it means?"

"I know what it ought to mean," cried Glyn mockingly; "a good flogging; but the Doctor won't give you that."

"No," whispered the lad piteously. "I'd bear that; but he'd send me back home in disgrace. There was a fellow here once, and the Doctor called it expelled. Severn, old chap, I am going to leave at the end of this half. It will be like ruin to me, for everything will be known. There, I confess. I was a fool, and what you called me."

"Then come like a man and say that to the Doctor."

"I can't! I can't! I—oh, Severn! Severn!"

The poor wretch could get out no more articulately, but sank down upon his knees, fighting hard for a few moments to master himself, but only to burst forth into a fit of hysterical sobbing.

The pitiful, appealing face turned up to him mastered Glyn on the instant, and he loosened his hold, to glance round directly in the direction of Morris, and then back.

"Get up," he said, "and don't do that. Come along here."

"No, no; I can't go before the Doctor. Severn, you always were a good fellow—a better chap than I am. Pray, pray, forgive me this once!"

"And you will never do so any more?" cried Glyn half-mockingly.

"Never! never! I swear I won't!"

"Well," said Glyn, whose rage seemed to have entirely evaporated, "I suppose that it would pretty well ruin you, at all events for this school. I don't want to be hard on you; but I can't help half-hating you, Slegge, for the way you have behaved to that poor little beggar Burton. Look here, Slegge, if you say honestly that you beg pardon—"

"Yes," cried the lad. "I do beg your pardon, Severn!"

"No; I don't want you to beg my pardon," cried Glyn. "I can take care of myself. I want you to tell that poor little chap that you are sorry you ill-used him, and promise that you will never behave badly to him again."

"Yes, yes. I will, I will. But you are going to tell the Doctor?"

"No, I shall not. I am not a sneak," said Glyn, "nor a coward neither. I have shown you that, and I am not going to jump on a fellow when he's down. But come along here."

"To the Doctor's? Oh no, no!"

"Be quiet, I tell you, and wipe your eyes and blow your nose. You don't want everybody to see?"

"No, no.—Thank you!—No," cried the big fellow hurriedly. "I couldn't help it. I am not well. I must go to my room and have a wash before the breakfast-bell rings. May I go now?"

"No; you will be all right. The fellows won't see. I only want you to come over here to where Burton is. No, there he goes! I'll call him here. There, don't show that we have been quarrelling.—Hi! Burton!" cried Glyn, stepping to the garden-hedge and shouting loudly, with the effect that as soon as the little fellow realised who called he came bounding towards him, but every now and then with a slight limp.

"Just a quiet word or two that you are sorry you hurt him; and I want you to show it afterwards—not in words."

"You want me, Severn?" cried the little fellow, looking from one to the other wonderingly as soon as he realised that his friend was not alone.

"Yes. Slegge and I have been talking about you. He wants to say a word or two to you about hurting you the other day."

The little fellow glanced more wonderingly than ever at his big enemy.

"Does he?" he said dubiously, and he turned his eyes from one to the other again.

"Oh yes," said Slegge, with rather a pitiful attempt to speak in a jocular tone, which he could not continue to the end. "I am precious sorry I kicked you so hard. But you'll forgive me and shake hands—won't you, Burton?"

"Ye–es, if you really are sorry," said the little fellow, slowly raising his hand, which was snatched at and forcibly wrung, just as the breakfast-bell rang out, and Slegge turned and dashed off towards the schoolhouse as hard as he could run.

"I say, Severn," said little Burton, turning his eyes wonderingly up at his companion, who had playfully caught him by the ear and begun leading him towards where the bell was clanging out loudly as Sam Grigg tugged at the rope, "do you think Slegge means that?"

"Oh yes. I have been talking to him about it, and I am sure he's very sorry now."

"Oh, I say, Severn," cried the little fellow joyously, and with his eyes full of the admiration he felt, "what a chap you are!"

Some one who sat near took an observation that morning over the breakfast that Slegge did not seem to enjoy his bread and butter, and set it down to the butter being too salt; and though the Doctor waited for days in the anticipation that the sender of the anonymous letter would come to him to confess, he expressed himself to the masters as disappointed, for the culprit did not come, and the affair died out in the greater interest that was taken later on in the matter of the belt.

Still, somebody did go to see the Doctor, and he looked at him wonderingly, for it was not the boy he expected to see, but the very last whom he would have ventured to suspect.

Chapter Thirty One
Glyn's worried Brain

"Is any one with the Doctor, Wrench?"

"No, sir," replied the man distantly, and he looked curiously at Glyn. "Aren't you well this morning, sir?"

"Yes—no. Don't ask questions," cried the boy petulantly.

"All right, sir," said the man. "I don't want to ask no questions. There's been too much of it lately. Suspicions and ugly looks, and the rest of it. I'd have given warning the other day, only if I had, the next thing would have been more suspicion and the police perhaps had in to ask me why I wanted to go. Shall I ask the Doctor, sir, if he will see you?"

"No," cried Glyn, and walking past the man he tapped at the study-door, and in response to the Doctor's deep, "Come in," entered.

"What does this mean?" muttered Wrench. "I don't like listening; but if I went there and put my ear to the keyhole I could catch every word; and so sure as I did somebody would come into the hall and find me at it. So I won't go. But what does it mean? Young Severn's found out all about it, as sure as I stand here. Then it's one of the boys after all. Well, I don't care about it as long as it ain't me or Sam, so I'll go on with my work."

Meanwhile Glyn had entered, closed the door after him, and stood gazing at the Doctor with a curious sensation in his breast that seemed to stop all power of speaking connectedly, as he had meant to do when he had obeyed the impulse to make a clean breast to his old preceptor.

"Well, Severn," said the Doctor gravely, as he laid down his pen, thrust up his glasses till they were stopped by the stiff grey hair, and allowed himself to sink back in his writing-chair, "you wish to speak to me?"

"Yes, sir, please; I—" Glyn stopped short.

That was all that would come, so the Doctor waited for a few moments to give him time to collect himself, and then with an encouraging smile: "Are you unwell, my boy? Do you wish to see our physician?"

Glyn uttered a kind of gasp, and then, making a tremendous effort, the power to speak returned, and he cried, "Oh no, sir; I am quite well, only—only I am in great trouble, and I want to speak to you."

"Indeed!" said the Doctor gravely, as he placed his elbows upon the table, joined his finger-tips, and looked over them rather sadly at his visitor. "I am glad you have come, my boy," he continued gently, "for I like my pupils to look up to me as if for the time being I stood in the place of their parents. Now then, speak out. What is it? Some fresh quarrel between you and Mr Slegge?"

"No, sir," cried Glyn. "It's about that dreadful business of Singh's belt."

"Ah!" said the Doctor, rather more sharply. "You know something about it?"

"Yes, sir. It's about that I have come. About people being wrongfully suspected, and all the unpleasantry."

"Indeed!" said the Doctor, and he now spoke rather coldly. "You know, Severn, where it is?"

"I—I think so, sir. Yes, sir," continued the boy, speaking more firmly, "and I want to tell you all I do know."

The Doctor fixed his eyes rather sternly now, for a strange suspicion was entering his mind, due to the boy's agitated manner and his hesitating, half-reticent speech.

"Well," he said, "go on; and I beg, my boy, that you tell me everything without reservation, though I am sorry, deeply grieved, that you should have to come and speak to me like this."

Glyn seemed to breathe far more freely now, and as if the nervous oppression at his breast had passed away.

"You see, sir," he began, "I have known all along that Singh had that very valuable belt. It was his father's, and the Maharajah used to wear it; and when he died my father took charge of it and all the Maharajah's valuable jewels as well."

"Yes," said the Doctor slowly. "He was the late Prince's executor and Singh's guardian."

"Yes, sir; and Singh was very eager to have it—oh, months and months before we came over here to school, and my father used to smile at him and tell him that he had far better not have it until he had grown older, and asked him why he who was such a boy yet should want such a rich ornament, and told him it was vanity. But Singh said it wasn't that; it was because the people had been used to see his father wear it, and that now he was dead and he had become Maharajah they would think more of him and look up to him if he wore the belt himself. You see, sir, Singh told me it was like being crowned."

"I see," said the Doctor gravely, and he kept his eyes fixed upon the young speaker. "Go on."

"Well, sir, father always put him off, and Singh didn't like it, and asked for it again and again; but my father would never let him have it till we were coming slowly over here to England. We stopped for a month in Ceylon, and when we sailed again to come here, one day Singh asked father again to let him have it, so that he could wear the belt as soon as we reached England. And then father said he should have it if he would make a promise not to wear it unless he had to appear before the Queen. Then he was to put it away again, and not make a parade of himself in a country where the greatest people in the land were always dressed in the plainest way."

"Your father spoke wisely and well, my boy," said the Doctor gravely. "Great men do not depend upon show, but upon the jewels of worth and wisdom with which they have adorned themselves in their careers. Well, I repeat I am very glad you have come. Go on."

"Yes, sir," said Glyn, clearing his throat. "Singh promised father that he would do exactly as he was told, and the next day my father told me to try and keep Singh to his word. He said it would be very absurd now that we were going among strangers and a lot of boys of our own ages if Singh were tempted to make a show of the royal belt. 'You be watchful,' he said, 'and help him when he seems weak, for he has naturally a good deal of Eastern vanity and pride in him.'"

"Quite true," said the Doctor softly; "but he has improved wonderfully since he has been here."

"Yes, sir; but every now and then he has bad fits, and has wanted to show off; but I was always able to stop him. Then, you see, sir—"

Glyn broke down, and as he met the Doctor's steady gaze he seemed to make effort after effort to proceed, but in vain.

"I told you, my boy," said the Doctor encouragingly, "to speak to me as if I were your father."

"Yes, sir, I know," cried Glyn passionately, "and I want to speak out plainly and clearly, but it won't come."

"Yes," said the Doctor gravely; "it will, my boy. Go on to the end."

"Yes, sir," cried Glyn. "Well, sir, there has been all this trouble about the belt when it was missed out of Singh's box."

The Doctor bowed his head.

"I seem to have been able to think of nothing else, and I couldn't do my lessons—I could hardly eat my meals—and at night I couldn't sleep for thinking about the belt and what my father would say about it being lost."

The Doctor bowed his head again very slowly and solemnly, and fixed his eyes once more upon Glyn's flushed face.

"You see, sir, my father said so much to me about Singh being as it were in my charge, and told me how he trusted in my example, and in me being ready to give Singh a sensible word whenever he was disposed to do anything not becoming to an English lad."

"Exactly, my boy," said the Doctor. "Your father is a worthy trustee of this young ward, and it will be a terrible shock to him when he hears of this—er—er—accident and the loss."

"Yes, sir, for you see, as he is the old Maharajah's executor, the royal belt was in his care till Singh is old enough to be his own master; and father will feel that he is to blame for giving way and letting Singh have it so soon."

"Exactly," said the Doctor; "but, my boy, it seems to me that you are rather wandering away from your purpose, and are not telling me everything exactly as I should wish."

"It's because, sir, it won't come; something seems to stop me. But I am trying, sir."

"Well, I believe you, my boy," said the Doctor. "Go on."

"Yes, sir. Well, I told you that I could hardly eat or sleep for thinking about it."

The Doctor sighed.

"And it seemed so horrid, sir, that so many people should be suspected for what one person alone must have done."

"Yes," said the Doctor, fixing him with his eyes again; and then as he met the boy's frank, unblenching eyes his brow began to wear a curious look of perplexity, and he disjoined the tips of his fingers, picked up his quill-pen, and began slowly to litter the table-top by stripping off the plume.

"Well, sir," continued Glyn, speaking very hurriedly now, "I have always been dreaming about it, and waking up with starts, sir, fancying I heard some one creeping into the room to get to Singh's box; and one night it was so real that I seemed to hear some one go to Singh's bedside, take out the keys from his pocket, crawl to his box, unlock it, and lift the lid, and then shut it and lock it again. And I lay there, sir, with my hands and face wet with perspiration, wanting to call out to Singh; but I couldn't stir. But when all was silent again I crept out of bed and went to his box to find the keys in it; and I opened it quickly and felt inside, feeling sure that it was one of the boys who had stolen the belt and who had repented and come and put it back again."

"And had he?" cried the Doctor, startled out of his grave calmness.

"No, sir; I think it was only my fancy. But I have been something like that over and over again."

"Ah!" said the Doctor gravely once more. "The workings, my boy, of an uneasy mind."

"Yes, sir, and that's what held me back from coming to you to speak out."

"Go on," said the Doctor; "and speak plainly and to the point, my boy. What more have you to say?"

"Only this, sir," cried Glyn huskily, "that the night before last I lay awake for a long time, thinking and thinking about the belt and about Singh lying there sleeping so easily and not troubling himself in the least about the loss of the emeralds; and then all at once, when my head was so hot with the worry that I felt as if I must get out and drink some cold water.—I don't know how it was, but I began going over the big cricket-match in the field, and it was as if it was the day before, and I was fidgeting and fidgeting about the crowd there'd be, and a lot of strangers walking about the grounds and perhaps finding their way into the empty dormitories; and it all worried me so, sir, that it made me think that somebody dishonest might go to Singh's box and carry off the emeralds, and they would never be found again."

The Doctor leaned forward a little to gaze more fixedly in his pupil's eyes. Then rising slowly, he reached over and placed his cool white hand upon Glyn's forehead.

"Yes, sir," said the boy quickly, "it's hot—it's hot; but it comes like that sometimes. I believe it's from thinking too much."

"Ah!" said the Doctor, subsiding again into his chair.

"Well, sir, I was so worried about the belt that I thought I wouldn't say anything to Singh, but that I would take his keys, get out the case, and bring it to you in the morning."

"Ah!" cried the Doctor excitedly now. "It would not have been right, my boy. But you did not do that."

"No, sir," said the boy, with a bitter laugh; "for the next minute I thought you would put it in your table-drawer, and that it wouldn't be safe there, for strangers might come into this room, so I—" Glyn stopped, and the Doctor waited patiently. "It seemed so weak and foolish, sir," continued Glyn at last, after moistening his parched lips with his tongue, "but I must tell you. I seemed to be obliged to do it. I took out the case and went downstairs past all the boys' rooms, and got out through the lecture-hall window to go across the playground to the cricket-shed where the boys' lockers are, and there I opened our locker and took out a ball of kite-string."

"Yes," said the Doctor. "Go on, go on."

"Then, sir, I came back across the playground and turned into the yard to go into the well-house, where I tied the end of the kite-string round the case very tightly and safely, and then leaned over and lifted one of the flaps of the well lid—"

"And lowered the case down into the well?" cried the Doctor excitedly.

"Yes, sir," said Glyn; "and I could smell the cool, damp sides of the place, and hear a faint dripping of the water as I let the string run through my fingers, till at last the case splashed and it ran down more slowly, seeming to jerk a little to and fro as a flat thing does when it sinks, till I felt it touch the bottom. And then I leaned over to feel for a place where I could tie the string to one of the loose bricks at the side."

"But there are no loose bricks at the side, my boy," said the Doctor.

"No, sir," said the boy. "I couldn't feel one; and then all at once, as I was feeling about, the ball slipped out of my fingers and fell below with a splash."

"So that you could not pull the case up again?" cried the Doctor.

"Yes, sir," said Glyn very slowly, and looking at him in a peculiar manner.

"And then," said the Doctor, "what did you do?"

"Nothing, sir," replied Glyn, "for just then the first bell rang."

"What?" exclaimed the Doctor.

"And I started up in bed, sir. It was all a dream."

"A dream!" cried the Doctor angrily. "Why, my good lad—"

"But it was all so real, sir, and I was thinking about it all day yesterday, and that perhaps it's possible that I really did do it walking in my sleep."

"Oh, impossible!" cried the Doctor.

"I don't know, sir," said the boy; "but you see, I might have done so."

"Well—yes, you might," said the Doctor slowly. "I did have a pupil once who was troubled with somnambulism. He used to walk into the next dormitory and scare the other boys.—Oh, but this is impossible!"

"I thought you'd say so, sir."

"Yes," said the Doctor, "impossible. Why, if it were true the belt must have been lying at the bottom of the well ever since the cricket-match weeks ago."

"Yes, sir, and I must have done it then in my sleep; and the night before last I dreamed again what I dreamed before."

"Tut, tut, tut, tut, tut, tut!" ejaculated the Doctor, rising now from his chair and beginning to walk to and fro excitedly. "Strange—most strange, and I feel sceptical in the extreme. It must all be imagination. An empty dream, brought about by the worry and anxiety of this unfortunate loss. Well, I am glad you have come, my boy, and—er—er—I must be frank with you. Your manner and the strangeness of your words half made me think that you had come, urged by your conscience, to make a confession of a very different kind."

Glyn started; his lips parted, and he looked wildly in the Doctor's eyes.

"Don't look at me like that, my lad. Your manner suggested it, and I cannot tell you how relieved I feel."

As the Doctor spoke he leaned over his writing-table and caught the boy's hand in his, to press it warmly.

"But," he said, as he subsided once more into his chair, "this must be a hallucination, an offspring of an overworked brain; and yet there are strange things in connection with the mental organisation, and I feel as if I ought to take some steps. What a relief it would be, my boy, to us all, the clearing away of a load of ungenerous suspicion. But one word: whom have you told of this?"

"No one, sir," said Glyn.

"Not even Mr Singh?"

"No, sir. I have been ever since yesterday thinking about what I ought to do, and I came to the conclusion at last that I ought to come to you, sir."

"Quite right, my boy; quite right."

"But it was very hard work, sir—very hard indeed."

"Yes, yes; so I suppose," said the Doctor thoughtfully; "and you have placed a problem before me, my boy, that I feel is as difficult to resolve. I am very, very glad that you have kept it in your own breast, Severn; and the more I think of it the more I feel that it is only an intangible vapour of the brain. But, all the same, the matter is so mysterious and so important that I should not be doing my duty if I did not have the well examined."

"You will, sir?" cried the boy eagerly.

"Yes, Severn, I will," said the Doctor firmly, "and at once. But this must be a private matter between us two. Let those who like consider the act eccentric; I shall have it done, and I look to you to take no one else into your confidence over the matter."

"No, sir; I'll not say a word," cried Glyn. "But,"—he hesitated—"but—"

"Well, Severn; speak out."

"If it all turns out fancy, all imagination, sir, you will not be angry?"

"No, Severn, not in the least," said the Doctor, smiling. "Now go and send Wrench to me."

As he spoke the Doctor turned and rang, with the consequence that Glyn met the footman in the passage coming to answer the bell, and half an hour later, when the boy made it his business to casually stroll towards the well-house, he heard voices, and on looking in found Wrench, who had changed his livery for an old pair of trousers and vest, talking to the gardener and making plans for the emptying of the well.

Chapter Thirty Two
The Doctor's Dictum

"It'd take a month," said the gardener, as Glyn was coming up. "Don't tell me! Should think I know more about wells than you do. Fast as you take a bucketful out another one runs in. You go and tell him that if he means to have the old well emptied we shall want half-a-dozen men, for we could never do it by oursens."

"Yah!" cried Wrench; "such fellows as you gardeners are. It's always the same old tune: more help, more help.—Hear him, Mr Severn, sir? I expect the water isn't so clear as it has been, and the Doctor says he will have the well emptied and cleaned out.—Look here, Taters, you can go and tell the Doctor that if you like; I am going to work."

"Oh, I shan't tell him," growled the gardener. "I aren't afraid of a bit of wuck; only, mark my words, as I says again, it'd take a month."

The unusual task did not take a month; but after a hard day's toil so little progress had been made, and Wrench's indoor work had come to such a standstill, that the Doctor gave orders for the gardener to get the assistance of a couple of labouring men, when the water was so much lowered at the end of the next day that unless a great deal filtered in during the coming night there was a fair prospect of the bottom being reached before long.

By a tacit understanding with the Doctor, Glyn was excused from lessons during the clearing out of the well, and spent his time watching the emptying of every bucketful as it was wound slowly up; and it was put about by Slegge that Glyn had been planted there by the Doctor to keep the juniors off for fear any of them should tumble down.

It was an anxious task for the boy, who had to resist appeal after appeal made by Singh to come and join him in some sport or go for a walk. But Glyn kept fast to his post, watching in vain, and without much hope, for if the case was there it would probably be sunk in the mud. One hour he found himself full of faith in the belief that there was something in his dream, and the next he thought that it was all nonsense.

The lowering and drawing up of the big buckets had a peculiar
fascination for some of the youngest boys.

And so the days passed on, with Glyn paying constant visits to the well-house, where Wrench went on toiling away; while, in spite of the sloppiness of the place, his big tom-cat came regularly to perch himself upon a shelf, and with his big eyes looking fierce and glowing in the semi-darkness of the building, he seemed to look upon it as his duty to see that all went on steadily and well.

The sixth day had come round, and the gardener reiterated with a grin, as he stared grimly at Glyn, "Ah, we shan't be done yet. It's my opinion that it will take a month; and that's what the ganger thinks too."

"The ganger?" said Glyn. "Who's he?"

"Him," said Wrench, with a sidewise nod in the direction of his feline favourite, who was crouched together in the spot he had selected for looking on.

"Oh, nonsense!" cried Glyn.

"Ah, you may call it nonsense; but you know, Mr Severn, I shouldn't be at all surprised if that cat thinks. It's my opinion that he knows there's holes somewhere down below, just above where the water used to be, and that sooner or later if he waits patiently he will see some of them as lives there come up in the empty bucket for him to hunt."

"And what are they that live down there?" said Glyn.

"Rats, sir—rats."

There was some colour given to Slegge's assertion that Glyn was there to keep the juniors from tumbling down; for the slow, steady lowering and drawing up of the big buckets had a peculiar fascination for some of the youngest boys, notably the little set whose playtime was nearly all monopolised by hard work—to wit, the bowling and fielding for Slegge. Their anxiety was wonderful. If Glyn was not constantly on the watch, one or other would be getting in the men's way, to peer down into the darkness or rush to where the full buckets were emptied into a drain.

On commencing work upon the sixth morning the water was found to be so lowered that the big buckets had to be removed from rope and chains, for they would not descend far enough to fill. So they were replaced by small ordinary pails; and, the work becoming much lighter, they were wound up and down at a much more rapid rate.

"We shan't be long now, Mr Severn, sir," said Wrench, for each pail as it came up had for its contents half-water and half-mud, the sediment of many, many years. And at last Glyn's heart began to throb, for hanging out over the side of the last-raised bucket was a long length of muddy string.

"Then I am right," he said to himself. "How strange!" And as he followed to the mouth of the drain into which the contents of the pail were to be poured he caught hold of the string.

"Here, don't do that, sir," cried Wrench. "You'll cover yourself with mud. Let me," and before the boy could stop him the man had snatched the string from his hand and drawn it out.

"Broken away," said Glyn to himself, as the end was drawn from the bucket, and he now peered anxiously into the pail, expecting to see one end of the long morocco case standing up out of the thick contents.

But as the half-fluid mud was poured away the empty bucket went down and its fellow rose similarly filled.

Glyn expected to see the rest of the string, for nothing like half of that which he believed he had lost had come up.

Again he was disappointed, for there was neither string nor case, and for some time bucket after bucket rose, at first full of mud, but by slow degrees containing half, a quarter, and then only a small portion of mud and water at a time, while each time the empty ones reached the bottom a hollow scraping sound arose, as by clever manipulation of the rope by Wrench they were dragged along the bottom.

"I say, Mr Severn, sir," he cried, "who'd ever have thought that there was all that mud under the beautiful clear water? Ah, it must be a mort of years since it was cleared out, and now we are at it we will do it well—let the water come in a little and give it a good wash out two or three times over. I won't let it fill up at all till we have scraped this all clear. That's the way to do it," he continued, giving the rope a swing so as to turn the bucket on its side and scrape it along the bottom. "Hear that, sir? All hard stone at the bottom down there, and mud and mud. Now, I half-expected to find a lot of things that had fallen down, and the hoops of some old bucket that had been lost."

Glyn started at the man's words, and saw in his mind's eye the long red morocco case, blackened now and saturated with water, while he wondered what effect the moisture would have had on the beautiful gold-embroidered leather of the belt.

"Yes," continued Wrench, giving Glyn as he stood close beside the mouth of the well what seemed to the boy a malicious grin, "I did expect to find something curious down there; but the buckets run easily over the bottom, and there don't seem to be—yes, there is," he shouted excitedly. "Nothing like patience in fishing. I have got a bite."

Glyn's heart seemed to stand still as the man gave a snatch at the rope.

"That's the way to strike," he cried excitedly. "I've caught him, and a heavy one too."

Glyn's heart sank with disappointment, for there was no heaviness about the belt, and he stood waiting now as the winch was steadily turned and the bucket began to rise.

They had not been observed before, but a little party of about a dozen of the younger boys had been hovering for some time about the well-house-door, and first one and then another made a dash in from time to time when Wrench was too busy with the buckets to take any notice of them.

Burton had come inside now, to range up close to Glyn, and in an affectionate way passed his arm round that of the lad who had been his defender more than once.

Glyn responded by withdrawing his arm, placing both hands on the little fellow's shoulders, and thrusting him in front so that the boy could have a good view of all that there was to see.

"I say, Severn," he cried, turning his head to look up, "no larks—no shoving me down the well!"

"Why not?" said Severn merrily, as he gripped the little fellow tighter.

"Because old Slegge will want me to bowl for him, and he likes kicking me."

"Likes kicking you? Why?" said Glyn, speaking almost mechanically, for he was anxiously watching the dark hole for the ascent of the next bucket.

"Because I'm so soft and don't hurt his feet."

"Don't let it drop out, mates," cried the gardener, who was on the other side of the well, turning one winch. "Hold tight now you have got him. Do you know what it is?"

"No," replied Wrench; "but I think by the feel of it when I got it slithered into the bucket that it must be an old brick out of the side somewhere."

"Yah! Not it!" said the gardener. "I'll tell you what it is: it's that big old tom-cat of the Doctor's that used to be about the garden and was always scratching up my young plants. He was missing four or five years ago, and I dare say he got into the top bucket to curl up for a nap one night, and went down in it and was drowned."

"If it is," said Wrench, "he's got to be pretty heavy with soaking up so much water down below. Maybe you know better than that how it was he did get drowned and left off scratching up your plants."

As the man said these words little Burton gave quite a jump, and made a peculiar sound.

"Here," said Glyn quietly, "what are you starting at? Did you think I was going to pretend to push you in?"

"N–n–no," said the little fellow in a peculiar tone.

"What are you laughing at?" said Glyn, tightening his hold on the boy's shoulders.

The little fellow squirmed.

"It—it—it—it—it," —he stuttered—"it does tickle me so!"

"There, there! Steady, steady!" said Glyn. "No nonsense, or I shall send you out of the well-house."

"No, no; please don't, Severn," whispered the boy excitedly. "Let me stay, please. I do so want to see."

"Very well, then, only no games now," and in rather a hopeless way, feeling as he did that there would be no morocco case and belt brought up this time, Glyn patiently waited till from out of the darkness the bucket came into sight, was wound up till it was well within reach, a thump and a scraping noise coming echoing up from the bottom to announce that its fellow had reached the end of its journey, and Wrench cried out "Wo—ho!" for the gardener to hold on tightly by the handle and prevent the heavy bucket running down again.

"Why, Crumpets!" cried Wrench, "what in the world have we got here?" while Burton reached both hands back behind him so as to get a good grip at the lapels of Severn's jacket, and began to dance with delight.

"Why, it's a cricket-bat!" cried Wrench. "Hanging over the side of the bucket by a string tied round the handle!"

At this Burton began to make uncouth sounds as if he were being choked in his efforts to suppress a hearty burst of laughter.

"Well, this 'ere's a pretty game," continued Wrench, as he took hold of the bat by the handle and ran his hand along the muddy string till at the bottom of the bucket his hand came in contact with a heavy brick. "Why, any one would think it was a tom-cat with a string round its neck and a brick at the other end of the string so as to keep him down. Four or five years ago! Why, that would be time enough for all the flesh and skin to have gone; but I never knowed that cats' skillingtons was shaped like a cricket-bat.—Here, steady, youngster!" he continued to the little fellow, "if you laugh like that you will have a fit."

"Oh, I can't bear it! I can't bear it!" panted the little chap, and wrenching himself free from Glyn's grasp he rushed out at the well-house door, ten or a dozen of his comrades bounding up to him as he shouted, "Oh, come and look! come and look! Here it is! They've pulled it up, drowned and quite dead."

There was a yell of delight from the little crowd, and all rushed up to the well-house-door, to begin performing something like a triumphant war-dance about the blackened and muddy bat.

"Here, I say, some one," cried Burton, "run and tell old Slegge that they have found his cricket-bat drowned in the well like a dead dog in a pond."

"Hush! Hush! Oh no. Hold your tongue!" whispered another of the boys excitedly. "Let him find it out for himself. Don't let the cat out of the bag."

"Bat out of the bag, you mean," said Glyn, who knew of the disappearance of the bat and began to see through what had been done. "Which of you did this?"

There was no reply.

"Do you hear?" cried Glyn, catching Burton by the collar of his jacket.

"I shan't tell," replied the little fellow. "Serve him right for loading the old bat with lead.—Chuck it down again, somebody."

"Nay," cried Wrench; "I am not going to have any more things drowned in my well. Now then, stand aside, some of you! Clear out, and take that bat away."

"Here," cried Burton. "Come on, boys! Bring it along."

"Stop a moment," said Glyn. "Here's a painted wooden label here. What's this on it?"

"B—e—a—s—t," said Wrench, "only it's turned nearly black with being in the water, and very badly done; but that's it, sure enough, sir—*beast*."

"Yes, that's it—*beast*," said another of the boys, snatching the bat from Glyn's hand, while another boy got hold of the brick.

"Come on, boys," cried Burton. "Let's get a spade from the potting-shed and bury the beast before old Slegge knows." And away they galloped, followed by a shout from the gardener:

"Here, I say, you mind you put that there spade away again!—They're nice uns, Mr Severn, sir, and knew about it all the time."

"Yes," said Wrench; "that young Burton was chuckling and laughing so that he could hardly bear himself while he was waiting to see it come up.—Now, then, twist t'other bucket over, mate, and give it a drag round the bottom. What are we going to catch next?"

Glyn started once more, his heart beginning to beat fast with expectation; but it gradually calmed down as the time went on, bucket after bucket after a careful scraping along the bottom bringing up nothing but a very little mud, and he began to feel convinced that if there had been a morocco case down at the bottom of the well it must have been felt in the careful dredging the live rock received, even if it had not been brought up.

"There," said Wrench, "that'll do for to-day. It's only scraping for nothing to get a little mud like that. I dare say there'll be six inches of water in the bottom by to-morrow morning, and we will give the whole place a good scraping round in getting that out; then another the next day, and it ought to do."

"But do you feel sure there's nothing down there now?" said Glyn.

"Certain, sir. What do you say to going down yourself to see? You could stand in the bucket, and we'd let you down. You wouldn't mind turning round as you went down?"

"No," cried Glyn eagerly; "and there's no water there now."

"Not much more than enough to fill a teacup, sir. What do you say?"

"I'll go," cried Glyn excitedly. "I could take a lantern with me so as to make sure there was nothing left."

"Well, yes, sir, it would be wise to take a candle," said Wrench.— "Wouldn't it, gardener?"

"Nay, my lad; you ought to send the light down first. Then, if it didn't go out, him as went down wouldn't go out."

"What do you mean?" said Glyn.

"Foul air, sir. Like enough there's some down at the bottom of that well."

"Oh, there couldn't be any to hurt," cried Glyn eagerly. "I'll go, Wrench. Get a candle."

"Not I, sir," said the man sturdily. "If any one was to go down that well it would be me; but there ain't no need for it. I could swear there's nothing down there, and I shan't go."

"Nobody wants you to go," cried Glyn. "I'll go myself."

"That you don't, sir, if I know it," said Wrench sturdily. "Pst! Here's the Doctor."

For at that moment the entrance was darkened and the Doctor came in, picking his way very carefully lest he should step into one of the puddles of the muddy floor.

"Well, my men," he said in his slow, pompous way, "have you nearly emptied the well?"

"Quite, sir," said Wrench.

"Was there any mud?"

"Yes, sir; we got out about two cart-loads, and scraped out all we could. To-morrow, when there's a little more water come back, we're going to try again."

"Yes," said the Doctor; "clean it out thoroughly while you are about it; and mind and carefully secure the door when you come away. You had better lock it, so that nobody can get in.—Well, Mr Severn, you must be tired of watching here. Come and walk down the garden with me."

Glyn followed the Doctor, who made room for him to walk abreast till they were half-way down the main path, when the latter said quietly, "Well, Severn, what have you found?"

"Nothing, sir," replied Severn, who did not consider it necessary to allude to the bat.

"No," said the Doctor; "I did not expect you would. Of course, you see, my boy, that it was only a dream."

Chapter Thirty Three
Between Boys

"Oh, I say, what a lovely morning!"

Glyn, who had lain awake half the night, woke up with a start, to see Singh standing barefooted by the window, which he had just thrown wide open to let in the joyous sunshine and the soft sweet air. "Yes, jolly," he cried, inhaling a deep breath. "No! Most miserable morning I ever saw," and he sank back sitting on the edge of his bed, to utter a deep groan.

Singh sprang to his side in an instant. "Glyn, old chap, what's the matter? Are you ill?"

"Yes, horribly. In my head. Oh, I say! I couldn't sleep for ever so long last night for thinking about it."

"Then why didn't you wake me, old fellow? I'd have dressed directly and gone and told the Doctor."

"What about?"

"You being so ill."

"Bah!" cried Glyn angrily. "It isn't salts and senna. What a fellow you are! You don't mean to say that you'd forgotten that the dad's coming down to-day?"

Singh plumped himself down on the carpet like a native of Dour, untroubled by clothes, with his knees nearly to his ears and his crossed hands before him resting on the floor, while his face lost its sympathetic expression and puckered up into one of misery and despair.

"Yes, I had," he said, with a groan; "all about it. Here," he cried passionately, "I won't be treated like a schoolboy! I am a prince and a chief, and the belt was mine. It's gone, and I won't be bullied about it by any one."

"Not even by your guardian, eh?"

"Not even by my guardian," cried the boy haughtily. "If Colonel Severn says anything to me about it I shall tell him I won't hear another word, and that he is to go to the best jeweller in London and order another exactly like the one that has been stolen."

"Of course," said Glyn solemnly. "It'll be as easy as kissing your hand, and they'll know at once how to engrave the emeralds with the old Sanskrit inscription, and make the belt of the same kind of leather, so beautifully soft, dull, and yellow; and there are plenty of people in London who can do that Indian embroidery."

Singh nodded his head shortly.

"Bah! You jolly old Tom Noodle!" continued Glyn; "why, even if they could get as big emeralds and manage somehow to have the exact words of the inscription cut, would it be the same old belt and stones as came down from the past, and that your father used to wear?"

Singh's eyes dilated and his lips parted.

"No," he said with a groan. "Oh, Glynny, what a beast you are! And you call yourself my friend!"

"Never," cried Glyn. "It was you said I was."

"Yes, and instead of helping me in my trouble, and saying a few words to comfort me, you call me names."

"Yes, but I didn't call you a beast. Is it being a friend to hide the truth from you and let you snuggle yourself up with a lot of sham? Answer me this: would a fresh belt be anything more than an imitation?"

"No, I suppose not," groaned Singh. "I am a prince, and going to be very rich some day, and rule over my people, with a little army of my own, and elephants, and everything any one could wish for; but I am not a bit clever, except at wicket-keeping. I haven't got half such a head as you have, Glyn, and such a head as I have got is now all muddled and full of what you may call it."

"Brains," said Glyn cynically.

"No, no; I don't mean that," said Singh piteously. "Don't tease me, old chap; I am so miserable. I mean, my head's full of that stuff, I don't remember what you call it—I mean what you have when you are very sorry for something you have done."

"Misery?"

"No, no. Here, I remember—remorse. I know well enough now, though I don't like owning it, that if I had done as you told me, and taken care always to lock it up, that belt wouldn't be gone."

"Well, it's too late to talk about that," said Glyn, "and it's no use to cry over spilt milk. You have got to face it all out with the dad when he comes, and take your blowing-up like a man."

"I can't. I shall do just as I said, and even if it isn't going to be the same belt," cried the boy passionately, "I shall give your father orders. Yes, I can see you sneering. Orders, orders," he repeated, with increased emphasis, "to have a new one made."

Glyn threw himself back on his bed, and gave his heels a kick in the air. "Ho, ho! ha, ha!" he roared with laughter. "What a game! Mind and do it when I am there. I should like to see you jump on a fence and cry 'Cock-a-doodle-doo' at my father. Fancy you playing the haughty prince to him! Why, he'd stare at you. You know his way. And he'd take a grab of his moustache in each hand and pull it out straight before he began; and then he'd get up out of his chair, take hold of you by one of your ears, lead you back, and put you between his knees as he seated himself again. And then he'd talk, and at the first word he said, he'd blow all the haughty wind out of you, and you'd curl up like a— oh, I don't know what. It's nonsense to try and think of similes, for you'd never say what you pretend."

"Well, then, I shall bolt, as you call it," cried Singh. "I won't face him. I can't face him."

"Why?"

"Because I am too proud I suppose, and the Colonel isn't my master."

"I say, Singhy, get off the stilts, old chap, and be a man over it. You know what the dad always used to say to both of us: 'A fellow who has done wrong and owns up like a man is half-forgiven at once.'"

"Oh yes, I recollect. But do help me now, I am in such trouble."

"You are in no worse trouble than I am."

"Oh yes, I am. You are not to blame, for you did tell me to be careful; and though I didn't like it at the time, I can see now how right you were."

"Yes; but I wasn't half right enough. I ought to have made you tell the Doctor what you'd got in the box, and then he'd have insisted upon its being kept in a safer place."

"But I wouldn't have given it up," cried Singh angrily.

"Oh yes, you would," continued Glyn; "and I feel now that I ought to have gone straight to the Doctor and told about your going to see Professor Barclay."

"No, you oughtn't, and you wouldn't have been such a sneak. Besides, it would have been getting poor Mr Morris into trouble, too, for taking me there. Did you want him to lose his place?"

"Well, no," said Glyn thoughtfully.

"And as to my going to see Professor Barclay and lending him a little money now and then—I mean, giving it—it was my own money, and what's the good of having money if you don't do good with it?"

"Well," said Glyn thoughtfully, "there is something in that," and the boy seemed yielding to his companion's attack.

Singh realised this, and pressed it home.

"I am sure it was doing more good with my allowance than you do with yours, always stuffing yourself with fruit and sweets and things."

"That I am not!" cried Glyn indignantly.

"Yes, you are. Why, you have got quite half of that big three-shilling cake in your box now."

"Oh, but that was to eat of a night when we came to bed and felt as if we ought to have a little more supper."

"Oh, bother!" cried Singh angrily. "What shall I do. Here, I know. I shall go."

"What, run away?"

"Yes," cried Singh, "and stop away till my guardian writes to me and begs of me to come back; and then I shall make terms, and not give way till he promises that he won't say another word about the belt."

Glyn chuckled to himself softly. "How are you going to make terms?" he said.

"I shall write to him," cried Singh importantly.

"Without giving any address?" said Glyn, with a mirthful look dancing in his eye.

"What rubbish! Why, of course I shall put my address, so that he can write to me again—"

"And then he won't write to you," said Glyn. "He'll come to you and fetch you back with a flea in your ear."

"Oh, you are a brute!" cried Singh viciously. "And I feel as if I could— No, I won't. I shall treat you with contempt."

"That's right; do. I say, you are comforting me nicely, aren't you? Pig! disagreeable old jungle-pig! That's what you are."

"Well, why don't you help me then? What am I to do?"

"Get dressed, I think," said Glyn. "Don't be what old Brohanne calls a *bête*—big fool. Do as I do. Go and have it out with the dad, and get out of one's misery. He won't be very hard."

"Oh, if it was only a good—good—good— What's that you say?"

"Bullying?"

"No, no. It was a bit of slang, and I like to use bits of English slang when I can; they'll be so useful to know by-and-by when I am scolding my people. Not bullying, but—"

"Oh, you mean tongue-thrashing?" said Glyn.

"Yes, that's it, tongue-thrashing. I wouldn't mind then. I feel so ashamed of myself."

"All right. So do I, I suppose, for making a mess of it when I wanted the dad to think that I had managed you so well that I was making myself fit to be your friend and companion when we both grew up to be men."

The next minute the lads were busy making their preparations to descend for a little study before the breakfast-bell should ring; and as he washed and dressed, Glyn's brow looked wrinkled and cloudy, for he was thinking very seriously all the while.

On the other hand, Singh dressed himself as if he had a quarrel with everything. He chipped the edge of the basin as he handled the ewer, dropped the lid of the soap-dish with a clatter, and as he washed himself he burst out with an angry ejaculation, for the wet soap was gripped so tightly and viciously that it flew out of his hand as if in fear, and dived right under the bed to the farthest end, where it had to be hunted out and retrieved, covered with the flue that had been forgotten by one of the maids; while the way in which he finished off with his towel was harsh enough to produce a smarting sensation upon his skin.

Chapter Thirty Four
A Witness called

Neither of the boys enjoyed his breakfast that morning, and their studies afterwards fared very badly, for their attention was principally directed from their books to the door, which opened again and again for some reason or another, but not for the delivery of the message they expected.

Knowing the military precision of the Colonel, both boys began to wonder at a quarter-past eleven why they had not been summoned, for the Colonel had said in his curt epistle to Glyn—which "looked cross," so the boy said—that he would be at the Doctor's at eleven.

Half-past was marked by the hands of the big dial, quarter to twelve, and then five minutes to mid-day, and in a few minutes the masters would rise; but there was no summons, and, what was more, the Doctor had not been in the class-room that morning.

It was exactly one minute to twelve, and just as Singh's spirits were rising fast from the effect of having fully settled in his own mind that the Colonel would not come down that day, that his heart sank with a rush, for Wrench entered with the familiar announcement that the Doctor wished to see Mr Severn and Mr Singh in his study.

The boys followed the footman, and as soon as they were outside Glyn began to question him.

"Has my father come, Wrench?"

"Yes, sir," said the man coldly, for since the beginning of the trouble and the sharp examinations that had taken place, the behaviour of the servants had been distant in the extreme, and such friendly intercourse as had existed between the pupils and masters had received a decided check. In fact, as the days glided away, the Doctor's establishment had become more and more haunted by the evil spirit, suspicion.

"How long has my father been here?" asked Glyn.

"About an hour, sir," replied the man shortly. "I didn't look at the clock. This way, please, sir. I am busy."

It was so different from the Wrench of the past that it sent a chill through the boys, as they followed on and began whispering so that the man should not hear.

"Go on first, Glynny," whispered Singh.

"Get out! I haven't lost my belt," was the reply.

"But the Colonel's your father."

"Well, I can't help that, can I? It's about your business. You go on first."

"I shan't. I have got something wrong with my legs," said Singh. "They feel quite weak."

"Come on together," cried Glyn, and he thrust his arm through Singh's, as the door was opened and the boys uttered a sigh of relief in concert, for the Doctor was not present, and at first they had to see the Colonel alone.

It was a strange sensation that ran through both, a mingling of dread, despair, and misery, as they gazed in imagination into the stern, threatening countenance of the fierce-looking old soldier, and wished themselves a thousand miles away. For Glyn felt more uncomfortable than ever before in his life, and as he darted a quick sideways glance at his companion it was to see no haughty indignant prince ready to stand defiantly upon his rights, but a fellow-pupil appearing as mild and troubled as could be.

All this was little more than momentary, and the fierce threatening face they had come to encounter was all fancy made; for the Colonel's looks as he held out his hand was very much the same as when they had dined with him the last time at his hotel, and his salute was just a hearty English:

"Well, boys, how are you? But you two fellows have been making a pretty mess of it over that belt!" And before either of them could reply, he continued, in his short, giving-order style, "Great nuisance and bother to me. I have had quite two months taken up with your affairs, Singh—Dour business, you know—and I shall be very glad when you are old enough to take the reins in your hand and drive yourself."

"But, guardian—" began Singh, who was breathing more freely, the warm pressure of the Colonel's hand having thrilled him through and through.

"Oh yes, I know, my boy; I didn't mean that. I am not going to be pensioned off. I am going to be a sort of House of Lords to you two commoners, and you will come and refer all big matters to me. Let's see, what was I saying? Oh, I've been busy two months over the Dour affairs. Got them pretty straight, and I was going up into Scotland for a month's rest. I meant to write from there if you had been doing your sums a little better, Glyn, and if you, Singh, had improved a bit in your spelling, for the way in which you break your shins over the big words in your letters is rather startling."

"Oh, guardian, aren't you rather too hard?" said the boy appealingly. "But you weren't only going to write to the Doctor about that?"

"Humph! No. I had some idea about salmon-fishing when the season comes on."

"Oh, fishing!" cried the boys in a breath.

"Yes," said the Colonel. "It won't be like getting up in the hills amongst the mahseer. Bah! Here am I running away about fishing! I caught a forty-pounder last time I tried, and a big fight too. But the Doctor wanted me to come out here about this wretched belt business, and I have had to leave my club and put off my journey to come down and see about this.—It's a bad business, Glyn. I am afraid you have not been so sharp as you should have been."

"I have tried my best, father."

"I suppose so; but the best's bad."

"Don't be hard on him, guardian," said Singh, laying his hand affectionately on the Colonel's shoulder. "It was all my fault, and I know better now."

"Know better? What do you mean by that, sir?"

"Well, sir," said Singh hesitatingly, "I know it was weak and foolish of me to want to have a showy thing like that to wear; but I was not so English then as I am now."

"Showy thing like that, eh?" said the Colonel. "Ahem! Well, I don't know that you need excuse yourself about that. It's rather natural. A soldier likes showy regimentals. I was always proud of my uniform, boys. No, I am not going to fall foul of you about that, Singh, so long as you didn't make a goose of yourself with it. But when you had such a showy thing, you ought to have had gumption enough to know how to take care of it. Well, it will be a lesson to you to know how to behave by-and-by when you come out among your own people as a prince. You won't go pitching your jewels about then as if you were asking people to come and help themselves."

"But it was like this, father—" began Glyn.

"Halt!" cried the Colonel sharply. "Wait till the Doctor comes. He is going through it all quietly with you, and he has asked me to sit like a judge till it has all been put before me, and then I am to give my verdict. He asks me to say whether the matter shall be placed in the hands of the police. Well, one of you had better ring, and—"

As he was speaking, there was a tap at the door, which was gently opened, and the Doctor said, "May I come in?"

"Yes, sir. Come in, come in. I have had my say to the boys, and told them what I think about their carelessness, and to a certain extent our young friend here, Singh, agrees, I believe, that it was rather a mistake for him to have that piece of vanity at school."

"I am glad, Colonel," said the Doctor, seating himself, "that they are ready to confess a fault; but as one who seeks to hold the scales of justice evenly, I hope you will excuse me for saying that I think my pupils are not entirely to blame; for—I beg you will not be offended—I venture to think it was rather indiscreet on your part to give way to my young friend Singh, however much he may have pressed you, and placed in his hands so valuable an heirloom."

"Humph! You think so, do you?" grunted the Colonel. "However, it is not of so much consequence. He has got plenty more valuable jewels—enough to make himself look as gay as a peacock by-and-by."

"Excuse me, Colonel Severn," said the Doctor stiffly; "I think the matter is of very great consequence. Not only is it a serious loss—"

The Colonel grunted again.

"But I feel as if the honour and reputation of my school are at stake, and it was for that reason that I wrote and asked you to come down to consult with me as to what steps should be taken now towards the recovery of the belt. This, before placing the matter in the hands of the police."

"Oh, hang the police!" said the Colonel shortly. "We can settle this little matter, I am sure, without calling in the help of policeman A or Z."

"I am very glad to hear you say so, Colonel; for it would be most repugnant to me, and painful to my staff of assistants, and for my pupils, I may add. There are the servants too, and the publicity in the town, where I am afraid the matter is too much talked about already. You think, then, that we may dispense with the police?"

"Certainly," said the Colonel; "unless," he added drily, "Singh here wants the business carried to the bitter end."

"I, sir? Oh no!" cried Singh. "If I could do as I liked I wouldn't have another word said about it. I hate the old belt. Can't even think of it without seeming to have a nasty taste in my mouth."

"Oh," said the Colonel; "but we can't stop like that. I think, for every one's sake, the shoe should be put on the right foot. — What do you say, Dr Bewley?"

"I quite agree with you, sir. We have talked the matter pretty well over this morning, and I have told you what I have done. I was bound to question the servants, though all of them have been with me for years, and I have perfect confidence in their honesty. As to my pupils, I could not examine and cross-examine every boy. It would have been like expressing a doubt of every little fellow's truth. It has been a most painful thing for me, sir; and if you can help me or advise me in the wearisome business, I should be most grateful."

"Very well, sir. I suppose I have had a little experience acting the part of magistrate in India, where petty thefts are very common; and I have attended trials in England, and have been vain enough to think to myself that I could examine a witness or cross-examine more to the point than I have heard it done in some of our courts."

"Then," said the Doctor, "you were good enough to suggest two or three little things this morning. What should you do first?"

"Well," said the Colonel thoughtfully, "I think, first of all, it is due to those gentlemen who act as your ushers that they should be asked to join in our consultation."

"Certainly. Quite right," said the Doctor, and, ringing the bell, he sent a message by Wrench to the class-room, and if the masters were not there, bade the man find them in the grounds.

There was a pause in the proceedings here, during which the Doctor and his visitor chatted about political matters, and the boys sat whispering together about the last match.

But they had not long to wait. Morris came bustling in to bow to the Colonel and take the seat to which the Doctor pointed, while Rampson and Monsieur Brohanne came in together from a walk round the grounds.

Then, after a very few preliminaries, forming a sort of introduction to the masters of the boys' father and guardian, the Colonel spoke about the great unpleasantness of the matter and the Doctor's desire to have what seemed like a cloud hanging over his establishment swept away.

He addressed a few words then to Rampson, who had nothing more to say after declaring his perfect certainty that not one of the boys he had the honour of instructing would have been guilty of such a crime.

Monsieur Brohanne, too, declared himself as lost in astonishment at the trouble which had come upon them like a sudden tempest. No, by his faith, he said, he could not think how such an outrage could have taken place.

Morris was disposed to be more voluble, and the Colonel more ready to examine him, while the master was prompt and eager in his replies, sighing as if with relief as the Colonel at length stopped short and sat patting the carpet with his right toe. "Well, sir," said the Doctor at last, "seeing that, as I told you, I carefully examined the servants, I had plunged as far as this in the mystery before."

"Humph!" grunted the Colonel, with his eyes closed, and Glyn and Singh exchanged glances.

"The servants," said the Colonel softly; "the servants. Doctor, I should like you to ring for that man of yours."

Morris glanced at the Doctor, who bowed his head, and the usher stepped to the bell.

"Oh, father!" cried Glyn excitedly, "pray don't suspect Wrench!"

"Hold your tongue, sir," said the Colonel sternly. "Wait and hear what is said, and don't jump at conclusions."

Chapter Thirty Five
Under Examination

Then there was a tap and Wrench appeared. "Come in, my man," said the Colonel, "and close the door."

Wrench started, turned pale and then red, as he looked sharply at his master, who sat perfectly still and avoided his gaze.

"Come a step nearer, my man," said the Colonel. Wrench gazed at him defiantly, shook himself, jerked up his head, looked hard at the two boys, who were watching him, tightening his lips the while, and then, after taking two steps instead of one, stood facing the Colonel, as much as to say: "Now, ask me as many questions as you like."

"Your master has deputed me, my man, to carry on this investigation, and I should be obliged by your replying in a straightforward, manly way. You are not before a magistrate, and hence are not sworn. Doctor Bewley gives you an admirable character for honesty and straightforward conduct, and if I ask you questions that sound unpleasant in your ears, don't run away with the idea that it is because you are suspected."

Wrench's manner changed a little, for the references to his uprightness and rectitude sounded pleasant in his ears.

"I give you credit," continued the Colonel, "for being as desirous as these gentlemen here and I am to find out the culprit."

"Yes, sir; certainly, sir, and Mr Singh and Mr Severn, sir, will tell you that I have been as much cut up about it as if the blessed—I beg your pardon, gentlemen—as if the belt had been my own."

"Exactly," said the Colonel. "Now then, it seems that the time when the belt was lost cannot be exactly pointed out, since it may have been taken at one of the times when Mr Singh's travelling-case was left unlocked."

"Oh, sir, but nobody ever goes up into his room except the maids and Mrs Hamton and me; and, bless your heart, sir, the Doctor will tell you that he wouldn't doubt any of us to save his life."

"Hah!" said the Colonel. "A good character, my man, is a fine thing. Now, what about strangers—people from the town—peddlers, or hawkers, or people with books to be subscribed for? You have such people come, I suppose, to the house?"

"Lots of them, sir; but they never come any farther than the door," cried Wrench, laughing. "You see, sir, Mr Singh's dormitory is on the first floor of the new building, over the little lecture-hall. Nobody ever went there."

"Could any strangers come up through the grounds and get into the passage or corridor after dusk?"

"No, sir; not without coming through the house. I have laid awake lots of times, sir, trying to put that and that together; but it's all been like a maze, sir—a sort of maze, sir, made like with no way in and no way out."

"Humph!" said the Colonel, looking at the man searchingly. "I have heard of cases where people have come to a house and asked the servants if somebody was at home when the speaker knew that he was out, and then made an excuse to be shown into a room to write a letter to the gentleman, say the Doctor, whom he wanted to see; Did such a thing happen in your recollection? No, no; don't hurry. Tax your memory.—Ah!—What is it?"

"I've got it, sir!" cried Wrench excitedly.

"Oh!" said the Colonel quietly. "Well, what did happen?"

"To be sure, somebody did come just as you said, sir, as you asked me that question, once. But it hasn't got anything to do with the stealing of that belt."

"Perhaps not," said the Colonel; "but let us hear. You say somebody did once come and ask for the Doctor when he was out?"

"Begging your pardon, sir, no, sir. It wasn't to see the Doctor, sir. It was on the day when everybody was out, gone to the Strongley cricket-match, and there was nobody at home but the maids and me, for Mrs Hamton our housekeeper, sir, had leave from the Doctor to go and see a friend who was ill."

"Well," said the Colonel sharply, "what is it, Glyn?" For the boy had jumped up excitedly.

"That was the day, father, when Singh left the keys in the lock of his box."

"Exactly," said the Colonel. "Sit down, my boy.—Well, my man, whom did this stranger ask to see?"

"Please, sir, it wasn't a stranger; it was a gentleman the Doctor knew, and who came here to dinner once, and he asked for Mr Morris."

"Oh!" cried Morris, springing up. "Impossible!"

"Mr Morris, I must ask you to be silent," said the Colonel sternly.

"But—"

"I will hear anything you have to say, sir, when I have finished with this witness," said the Colonel firmly.—"Go on, my man. Who was this gentleman?"

"Pro— Professor Barlow, sir. No, sir; Professor Barclay, sir. And he said he was very much disappointed, as he had come down expressly from London to see Mr Morris. He said he couldn't stop, but he would write a letter if I would give him pens, ink, and paper."

"Go on," said the Colonel, as the hearers bent forward with eager interest. "Did you supply him with pens, ink, and paper?"

"Yes, sir. You see, he wasn't a stranger, but a friend of master's."

"And you took him to my study?" said the Doctor almost fiercely.

"I beg your pardon, Doctor," said the Colonel stiffly.

"I beg yours, Colonel Severn, for the interruption."

"Now then, my man," continued the Colonel; "you took this visitor, this Professor Barclay—"

There was a low, indignant murmur here, and the Colonel looked round sharply.

"You took this Professor Barclay into your master's study, I understand, and gave him pens, ink, and paper, and left him to write the letter?"

"No, sir, that I didn't," said Wrench, grinning with triumph. "I have been a servant too many years, sir, to go and do a thing like that. What, take him into master's room, where he keeps his cash-box and cheque-book in the little iron safe in the closet! And there's the presentation clock on the chimney-piece, and his old gold watch that he never wears in the table-drawer! No, sir. That gentleman was master's friend to some extent; but he was a stranger to me, and if he'd been a royal duke I shouldn't have done it."

"Then, what did you do?" said the Colonel.

"Took him into the theaytre lecture-room, sir, where there's little tables, and the young gentlemen writes out their exercises. That's what I did, sir," said Wrench triumphantly; and he looked hard at his master, who sat shaking his head at him solemnly.—"What! Wasn't that right, sir?" cried Wrench.

"Oh Wrench, Wrench, Wrench!" said the Doctor. "And you left him there, with the staircase close at hand leading right up to the corridor and the young gentlemen's dormitories?"

Wrench's jaw dropped, and one hand went slowly up to the back of his head and began to scratch.

"Well," continued the Colonel; "and how long did this gentleman stay?"

"I don't know, sir. Not half an hour—I'd swear to that. I gave him long enough to write a letter, and then I come back to see if he was ready to go."

"Let me protest," cried Morris indignantly. "No such letter was written for or delivered to me; that I declare."

"Pray be calm, sir," said the Colonel judicially. "You can ask this man any questions when I have done with him.—Now, my man, go on. Did you find this gentleman where you left him?"

"Yes, sir."

"And he gave you a letter to deliver to Mr Morris?"

"No, sir," cried Wrench sharply. "I'd forgotten all about it till you began arxing me questions like this. When I come in he got up in a disappointed sort of way and began tearing up the letter he had written quite small, and throwing it into the waste-paper basket. 'It's no use, my lad,' he said. 'I can't say in a letter one-hundredth part'—I ain't sure, sir, he didn't say a thousandth-part—'of what I want to tell Mr Morris. I'll stay in the town to-night, and come and see Mr Morris in the morning.'"

"And did he come and see Mr Morris in the morning?"

Morris half-rose in his chair, but sat down again.

"No, sir; and I haven't seen him from that day to this, though I had often seen them together before."

"That will do, my man," said the Colonel quietly.—"Now, Mr Morris; you wish to ask this man some questions?"

"Yes, sir," cried Morris springing up.—"Now, Wrench, did you ever tell me that Professor Barclay called when I was absent?"

"No, sir. I suppose it was the cricket-match put it all out of my head."

"Bah!" cried Morris.

"And then, you see, sir, I have so many things to think of about my work and the young gentlemen that I haven't got room to remember everything; and I always have to tick things off."

"Tick things off? What do you mean by that?" cried Morris.

"Well, sir, there's things to do and there's things that's done; things I have got to remember, and things I haven't. The Professor said that he'd come and see you, so that was his job and not mine; and if you'll believe me, gentlemen all, I never remembered about his coming until Colonel Severn here asked me about any one coming and wanting to write a letter."

"I believe you," said the Colonel quietly, as if speaking to himself; but it was sufficiently loud for Morris to hear, and he turned upon the speaker fiercely.

"I protest, sir," he cried indignantly, "partly against my name being dragged into this despicable theft, and partly on behalf of my friend Professor Barclay, a scholar, a gentleman, and a professor of Sanskrit and other Eastern languages; a gentleman, sir, though a poor and needy gentleman upon whom the world had frowned, but whom I considered it an honour and a privilege to know, as I should any gentleman whom I was introduced to by my revered principal the Doctor. I cannot sit still and hear such a man even suspected of being dishonest; and I beg you, sir, and the Doctor will go on with this investigation so as to prove to the world that Professor Barclay was a gentleman indeed."

Chapter Thirty Six
The Colonel opens Folk's Eyes

Morris sat down, panting, and began wiping the perspiration from his forehead. He looked very much agitated, and then he smiled with satisfaction, for Singh sprang up and cried, "Mr Morris is quite right, guardian. The Professor was a scholar and a gentleman, whom I knew too."

"Indeed!" said the Colonel.

"Yes, sir. He spoke Hindustani very well for an Englishman. Why, you saw him, sir!"

"I?" said the Colonel sharply. "Yes, sir; that night we were dining with you at your hotel."

"The Colonel forgets," said Morris quickly. "He was with me in the hall, sir, and wanted to be introduced to you."

"Oh," said the Colonel; "that man? No, I don't forget. I remember perfectly well."

"And, guardian, he took such an interest in my belt!"

"Indeed!" said the Colonel quietly.

"Yes, sir, when I showed it to him. He asked to see it, you know, when I told him about the Sanskrit letters."

"Naturally, as a Sanskrit scholar," said the Colonel drily. "Sit down, my boy.—Doctor, I am very glad you sent for me, and that I am able to clear up this miserable little mystery. You knew this Professor Barclay?"

"Only as coming to me with testimonials to prove that he had been one of the professors at Stillham College."

"Yes; and his name?"

"Barclay—Professor Barclay, Professor of Sanskrit and Hindustani. He applied for an engagement here."

"Humph! All wrong," said the Colonel. "I thought I knew his face when he tried to thrust himself upon me in the hotel; and I was right. I did know it, though thirty years had elapsed since we last met. A man who had been out in Calcutta and picked up a little Sanskrit and a pretty good smattering of Hindustani—a man who can chatter a bit in a foreign tongue always seems a big scholar to one who can't. This fellow, on the strength of his acquirements, came back to England and obtained an appointment near London where military cadets were in training for the Honourable East India Company's Service. I was there—not Stillham, but Barniscombe; name not Barclay, but Roberts. He was kicked out, Doctor, for blackmailing the students. He was not much more than a boy himself in those days."

"Colonel," cried the Doctor indignantly, "are you prepared to say you are sure, and that this is a fact?"

"Yes," said the Colonel coolly. "He blackmailed me."

"Oh, impossible!" cried Morris wildly.

"No, sir," said the Colonel, smiling. "Quite possible. But you don't offend me, sir. I admire the way in which you defend the man whom you seem to have made your friend.—Well, Doctor, there's your man.—Why, boys, you seem to have been babies in his hands. Glyn, I'm ashamed of you."

Glyn looked at the Doctor, and then at Morris, as he felt that his father was not treating him fairly; but he held his tongue, and then his eyes flashed with satisfaction as Singh gave him a quick look and then spoke out.

"Glyn had nothing to do with it, sir," he said. "He protested against it, and regularly bullied me for showing this man the belt and lending him money."

"Ha, ha!" said the Colonel. "Then he fleeced you a little, did he, my boy?"

"Well, yes, sir. I lent or gave him some money, because I thought that he was a poor gentleman. How was I to know that he was not honest, when—when—"

He was about to say "when my teachers were deceived," but the Colonel checked him.

"There, there, there," he said; "that'll do, Singh. You are not the first fellow of your age who has been imposed upon by a needy scoundrel."

"No," said the Doctor sharply. "If any one is to blame it is I, who pitied the position of a man out of employment and tried to befriend him. Well, Colonel Severn, I am very sorry; but it is forced upon me. I feel it a duty to you to try and make some recompense."

"Oh, nonsense!" said the Colonel rather haughtily. "I need no recompense."

"Indeed, sir," said the Doctor, "but I am answerable to Mr Singh here for his loss through my want of care and foresight."

"Oh, pooh, sir! pooh! The belt was not worth much; eh, Singh?"

"Oh no," said the boy contemptuously, and raising his head he walked up to the Doctor and held out his hand. "Don't say any more about it, sir, please," he added rather proudly. "I don't mind losing the belt a bit."

"Oh, but," cried the Doctor, catching at and pressing the boy's hand warmly, "this is very brave and noble of you, my boy. Still I must put aside all false shame and accept the punishment that may fall upon me from the want of confidence that people may feel in the future.—Colonel Severn, this must go into the hands of the police. Such a man as this must be run down; it is a duty, and before he imposes upon others as he has imposed upon me."

"No, no, no, my dear sir! No, no," cried the Colonel. "The swindling scoundrel has had his punishment before this, so let him go."

"I beg your pardon," said the Doctor; "he cannot have had his punishment; and such a man as this should not be allowed to be at large."

"There, there, sir," cried the Colonel, laughing pleasantly, and greatly to the annoyance of the Doctor that he should treat the loss of his ward's valuable belt in so light a way. "I find that I must make a confession. That belt really was not intrinsically worth more than a ten-pound note. It cost me about twenty; but I very much doubt whether the scoundrel would be able to sell it for a tithe of the amount."

"Guardian," cried Singh, "what are you saying?"

"Something in very plain English, my boy. Let's see, how old are you now?"

"Sixteen, sir."

"Well, it's about two years since you began to attack me about letting you have that part of the Dour regalia, and I wanted to satisfy you and do my duty in the trust my good old friend your father placed in me."

"I don't understand, sir," cried the boy, flushing.

"You soon will, my lad. I, in my desire to do my duty by you, felt that it would not be right to let a mere schoolboy like you come away to make your home at some place of education with so costly, and, from its associations, unique a jewel as the one in question."

"You used to say so to me, sir," said the boy quickly.

"Yes. But in your young hot-blooded Indian nature you were not pacified, and I felt bound to do something that I thought then would be right."

Singh looked at him and then at Glyn, while the rest of those assembled listened eagerly for the Colonel's next words.

"Do you remember, boys, our long stay in Colombo?"

"Yes!" they cried in a breath.

"Well, they are famous people for working in jewellery there, and I easily found a man ready to undertake the task of making a facsimile of the belt."

"Facsimile!" cried Singh, starting away from the speaker.

"Yes, my boy; and he did it beautifully—so well that I was almost startled by its exactitude and the way in which a few pieces of green glass resembled emeralds."

"But the Sanskrit inscription?" cried the Doctor.

"Exactly copied," said the Colonel; "cut in the glass. I tell you it was so well done that I was almost startled."

"Then—then—then," cried Singh wildly, "I have been deceived!" and his voice seemed to cut down that of Glyn, who was about to burst out in a triumphant "Hooray!"

"Well, yes, my boy," said the Colonel quietly. "I told you I must confess. I did deceive you in that, but with the best intentions."

A look of agony crossed the boy's face, and he turned from father to son and then back.

"Treated as a child!" he cried. "Deceived again! Oh, in whom am I to trust?"

"In me, I hope, boy," almost thundered the Colonel in the deepest tones. "I had the trust imposed on me by your dead father to care for you and your wealth until you came of age. Should I have been acting my part had I given up to you and let you treat as a toy that valuable jewel that was almost sacred in his eyes?"

"But to—but to— Then where—where is it now?"

"Lying safely with others, sir, in the bankers' vaults."

"Oh–h–h–oh!" cried Singh, and his whole manner changed as he stood for a few moments striving for utterance yet unable to speak. But at last the words came, hoarsely and with a violent effort, as in the reaction from his fit of indignation he almost murmured, "What have I done? What have I said?"

"Nothing, my boy," said the Colonel, holding out his hands, "but what had my son been in your place I would have gladly seen him do and heard him say."

One moment Singh's face, quivering with emotion, was hidden in the Colonel's breast; the next, he rushed from the room, closely followed by Glyn.

Chapter Thirty Seven
The Sore Place in the Fence

Time had gone on after his good old fashion, moving silently and insidiously, seeming to crawl to those who were waiting for something, till it suddenly dawns upon them that he has been making tremendous strides with those long legs of his which puzzled the little girl who asked her mother whether it was true that Time had those means of progression. Many will remember that the mother asked the child why she supposed that Time had legs, "Because," she replied, "people speak about the lapse of Time, and if he has laps he must have legs to make them of."

The troubles connected with the disappearance of the belt, and the unpleasant weeks during which masters, scholars, and servants seemed to have been mentally poisoned by suspicion and were all disposed to look askant at each other, had passed away, and, in his busy avocations and joining in the school sports, Singh was disposed to look upon the theft of his pseudo-heirloom as something which had never happened.

"Even if it had been real, Glyn," he said one night as they lay talking across the room in the dark, and the boy had grown into a much more philosophical state of mind, "what would it have mattered?"

"Not a jolly bit," said Glyn drowsily.

"I suppose it's being here in England," continued Singh, "where you people don't think so much about dressing up, and getting to be more English myself, that I don't seem to care about ornaments as I used. Sometimes I think it was very stupid of me to want to bring such a thing to school with me in my travelling-trunk."

"Awfully," grumbled Glyn.

"What!" cried Singh sharply.

Glyn started. "Eh! What say?" he cried, and a yawn followed.

"You said 'awfully.'"

"Did I?" said Glyn, more sleepily than ever.

"Why, you know you did," cried Singh petulantly.

"What did I say that for?"

"Ugh!" grunted Singh. "There, go to sleep. What's the good of talking to you?"

"Not a bit," replied Glyn; "it only sounds like *buzz, buzz.*"

"I haven't patience with you," cried Singh; "when I was trying to talk quietly and sensibly about losing my belt."

"Bother your old belt!" cried Glyn. "Who wants to talk quietly and sensibly now? I came to bed to sleep, and every time I'm dozing off nicely and comfortably you begin *burr, burr, burr,* and I can't understand you a bit."

"I wish we were in India," said Singh angrily.

"I wish you were," growled Glyn.

"I should like to set a punkah-wallah to pick up a chatty of water and douse it all over you."

"He'd feel very uncomfortable afterwards," said Glyn, "if I got hold of him. Oh, bother! bother! bother!" he cried, sitting up in bed. "Now then, preach away. What do you want to say about your ugly old belt?"

"Go to sleep," cried Singh, and there was a dull sound of Glyn's head going bang down into the pillow, in which his right ear was deeply buried while his left was carefully corked with a finger, and a minute or two later nothing was heard in the dormitory but the steady restful breathing of two strong healthy lads.

"What shall we do to-day; go out somewhere for a good walk?" asked Glyn the next morning.

"No; I want to have a quiet talk. Let's go down to the jungle, as you call it," said Singh.

"Thy slave obeys," cried Glyn. "But, jungle! poor old jungle! What wouldn't I give for a ride on a good elephant again—a well-trained fellow, who would snap off boughs and turn one into a *chowri* to whisk off the flies."

"Wouldn't old Ramball's Rajah do for you?"

"To be sure. I wonder what has become of the old boy. Roaming round the country somewhere, I suppose. What a rum old chap he was, with his hat in one hand, yellow silk handkerchief in the other, and his shiny bald head. Yes, I wonder where he is."

"Ramballing," cried Singh, with a peculiar smile on his countenance; and then he started in wonder, for Glyn made a dash at him, caught him by the wrist, and made believe to feel his pulse in the most solemn manner.

"What are you doing that for?" cried Singh.

"Wait a moment," replied Glyn.—"No. Beating quite steadily. Skin feels cool and moist."

"Why, of course," said Singh. "What do you mean?"

"I thought you must be ill to burst out with a bad joke like that."

"Oh, stuff!" cried Singh impatiently. "It's just as good as yours. Yes," he continued thoughtfully, "it is very nice here; but I should like another ride through the old jungle; and this old row of elm-trees—pah! how different."

The two lads remained very thoughtful as they walked slowly across the cricket-field, mentally seeing the wild forest of the East with its strange palms that run from tree to tree, rising up or growing down, here forming festoons, there tangling and matting the lower growth together, and always beautiful whenever seen.

Strange musings for a couple of schoolboys, who never once connected these objects of their thoughts with the stringent master's cane—the rattan or properly *rotan*-cane or climbing-palm.

They stopped at last in their favourite place beneath the elms, and stood with their hands in their pockets and their shoulders against the park-palings—the patch that looked newish, but which was gradually growing grey under the influence of the weather that was oxidising the new nails and sending a ruddy stain through the wood.

Neither spoke, but stood gazing up through the elm boughs, their thoughts far away in Northern India, dwelling upon active monkeys, peacocks and other gorgeously plumaged birds, tigers haunting nullahs and crouching among the reeds. All at once there was a strange panting sound, and a scratching behind them on the park-palings which made the two lads start away and turn to gaze at their late support, for the sound suggested, if not a tiger some other savage beast trying to climb the division between the Doctor's premises and the adjoining estate.

The next moment eight fat fingers appeared grasping the palings, there was the scratching of a boot on one of the supporting posts, and a round, red, fat face rose above the top of the fence like a small representation of the sun gradually topping a bank of mist upon a foggy morning.

'Hurt!' cried Glyn anxiously.

s.—Front.

Chapter Thirty Eight
His Great Attraction

"Mr Ramball!" cried the boys in a breath. "Aha! Good-morning! Only to think of me looking over here to see if I could catch sight of you two young gents, and hitting upon just the right spot, and— Oh my!"

There was a rushing sound as the wild-beast proprietor suddenly disappeared—so suddenly that, moved as by one impulse, the two lads made a dash at the palings, sprang up, and held on to look over, and see Ramball seated on the ground in the act of taking off his hat and extricating his yellow silk handkerchief to dab his bald and dewy head.

"Hurt?" cried Glyn anxiously. "Well, I—I don't quite know yet," said their unexpected visitor. "I haven't sat down as quick as that for a precious long time. Well, no, I don't think I am; it wasn't pleasant, though. But my toe might have given me notice that it was coming off that ledge. Well, how are you? If you'd come over here I'd offer to shake hands, but I would rather sit still for a few minutes to get my breath again. It seemed to be all knocked out of me at once."

The two lads glanced across the fields towards the orchard where the elephant had eaten his fill of apples, and, seeing nobody near, they both broke bounds by swinging their legs over the palings and dropping on the other side by the fat little man.

Glyn offered his hand to help him up, and Ramball took it and shook it.

"By-and-by," he said. "I am all right here.—And how are you, my hero?" he continued, extending his hand to Singh.

"Quite well," said Singh good-humouredly, looking at the showman but in imagination seeing the great elephant instead.

"That's right," cried Ramball. "You look it—hearty, both of you!"

"Where's the elephant?" said Singh.

"Oh, he's all right, sir. Fine."

"Is he coming into the town?" cried Glyn.

"What, here, sir? Bless you, no! He's in Birmingham, where we are doing a splendid business; crowded houses—tents, I mean—twice a day."

"And what are you doing here?" cried Singh.

"Oh, killing two birds with one stone," said the man, laughing.

"Where are they?" asked Glyn, laughing in turn.

"Get out! Poking fun at me! It was like this 'ere. The gent yonder,"— and the man gave his head a jerk backwards—"wrote to me and said that he'd had to pay a pound for a bit of damage to the fence about his orchard, and that he thought, as my elephant had done the mischief, and I had only paid him for the apples he ate, the money ought to come out of my pocket. Well, young gentlemen, I always pay up directly for any damage done by my beasts if the claim's made honest. This gent, your neighbour, sent in a very honest demand, and I set that down as one of the birds I wanted to kill. T'other was that I wanted to see my farm and how some of the young stock was getting on. So I nips into the train yesterday, travelled all night, and been to see the gentleman, paid up, and he was very civil—give me a bit of breakfast, and when I said I should like to look round the place again where my elephant went in for his apples he said I was quite welcome to look about as much as I liked. Well, we have been lately in the iron country and among the potteries; and bless you, it's quite a treat to be away from the smoke and to see things all a-growing and a-blowing. Then I catches sight of this bit of new fence, and that set me thinking of your school and you two young gents; and for the moment I thought that I would go back, say good-morning to the gentleman, and come round to the school and ask to see you two. But then I said to myself, 'Well, they are not their own masters yet, and the Doctor mightn't be pleased to have a common sort of fellow like me coming the visitor where I had no business,' and I says to myself, 'It might make it unpleasant for those two young fellows, and so I won't go.' Then I thought I should like to catch sight of you both again, for I took quite a fancy to you young gents. And here I am."

"Well," said Glyn, laughing, "we are glad to see you; eh, Singh?"

"Yes, of course. But hadn't you better get up, Mr Ramball? It seems so queer for us to be standing talking to you and you sitting there," said Singh.

"Oh, I'm all right, bless you, my lad. It makes me think about my Rajah."

"And me too. He's a grand beast."

"Isn't he, my lad? And the way he's been putting flesh on is wonderful. I won't say he weighs a ton more than when you saw him last, but he's a heap heavier than he was."

"But," cried Glyn mischievously, "his trunk's fine enough, only he's got such a miserable little tail."

"You leave his tail alone," said Ramball, wagging his head. "What he's got is his nature to."

"But I say, Mr Ramball," cried Singh merrily, "don't you want me to come and ride him in your show?"

"Well, no, sir; you chucked your opportunity away. I have got a new keeper now as fits exactly."

"What a pity!" said Glyn merrily.

"Well, that's what I thought, sir," said Ramball quite seriously, "when the young gent threw away his chance. You know we are common sort of people; but the money we earn sometimes ain't to be sneezed at. Why, of course I ought to tell you. Who do you think I have got?"

"Oh, how should we know?" cried Glyn.

"Friend of yours, gentlemen, that come to my show when it was here and wanted me to take him on."

"Friend of ours?" said Glyn.

"Yes; just after squire here had ridden Rajah. Said he was hard-up and couldn't get anything to do, but that he could talk Ingyrubber tongue as well as squire here. But I wouldn't have anything to do with him then, for I didn't believe in him."

"Professor Barclay!" cried Glyn excitedly.

"That's the man, sir. Well, he come to me, followed me up like, and I engaged him."

"But he's gone to India!" cried Singh excitedly.

"Gone to India, sir? Well, he's only got as far as the elephant, and that's in Brummagem town as sure as I am sitting here."

"Do you hear this, Glyn?" cried Singh excitedly.

"Oh yes, I hear," was the reply, and the two lads exchanged glances, while Ramball sat shaking and nodding his head like a mandarin image.

"It's no use, gentlemen. You threw that chance away. He come after me and followed me up all through the Midlands. Half-starved he was, pore chap. I never see such a gentlemanly sort of chap so hard pushed as he was; and at last out of charity like I took him on. And very glad I am, for he's turned out capital. He talks that Indian gibberish to the old Rajah, and the big beast follows him about like a lamb. Never have a bit of trouble with him now, only when he tries to shove one of the caravans over with that big head of his, just in play; and then Bah Klay—that's his show-name, and a very good one too—comes and says 'Hookah-bah-dah' and 'Shallahballah,' and the Rajah follows him as quiet as can be."

"Oh," said Singh.

"Ah, I wish you could see him, sir," continued Ramball, dabbing his head pleasantly with his yellow handkerchief. "Bah Klay is quite an addition to my show, and the people come in hundreds to see him and the Rajah alone. It was him himself as came to me one day and proposed it."

"What, the Rajah?" cried Glyn.

"The Rajah! Tchah! What are you talking about? No; Bah Klay. He said it wouldn't cost much, and that if I'd pay for the white cotton bed-gown sort of thing for him to wear and some scarlet muslin to roll up to make a muzzle to wear upon his head—"

"Muzzle! Over his mouth, you mean," cried Glyn.

"Who said anything about muzzle?" cried Ramball tetchily. "I said puggamaree—and that if I'd buy them, he'd dress up, and that he'd got a property to finish it all up fine. Well, I'd never seen any property that he'd got except a few things in a very shabby old carpet-bag that I wouldn't have picked up off the street. Still, I couldn't help thinking that him in a white bed-gown and a red turban on his head, cocked up there on the elephant's neck, wouldn't make a bad picture; so I said I would, and the very next week when we had paraded for a procession to go through one of the pottery towns and draw the people in, Mr Bah Klay came out in what he called his property. Ah, and he done it well! He'd washed his face in walnut juice, and his hands too. There he was in his white bed-gown and scarlet puggaree turban thing, and round his waist he'd got on a yellow leathern belt all dekkyrated with gold and buckled on with three great green glass ornaments that twinkled in the sun like hooray."

Singh started, his lips dropped apart, and he made a snatch at Glyn's wrist just as his companion clutched him by the arm, and the lads stood gazing into each other's eyes.

"Yes, gents, I tell you he looked fine, and it would have done your hearts good to see him. That there idea of his put steady vittles into his mouth and a few shillings a week into his pockets; but it always puzzled me why, him being so hard-up, he hadn't tried to sell that there belt. I said so to him one day, but he only gave a curious kind of grin and said he should have done so, but nobody would buy it, for it wasn't real. Well, of course I never supposed it was, being a theaytrical kind of property. Still, I don't suppose it was made for less than a five-pun note. Well, gentlemen," cried Ramball, rising slowly and giving his head a final dab, "I must be off. I go back to Brummagem again this afternoon, and all the better for seeing you two gents; so if you will shake hands, your sarvint to command, Titus Ramball, of the Imperial Wide World Menagerie."

The two lads shook hands heartily, but they were too full of thought to say much; and as the visitor went in one direction, they slipped over the palings and sat down with their backs against the fence to have a good long talk, for Fate seemed to have provided them with a subject upon which they could discourse; and it was this:

There was the criminal, almost within touch, for they had only to give notice to the police and the Professor would be lodged in jail for theft.

"And what then?" said Singh slowly. "I wouldn't have that belt again if it were brought to me. And what was it your father said about the Professor being punished?"

"Oh! about the punishment coming when he found that he had made himself a thief to get something that was not worth the pains."

"Yes," said Singh, "but not in those words. Then we don't want to punish the miserable cheat any more."

"And do harm to droll old Ramball," said Glyn. "My word, though, I should almost like to go to Birmingham and suddenly come upon the Professor riding upon old Rajah's neck!"

"Pah!" exclaimed Singh, with his lip curling and a look of disgust in his eyes, "I shouldn't like to see the miserable creature for the poor elephant's sake. Here, let's go and tell Mr Morris."

"No, no!" cried Glyn excitedly. "All that trouble is being forgotten, and it would hurt his feelings if it were brought up again."

"Think so?" said Singh.

"Yes. Promise me you'll never say a word to any one here."

"Well," said Singh thoughtfully, "I won't."

Salaam To All!